Archipelago

GW01463894

Gabrielle Barnby

ARCHIPELAGO © 2025 Gabrielle Barnby

Gabrielle Barnby asserts the moral right to be identified as the author of this work in accordance with the Copyright, Designs and Patents Act 1988

This is a work of fiction. Names, characters, places and incidents are either the result of the author's imagination or are used fictitiously.

All rights reserved. No part of this publication may be reproduced, stored in or introduced into a retrieval system or transmitted in any form or by any means (electronic, mechanical, photocopying, recording or otherwise) without the prior written permission of the author.

Isbn: 978-1-914399-41-1

This book is sold subject to the condition that it shall not be resold, lent, hired out or otherwise circulated without the express prior consent of the author.

Printed and bound in Great Britain by Clays Ltd, Elcograf S.p.A

Cover Design © 2025 Mercat Design, images courtesy of Dreamstime. All Rights Reserved

SPARSILE
BOOKS

Prologue

Before the meeting Harriet is many things. She is a lecturer, a tutor, a researcher, a mentor. She is a daughter, sister and friend. She has defined herself in many different ways. So have others.

This is how it changes.

~~~

The disciplinary committee begins at four o'clock. It is Thursday afternoon in the fourth week of Hilary term. Green spears are rising in the college flowerbeds. The weather is resolutely cold, yet the Old Library is stuffy, water decants lukewarm when poured. The polished surface of the table gleans reflections from above, colour enters the space, a vivid glow through the stained-glass emblem of the college. A bright blur strikes the wall, held aloft in the gothic crown of the high window arch, split in three, then two.

There is nothing spiritual about the ceremony, only ritualistic trappings. Academic gowns are worn by everyone present.

The committee is chaired by Professor Paul Molyneaux, head of ancient languages.

'Our task is to decide on a course of action following an alleged breach in the staff code of conduct. Copies of the college handbook and university staff handbook are before you. Mrs Hart will minute the meeting. The College Dean Doctor Calvin Neeley, Doctor Harriet Wolf, Professor Annette Bell, Professor Thomas Knight and Doctor José Blanco are recorded as present. Apologies are from Professor Dasgupta, Doctors Plumb and O'Connell.'

The secretary, dressed head to toe in navy blue, makes a note.

Professor Molyneux goes on.

'The handbook states that, "A personal relationship of a sexual or other intimate nature between a student and a member of staff with academic, pastoral or administrative responsibilities towards that student undermines the relationship of trust and confidence which is intrinsic to interactions between staff and students, and may give rise to an actual, or apparent, conflict of interest, risk of favouritism, or abuse of authority".

He takes a sip of water.

'Furthermore, "If such a relationship develops during the course of employment or study between a member of staff and a student for whom they have a professional responsibility, this must be disclosed by the member of staff to the Head of Department as early as possible".

The dean releases the index finger pressed into his lips and speaks.

'Doctor Wolf, you have elected not to have any representation. I have received an informal note from Professor Paracchini in reference to the matter. But it was received beyond the permitted submission time. It cannot be entered into proceedings.

Professor Molyneaux accepts a sheet of paper filled with slanted writing rich in curlicues and places it to one side.

'Dean, might you provide background as to how this committee has acted in similar circumstances.'

The dean obliges.

'The committee has been convened five times since foundation. Previous sanctions have broadly followed recommendations in the staff handbook. In this case, suspension from teaching duties is mandatory, as is a permanent letter placed on file.'

Professor Annette Bell, the only female member of the committee, grey hair neatly tucked, eyes sparkling blue, a trace of Ulster in her tone, speaks.

'Wasn't Craig Greyson reinstated to his teaching role almost immediately two years ago?'

'The student in question changed course,' answers the dean. 'So there was no longer a need for distancing within the department.'

'Wasn't it rather that the student withdrew,' says Professor Bell. She looks pointedly at the dean.

Professor Molyneaux, committee chair, speaks again. 'Our remit is to examine Doctor Wolf's current position, not revisit previously settled cases. There is no indication that the student in question wishes to change course. Dean, does the college have reciprocal agreement for Archaeology and Anthropology tutorial teaching with any other college?'

'No.'

'Professor Paracchini has agreed to teach tutorials if necessary,' says Harriet. 'He told me himself.'

'He has made no formal approach to the committee. It is a question of trust, not simply alternative arrangements that accommodate your failure to report the relationship. We cannot allow this to drag on.'

Professor Bell speaks again. 'The college has previously accommodated student-staff relationships. There have been changes in PhD supervision within the biochemistry department a number of times.'

The dean re-examines a page in the staff handbook.

'I'd like to know who reported the relationship,' said Harriet. 'Was it a member of college?'

'The reporting of student-staff relationships is not limited to members of staff, or even those matriculated in the university,' responds the dean.

'It is important such things remain confidential,' adds Professor Molyneaux.

'I want to know what I am being accused of? And who by.'

The dean speaks again. 'I regret you venture to ask. Rest assured, an investigation has been carried out of a discreet nature, following committee guidelines.'

'What about my privacy?'

Harriet cringes at the bitterness in her own voice.

'Do you wish to describe events yourself, Doctor Wolf? This is your opportunity if you wish to take it,' says the dean.

'I have had a consensual relationship with Art Rivers since the seventh week of Michaelmas term.'

'And is the relationship continuing?' says the dean.

'Yes.'

'It strikes me as extraordinary that you acknowledging this openly.'

'That is precisely what you are demanding,' says Harriet.

'Did you not think to approach this committee sooner? Or remove yourself from your professional duties?'

Harriet's molars grip. She answers, 'No.'

'In hindsight, does this strike you as an oversight?' says Professor Bell. She looks over the bridge of her glasses at Harriet.

'I did not expect to be treated fairly. My confidence in the procedures of this committee following previous information leaks and inconsistent actions is low. Its membership has recently altered. Annette, I am glad you are here at least. But I did not want its scrutiny.'

'That is exactly what we are here to provide,' says the dean. 'Scrutiny.' He glances across to Professor Molyneaux and the corners of his mouth twitch upwards.

'We're here to provide support as well,' says Professor Bell.

'How?' says Harriet.

'The dean will explain the options the committee can recommend,' says Professor Molyneaux.

Harriet sits back in her chair, cheeks flushed.

Professor Knight stirs awake. He peers at Harriet, suddenly breaks into rapid speech.

'If I could suggest, propose, postulate that this is simply a case of time going awry? If the student had been older or Doctor Wolf younger, this issue would not have the same significance? I ask this and bring it to the committee's attention with no particular motivation. But, do we not have to question how long must pass before Doctor Wolf can have consensual relations with an individual who has been an undergraduate at the college? Did not the Computer Scholar become engaged to a final year classicist? Did we not celebrate the event in the annals of the College Gazette? Did we not drink champagne?' He points to a row of green volumes then squints through half-moon glasses at Harriet. 'Will you be getting engaged? How old exactly are you, Doctor Wolf? In my opinion you don't look notably old.'

Professor Knight nods, rests his hands on his chest and resumes his supine pose.

Professor Molyneaux leans forward over his notes and rests his pen. There is a brief silence.

The dean speaks. 'If we can move on to the options before us.'

'Will the undergraduate in question be taking finals in Trinity term?' asks Professor Bell.

'Yes, of course he will,' says Harriet.

The gathering is quiet. Harriet sips tepid water.

'Cessation of teaching duties for a full academic year will begin immediately,' says the dean.

'I propose that this sanction only last until the end of this Trinity term,' rejoins Professor Bell. 'To be followed by full reinstatement.'

The dean replies swiftly, 'I think the college is vulnerable to criticism if they are seen to be dealing too lightly with the matter. We must be mindful of the student 'It Happens Here' movement.' He presses his index finger into the tabletop. 'We need to move away from accusations of past leniency as highlighted by Doctor Wolf. A higher standard must be set, beginning with this case.'

'This is clearly a decision based on a desire to improve committee reputation. Or are there other reasons?' says Harriet.

'You imply prejudice, Doctor Wolf? Are you accusing the committee of abusing the ethos of equality—an ethos central to all who have developed this process.'

'There has been no complaint from Art or any other student. This is an intrusion into a private relationship that is wholly unacceptable.'

'Given the differences in power, position and authority, and the vulnerability to duress or abuse, there is hardly genuine freedom to bring a complaint in this case,' says the dean.

Professor Molyneaux speaks. 'Doctor Wolf, you were fully apprised of your obligations when you signed your employment contract.'

Harriet lifts her gaze to the windows, lips pursed.

'Does anyone oppose the decision to suspend Doctor Wolf from all college duties?'

Doctor Blanco, who has been assiduously marking essays, looks up briefly and nods. Professor Bell bats her eyelids and submits. Mrs Hart takes note that there are no objections. The decision is made.

'A letter will go into your personal file and remain there for two years from the date of your return. I declare this committee closed.'

Professor Knight, opens his eyes sleepily and smiles at Harriet as she gets to her feet and exits the room. Her life is gone.

Ebb

1

Harriet felt another presence as she woke. The room was utterly black, yet there was an area of more intense blackness at the end of the bed. She reached over, then quickly withdrew her hand. It was fur. An animal. What was it? How had it got in?

She lay flat again and experienced a sensation of falling, her body pressing through the mattress towards the flagstone floor. She pushed upright, nausea rising as her feet went down onto the cold stones. This part of Erskine had grown organic with age, the smooth surfaces sloped to the old outer door of the ground floor.

She shivered. It had been six weeks since her last period, part of her wanted to give thanks for its arrival, but to whom? Another part of her wondered if this loss were more than the sloughing of blood. She had an unfamiliar desire to speak to her mother, her younger sister too. But Addie was chaos.

The ache in her abdomen sharpened. It reminded her of sunlight flashing through the windows of her abandoned study in Oxford. The diamonds of light faded on the black doctoral gown hung on the door and she was again in the dark.

Her eyes began to adjust further and subtle shapes emerged. Harriet looked towards a void in the inner wall and braced herself to stand.

~~~

'So, I'm staying in a stable?'

It was the night before, during dinner.

'The estate agent girl called it an old "firehoose". Don't you love it?' Anna had interlaced her fingers and rested her chin on her hands. 'It used to have an open hearth and an open chimney called a lum…oh dear. What is it now, Eveline?'

'I can't sleep.'

The child had wheezed softly through a half-open mouth.

'She's usually much better once we're here,' said Anna. 'London's killing her.'

'Killing us all,' said Martin with a resigned chuckle. 'I expect Oxford's just as bad pollution wise.'

He had poured more wine into Harriet's glass.

She saw his smile flicker curiously. She'd seen similar expression on other people's faces, the dean of her college included. In Martin's case there was nothing censorious in his expression. Was it an air of mild approval? Envy perhaps?

'I'll take her up,' said Anna. She had glanced to her husband, now filling his own glass. 'Please, don't encourage him, Harriet.' She rolled a tendril of her daughter's fair hair between her fingers. 'I suppose we'll have to resort to a puffer.'

'Sorry, Mum.'

'Don't be sorry, darling. It's why we're here.'

Anna's voice faded as they retreated upstairs.

'It's a beautiful house,' said Harriet.

'I've had nothing to do with it,' said Martin. 'You know Anna. She'll be bored now it's done. She hates working at the bank more than ever.'

Martin glanced towards the door.

'Still trading futures?'

'Derivatives, or is that the same thing? Anyway, it pays the rent.'

Harriet had sipped her wine, Martin's gaze slid to her legs. Without Anna the atmosphere subtly changed; it was the same as when they had been at university together nearly twenty years ago.

'So, tell me about your student.'

'Anna said I wasn't to get you excited,' said Harriet. Her eyes half closed.

'It can't be that uncommon.'

'The dean is calling it a sabbatical. So I can concentrate on conference papers, and complete the Nepali manuscript.'

'You'll be bored in a week,' said Martin. 'Who're you going to talk to?'

'I suppose it's what I need.'

'Isolation?'

Anna had re-entered the room, her movements lithe in the candlelight. Harriet yawned, the effect of travel and wine.

'Really, it's very kind of you to let me sleep in the stable.'

~~~

In the darkness, Anna's warning about a cat came back to her. Harriet edged around the bed and stepped forwards. She shouldn't have let the animal frighten her. What a fool she was to not turn on the lamp.

She felt a doorway, then a switch. The bathroom was crammed into a space six feet long by barely four feet wide. A single massive slab of stone braced the lintel and gave the incongruous impression of an ancient tomb entrance beside a modern door.

Anna insisted the property had found her, not the other way around. She had made a throwaway comment to her estate agent after a conversation about prioritising off-road parking: 'But really, I want a country house.'

The next day he had emailed her the details of Erskine.

While the renovations and extension were being completed Anna had gone to the Orkney Archives in Kirkwall to research the property. She'd told Harriet a raised sleeping platform had once been installed inside the small recess. The last couple to occupy the dwelling had been childless and the deeds passed to the Scarth family, owners of the neighbouring farm.

Harriet hesitated at the doorway, feeling claustrophobic, a sensation amplified by hormones and alcohol. In the mirror, her eyes were stone-coloured and flat, the skin on her neck ivory, her hair buoyant on one side and compressed on the other. The highlights looked yellow in the electric light.

The apple cheeks and bright eyes of the past months were gone.

'God, what a mess.'

She rummaged through a narrow set of drawers and gave silent thanks to Anna as she found the sanitary wear she needed.

What would her mother have said about her contraceptive carelessness? Harriet had an intuition that both her mother and sister would be sanguine about the relationship with Art, but to be pregnant by accident—that would be a dreadful lapse.

Their mother had been candid about her own experience of pregnancy termination. Not long after the procedure she had finished with the boyfriend. She had been upset and left him standing in a bar, forgetting her coat. Their father had watched, sensed something beneath her grief, and followed her out in the rain, hardly knowing her, and held out the left-behind jacket. He had walked her to the tube station, and a few days later he discovered the interior design store where she worked and ordered curtains he didn't need. Once, after her mother retold the story, she had said, 'I still imagine a parallel life, even though I cannot live it or change it.'

The heavy scent of tuberose filled the air as Harriet opened one of the creams on the vanity shelf. The musky sweetness reminded her of kissing Art, being infused with warmth by his touch.

'You know I don't feel younger,' he had said one afternoon. 'You are who you are. It doesn't matter.'

She'd raised a finger to his lips, her thoughts ahead of his. He wanted to ask, did she feel older?

He shouldn't ask.

They had driven out of town so they could eat out, to The

Bull, a pub set in a ring of cottages. Its saloon was smaller than her tutorial room; Art had to duck to avoid the brass tack hanging on the iron-hard black beams. An extraordinary painting of a bull with prominent sexuality hung above their table.

The barman, moustached and rectangular, had poured generous measures, rum and coke and a red wine. He stepped around the bar and sat on a stool like a customer, one hand contentedly folded around a pint.

Harriet's recently cut hair had felt too short and too blonde, her lips too glossy, her coat too expensive. Art, understated in manner, could not help being conspicuous in an Oxfordshire village. Did he notice the barman looking at his hands as he received the menu? What did he feel being told that the dishes were spicy?

The timing of their visit had coincided with a motorcycle meet. Dozens had been parked on the common beyond the pub's garden. A barbecue had been set up and the smell of onions and meat rolled across the green. Moths rose from the grass as they inspected the machines and enjoyed mixing with the enthusiasts. Art had told her how he missed market food in Port Louis.

'In the house, Nounou baked every day. Even my mother would sneak macarons from plates in the kitchen. I'd take them as gifts for Madame Ramdin, my piano teacher. Every colour you can think of, like the jockey silks on the Champ de Mars. I always wanted to be one of them, thundering along. But it was not a worthy ambition.' He'd looked over to the ranks of motorcycles. 'I had one of those.' He laughed, pointing at a scooter. 'We'd all ride out of Port au Prince, 'The Bluebottles' we called ourselves.' Art had gazed down the hawthorn-edged lane, his thoughts a thousand miles away.

They had walked, hands loosely held, words occasionally exchanging as their thoughts diverged and intertwined.

How could she have known they were seen?

2

Addie's phone call had come in the early evening, a river of fragmented instructions, flippant and pressing. The result was a detour to Chipping Norton in the dusk at the end of Hilary Term.

Addie had leaned over the passenger seat and pushed a spilling folder towards Harriet.

'How was I to know there was no train station?' she said.

She had gone back into a boutique and returned with a canvas packaged for transportation.

'It has to be in position for the final insurance inspection.'

She balanced the frame against the dashboard, then reached round for her seatbelt. 'Oh?'

Art's raised his fingers in greeting and nodded his head a fraction, lips resisting a smile.

'This is Art,' said Harriet.

'That's funny,' said Addie. 'Don't you see? I'm picking up art and you arrive with Art.'

Addie had let out a ripple of laugher.

'It's not that funny,' said Harriet. 'How is it never your fault?'

'I had a lift, well, someone gave me a ride. Then they left. I can get the train to Paddington from Oxford.'

Harriet had pushed the folder back to her sister and started the car. Addie strapped herself in, then tucked her hair to one side and peered more closely at Harriet's passenger.

'Who are you, then?'

Art made eye contact with Harriet in the rearview mirror.

'I know Harriet through college.'

'Another musician?'

'What do you mean by another?' said Art.

'She means nothing,' said Harriet.

Addie's lip had twitched upwards. She had taken a deep breath and launched into a flood of people, places and drama that Harriet cared nothing about. For once it had been a relief just to let her sister talk.

At one point she'd mentioned a North African jazz pianist and turned to the back seat.

'Where are you from?'

'Kensington,' said Art.

Addie had arched an eyebrow.

'Art plays the piano,' said Harriet.

'But you said he wasn't a musician.'

Addie had turned around in her seat and looked sideways at her sister.

'Go on, tell me about what's-his-name and the exhibition,' said Harriet. 'Are the press going to be there?'

Addie had restarted her narrative, the hawthorn hedges darkened and the sky had released its last shades of red and became a deep, petrol blue.

At Oxford station Addie had collected together her possessions.

'I knew I could depend on you,' she said, kissing Harriet on the cheek. 'I would do the same.'

'I'll hold you to that,' said Harriet.

Addie's gaze had travelled to where Art was standing by the bonnet.

'He's very nice.'

Harriet's cheeks flamed.

Addie had blown them both a kiss as she tripped up the steps through the automatic doors. When she was gone Art came around to the open car door.

'Sorry,' said Harriet.

'She's your sister,' he said.

He had scanned the stream of pedestrians heading past the Saïd Business School.

'I'm going to walk back to college'

'Not coming back to the flat?'

He had hesitated.

'No, not tonight.'

'Never mind then, I'll see you Tuesday afternoon with Gregory.'

Art had turned up his collar, glanced at the red traffic lights and stepped into the road.

She had eased into the stream of traffic, a charge running through her body, pulling her to him even as she drove away, urging her to seek him in the rearview mirror.

Over time the lines had gradually been redrawn.

Each week of term they met between three and four o'clock. A new cafetière was always made. She had poured cups for herself and Art. Gregory gauchely refused, although from the sour alcoholic smell he was often in need of it most.

The two o'clock tutorial pair left her in need of refreshment, beneath her hijab Zineb had ambition and challenged everything—as she should.

Gregory barely had stomach for his own sentences. He regurgitated ethical dilemmas like old news, but there had been something personal in Art's responses. Harriet had gone away and researched some history of Mauritius, the layers of power, cultures settled like sediment, some crushed others transformed.

'Only their lives,' that was how Gregory had summed up ethnographic research.

'But what is so only about their lives?' she had said.

She smiled at the phrasing that came to her lips.

Art had been perceptive. She had been provocative. The sun had dipped beneath the clouds and the tessellated light through the lead windows had softened and blurred.

'Someone could study us, right here and now. Couldn't they? From the outside. See something we've not perceived,' he'd said.

'So, you think we don't know the social norms we act according to?'

'They are invisible,' he'd replied. 'Like all important things.'

Gregory had looked at the clock on the wall and began to tidy his notes.

'Yes, time is up,' said Harriet, 'Although I feel we were just getting started on something interesting. Art, if you are not in a hurry, I have a book that might interest you. I have no further tutorials anyway this afternoon.'

She had performed a small catlike stretch to ease her back, felt his gaze on her, felt her heart beat faster. Gregory's downwards tread on the spiral stair disappeared. They had been alone. The book had been found and lent—that was all.

It had only been a moment.

She was brought back to the Ashmolean Museum and the lines of traffic, the lines of trees and the lines of buildings, the buses pulling to a stop and horns sounding. The light ahead had turned green, but she missed the chance to turn.

3

In the morning, warmth of sleep and menstruation held Harriet captive. A restless rummaging sound, distant yet pressing, rolled, scattered and swept with rising tension then dropped into sudden abeyance. She briefly wondered if she were in danger from the sea and then sank back into the labyrinth of sleep.

When Harriet finally opened her eyes, soft light from an overcast morning filtered into the room. Where there had been an open chimney there was now a piece of glass. It shone like an eye. Noise penetrating through from the modern part of the house indicated activity.

The shifting presence of water had been disorientating as they had driven to Erskine from Kirkwall airport. The invaginations of coastline gave an illusion that the distant, low hills were islands or that tails of land were connected, when they were in fact separated by miles of water. Blurred edges of grey stretched around the horizon and rose overhead in an opalescent dome as if tent-pegged to the unseen edges of the earth.

No aspect of the landscape was familiar to Harriet. Everything was seen at once in one long sweep. Nothing manmade consoled her to the sense of scale, no spires with gothic embellishments, no stout academic departments. There was an incalculable breadth of vision. Yet still she sensed it was a place only partially revealed; a surface withholding invitation.

The door opened.

Anna entered and opened the curtain of a small, deep-set window.

'We're off out. The stoat team might call. Oh, Sleekit, how did you get in here?'

Anna lifted the cat from the end of the bed and took him to the old farmhouse door.

'I don't know how he gets in. I suspect it's Oscar. I'll have to start locking more doors until I get the garden secure.'

'You don't lock the house?'

Anna slid the latch and opened the wooden door to reveal a rectangle of light. There was nothing to indicate the presence of land outside, the cat could have been cast gently into an abyss. Air fragranced with salt and tang pushed into the room. Harriet wrinkled her nose.

'I found him halfway down the lane last time we came.'

'The cat?'

'No. Oscar. Martin forgot he was meant to be supervising.'

Anna stayed at the door looking towards a crenelated line of yellow-green bladderwrack on the shore. A group of birds with white breasts and chevroned black and white wings picked their way over the stones.

Harriet pushed up onto her elbows and watched her friend's expression soften. It was so unlike the city, yet Anna fitted.

'Is that the Casini?' said Harriet.

The light from the doorway caught the curves of a string instrument hanging on the wall. Anna glanced towards the violin..

'It isn't getting played in London,' she said. 'The fiddlers here are something else. Maybe one day I'll have courage and go to a session.'

Harriet's eyebrows rose. 'Hardly your skill set.'

Anna waved her away as Oscar bounded into the room and collided into her legs.

'Shoes first,' said Anna, closing the door firmly. 'Sleekit must stay out.'

'No,' cried the boy. 'Sleek in!'

Anna lifted the toddler. He leaned away, arching and falling backwards, but she caught him and held tightly. The flagstones would be unforgiving.

'We'll be back for lunch,' said Anna. 'You're here to rest.'

Harriet shook her head. 'I'm not an invalid, just a…'

'…castaway,' finished Anna.

~~~

An hour later, Harriet had made it as far as sitting in the kitchen, still in nightwear. The tall windows of the living area stretched up into a triangular mezzanine like the prow of a glass boat.

She saw herself reflected in the windows, all folded limbs

like an insect emerging from a cocoon of grey silk. There were rings under her eyes and dark roots showed in her hair. She ran her tongue over dry lips.

Behind the window, strips of leaves belonging to an unknown plant flattened and then flashed upwards as the breeze rebounded from the house.

So this is it, she thought. The end.

Anna had warned Harriet that she would have to roam for phone signal.

Would there ever be another message from Art? If he died, would anybody call her?

She stared at the trembling plants absorbing the wind's energy, a silent film, endlessly running, while she sat sealed away. Harriet's gaze trained towards the shrubs that lined the stone dyke.

A slim animal hunkered in the grass, larger than a squirrel, with a dark tip on its tail. She watched as it edged beneath the dog roses.

The stoat's head rose slightly for a a better vantage point, then the animal bounded to the gatepost and disappeared.

Harriet had never expected to see one in the wild, yet she felt its absence acutely when it had gone. She roused herself and moved to the bathroom and turned on the taps. She lowered her body into the water and ceased the flow, then watched the surface rise and fall with her breath. If she stopped breathing the surface remained level. She had no desire to wash, only dissolve.

The steam condensed on the stone walls, drifting through to the bedroom, and the wind beat out its irregular rhythm in her temples, whistling through the tiny gap over the old lum. Her body stopped calling for breath. Her vision blurred, clouding at the edges and becoming mauve then inky black, drifting dark spots flocked like jellyfish, denser, darker.

There was a male voice calling.

Harriet pressed her hands against the smooth sides of the bath, raised her face from beneath the water. The bathwater rippled and she shivered at the influx of cold air pimpling her skin.

Antipodean vowels rolled together.

'In ya go buddy.'

Harriet became aware of carelessly dropped clothes, her suitcase, laptop, painkillers, books.

'Don't do anything I wouldn't.'

The footsteps retreated and the latch of the old door clinked shut. Through the open bathroom door she watched a windswept black cat pad over to a pool nightwear. It stretched out its front paws, turned a circle then curled up to sleep.

Harriet leaned back into the water. The sound of wind mingled with the bubbling cry of a bird. The haunting sound reminded her why she had finally accepted Anna's invitation.

She had nowhere else to go.

4

On the dashboard, a clipboard held laminated ordinance survey maps and leaflets in waterproof pouches. Clem had watched Uncle Ernest working with Kieran, but now they were out of sight and time was slowing. Clem lifted an index finger and began to tap the rhythm of the wind on his leg. The stoats shouldn't be on the islands. Clem had been told it was wrong to feel sorry for them. It was wrong to like the skip and weave as they ran. They were killers. Kieran was the expert at eradication, that's why he'd come half way around the world. Kieran told them how it was done.

Rats came decades ago, Uncle Ernest said, about the time

he was born, found their way over in fodder. It only took a breeding pair. Clem understood that.

The new woman at Erskine was moving around the kitchen. He'd never seen a pattern like the shirt she wore. Gold and black, like her hair out of the towel, the sea at winter sunset. He could see her face clearly, a pale oval with dark, sliding eyes. A smile spread across his face. The finger on his leg paused. Maybe he should get out and say hello.

Before the thought finished the van's back door opened. The smell of fresh spread slurry carried into the cab. Uncle Ernest was there in blue overalls, matching Clem, with a black plastic box with an entry hole for a rat under his arm.

Clem twisted in his seat.

'Bide where you are,' said Ernest. 'Thir's somebody hame.'

Clem turned back around.

No one liked a rat. Rats spread on nearly every island from one breeding pair. They were a pest. It was Westray that was still clear of them.

The stoats were worse killers though, never anything like them. Even when the creature was dead the pelt was soft and alive. They were held in high esteem in other places, he liked to know that fact.

Kieran had stubble, wore khaki shorts and hiking shoes whatever the weather. Never overalls and black rubber boots. Too tall and thin, Uncle Ernest said.

When Kieran passed the windows the woman stood upright and then moved away.

Clem saw they politely looked away from each other. Not like him. He stared too much. And he spoke when he shouldn't. Words didn't go where he wanted, he had to watch them carefully. He had to understand people were saying meanings underneath the words. His uncle had lost a great deal of money by not understanding what was said on a telephone call.

~~~

In the shelter of the van Ernest was working away at the trap. A clasp gave way and revealed a stiff, brown body. It came away with a shake into a catering-size mayonnaise bucket with tight-fitting lid.

Kieran arrived.

'Anythin?' said Ernest.

'Nah,' said Kieran. 'I let in the moggy that hangs around.' He looked over his shoulder. 'Wouldn't do any harm to get rid of them as well. Hundreds caught in Canterbury.'

Clem's thoughts switched to cats. Their secret lives, trails and tracks. Fine to be a cat. He didn't want to get rid of cats.

Kieran interrupted the thought.

'Pass the clipboard, mate.'

'The clippy,' repeated Ernest. 'Pass hid back.'

Clem nodded. He balanced and stretched backwards.

'Gonna leave a calling card,' said Kieran.

'Someone's hame,' said Ernest.

Kieran shrugged and held out a leaflet.

'Knock on the door if you like. I'll finish cleaning up.'

Ernest laid down his wire brush, tapped the top of a plastic pump connected to a large bottle of sanitising gel, rubbed his hands, and took the leaflet and calling card.

No one would argue it was a bad thing that Erskine had become hard to recognise. For years there had been nothing but a rutted track to a ruin. Steven Scarth had let the place rot and Ernest couldn't think why anyone would want to renovate, never mind go to the bother of reusing slates. The sign for Erskine was long lost at the bottom of the lane rising from the coast road. On the seaward side another croft, Storrtang, slowly eroded into the shore.

The lane had a broad ditch where a burn trickled to the lochan at Kingsgarth. Crowns of daffodils were emerging on the banks, the shoots retarded according to exposure to the west. In the summer, the bank facing east would be invaded with red campion, hogweed and clover. Ernest saw the lane was badly in need of offlet cutting to drain surface water.

Crows flew overhead. Ernest slowed his steps as he approached, remembering what had happened at Erskine. It haunted him more than it had ever done. He drew breath and steadied himself at the new door.

He had painted Clem's door on Balfour Rise a good Lighthouse Board red. Even as it faded Clem always said it was bonny.

Ernest knocked, ignoring the bell. His gaze caught on a crow stalled in the breeze as he waited until a woman tidying her hair came stood for a moment and opened the door. In defiance of the new expanses of glass and wood the roof of the original building gently echoed the line of the hill behind.

The woman greeted him with a formal smile.

'You must be the stoat man. I'm Harriet, friend of Anna's.'

Ernest's glance fell to Harriet's bare feet as she took the leaflet. They were handsomely formed. His wife Meg had fine feet, still fitted her wedding shoes once a year. His stomach knotted as the thought came.

Ernest lifted his head. He couldn't place the woman's age. She was pale, stretched out. Maybe it was an illness, or something in her constitution that reacted badly to being so far north.

'I'll pass it on,' said Harriet.

The neat-limbed black cat walked towards the base of a wooden staircase. The direction of Ernest's gaze caught Harriet's attention.

'I don't think he's meant to be in here,' said Harriet. 'But he won't let me touch him.'

'Always a black cat,' said Ernest.

No matter how many were caught and taken away, one returned; small bodied and black, with sea-glass eyes. It gave him a queer feeling to see the spry animal near the ailing woman.

Ernest turned and walked away. As he slid into the van next to Clem he looked back. The front door was still open, but there was no sign of the woman.

'A new sighting on Burray,' said Kieran. 'Roadside carcass. They've taken it home.'

Ernest untwisted Clem's seatbelt and clipped it securely while Kieran slid his phone onto the dashboard and fitted the key in the ignition. Clem's fingers fluttered over the radio. The hiss and squawk of distant frequencies pierced the cab.

'Leave hid, Clem,' said Ernest.

Ernest leaned forward to correct the frequency.

'No worries,' said Kieran. 'Switch it off.'

A black-backed gull, white bellied with a hooked yellow beak and fanned tail, slipped through the air ahead of them. It stood out briefly against the clouds, then flashed over the water. For a moment, Kieran forgot where he was, and imagined an albatross and felt a rush in his veins.

Mish came to mind and he felt the distance from home grow in his gut. She'd been a volunteer when they first met, they'd spent a lot of time together, sampling and trapping, checking fences to protect the albatross reserve.

Orkney and Otago had similarities, stoical people, testing weather, rich birdlife, and now the problems with stoats. There were neighbourhoods on the peninsula where doors were left open.

It would all change in time.

He'd left, he'd ended all that, and he didn't know when he'd return.

5

The cat easily outstripped Harriet on the top landing.

'Come here cat. Sleekit…'

Her tone was wrong, and calling was ridiculous given her intention. She looked at the cream walls and carpets and sighed. The cat's tail curled and stroked the carpet. It should definitely not be upstairs.

The animal stared back at her, and in the impasse she became lost in her own thoughts.

Who had spoken to the college authorities about Art? What did public opinion matter on a personal relationship?

An age gap of a decade was nothing in the past. An avuncular aged husband was not taboo. Her own great uncle had married a girl of eighteen when he was fifty. It was even more astonishing because the entire family had assumed his habitual shyness and obsession with reptiles of the British Isles (particularly slow worms) indicated a desire for permanent bachelorhood. There had also been conjectures based on his preference for music hall. Yet, he had proudly presented the girl to the family on the wedding day—Eliza Smith from Brighton whose family made a living in wholesale wines and spirits.

The couple had no children and rarely attended family gatherings, yet when they did the physical tension between them remained curious to her in a way other adult relationships did not. She had felt a small physical thrill in their presence.

Addie had once asked, 'Are you her father?'

The uncle had roared with laughter and said, 'No child, but I am old enough if that's what you mean.'

Harriet had shivered. Addie had giggled behind her hand.

The cat proceeded to a group of Eveline's toys tucked beneath a white crochet blanket and lowered its haunches. The calculating expression in the animal's eyes reminded her of Dean Neeley.

'Sleekit…'

There was the sound of fluid under pressure hitting the carpet. An ugly toy with hooded eyes toppled sideways away from the sodden blanket. Harriet lunged, hands outstretched as the cat sprang nimbly to one side. In two strides the animal was at the top of the stairs. It fled, pausing momentarily at the bottom to watch Harriet scurry downwards, then walked unhurriedly out of the open door into the garden.

Harriet stood looking out at the outbuildings and stunted scrub, and wondered how anything could survive outside if Anna's description of the climate were true.

6

A hundred years ago, James Poke made a pact with the soil at Erskine. In exchange for fertile seed he gave his labour and life. He was bound to the promise, for good or bad.

He dragged seaweed tangles up from the shore by Storrtang, where piles of kelp smouldered in heaps. He resisted the lure of cash that made his brother-in-law neglect his croft and took stinking bales to Erskine. Seaweed, thick with flies, lay on the banks at the top of the lane, waiting to be washed by the spring rain.

Weeks later, when curlew calls bubbled through the dusk, James dug the mass of dark fibres into the soil. The earth was dry enough to crumble between his fingers, warm to touch.

His wife Gudrun had been awake since before sunrise, milking, skimming and churning. A bright yellow pat of butter and squeaky farmhouse cheese waited with bannocks inside. If they'd had a boy the year they were first married he'd be helping now. If they'd had a girl the house would echo with more than the sound of song and labour.

Year after year the sunset moved along the horizon from the shores of West Mainland to Flotta without a birth. Gudrun counselled him to be patient.

'James, come in now.'

James finished thinning a row and then pulled upright, his head and shoulders framed against the fading blue. Sweat broke on his forehead and his breath was quick. He took his hoe into the outhouse where chickens roosted and ewes and lambs were penned.

Gudrun was strong and comely, with quiet confidence. She had been queen of the lasses that came at shearing time, with an ancient name, one never said with the sing-song air like other names. Her eyes shone like they'd been stolen from Spanish shores.

The days stretched and declined and still Gudrun never fell with child.

They sat together, and bannocks were shared and slices of salty cheese cut.

'I want to get the boy up here.'

'Boy?' said Gudrun.

James nodded.

'Thorfinn. Thorn as the baby calls him.'

He picked up a slice of cheese. Half way to his mouth it crumbled into two pieces, one falling to the floor. He ate the portion he held, then stooped down and picked up the fallen piece and put it into his mouth.

'You can give over some dairy work, pick up books again. If you want.'

Gudrun's gaze travelled to a shelf where a handful of volumes rested with the rare newspapers James brought back from town. Most of the pages were filled with commercial advertisements and announcements, but there were fragments of news. It might have been fiction for all they saw of the world.

James's sister Janet was fertile as Mither o the Sea. Her man, Robert, was an eager tup for work, even as grey advanced at his temples. There would be another baby by Michaelmas.

Storrtang was hard by the shore, and all the time poorer for being assaulted by the sea. At high-tide with a southerly blow, boulders the size of a man's head were thrown over the crumbling dykes, saltwater bleached the soil and the animals suffered miserable shelter.

His brother-in-law, Robert, would stand glaring at the bursting foam as it rose, rain bouncing on his shoulders, daring it to breach the dyke. He vented fury at the water, cursing its trespass and telling anyone who would listen that he was leaving for Canada to find a decent piece of land. Time after time, the morning came and the storm cleared, and he forgot the promise.

James kenned Janet cared for her children, but knew she might spare the one she loved most. A child might act as a good omen and Gudrun fall with her own. Hadn't a woman in Burray had twins at forty-five. Gudrun was a decade younger still, even though they lay together less frequently and his patience with the act was short.

Thorn was first born, a set-apart boy, lean and sinewy with eyes the colour of ash. He had been christened Thorfinn, but was never called by name since his sister lisped out "Thorn" for the first time to call her brother. He had a coolness that drew Robert's anger like none of the other bairns. A minor offence that would be overlooked in his other children would ignite violent disputes. He had seen it himself one evening when Thorn was ladling out supper.

'Put that down, boy,' said Robert.

'I'm hungry,' said Thorn.

'You think you're hungry after doing next to nothing all day?'

Thorn had kept spooning stew onto his plate.

'How hungry do you think I am?' said Robert.

Thorn paused and held out the plate to his father.

'Take it then.'

Robert tucked his finger beneath the rim, looked his son in the eye then flicked the edge. The boy flinched as the scalding contents hit his chest. He stood with a placid face. 'Sorry, Fither.'

Rather than strain or resist he became limp as a rag when he was seized; slack as unanchored kelp. Robert seized the paddle for shaping butter and clobbered it around Thorn's body, as if reshaping his son until the peedie sister began to whine.

Janet waited until her husband was away, then took Thorn in her arms. Janet had that tenderness for Thorn even when he'd long outgrown her lap. Any injury would be gently compressed, bruises cooled with water from the burn.

Thorn gave small protest and relaxed to her touch. There was a warmth between them neither from sun or peat, nor the whisky taken from the drawer in Robert's high-backed chair.

A terrible beating had come Thorn's way after he'd left the new Cheviot ram untethered. The animal had wandered and drowned itself, ending its own life, heedless of the consequences to Thorn. The next afternoon Thorn stayed inside, leaning against the rounded hood of his father's chair nursing a swollen eye and cut lip, a blanket over his knee and a dram from his mother in his hand. He watched the twirls of smoke climb from the red hearth to the lum above. Occasionally, Janet looked over from her work and smiled sadly at her son. She swore Thorn would have been the brightest in school if his father had let him stay on.

The latch clicked, released from its hold the door flew open from the wind. Robert, agitated by the enemy chewing his land, was in no mind to catch Thorn in his chair. A black veil dropped over his eyes.

'Should you like that chair from now on?'

Robert's voice had cut under the wind like a travelling wave. Janet watched in silence, hands paused.

'Think you're a man, do you?'

Thorn had knocked back his dram, sending fire through his body. Robert roared and jolted Thorn onto the floor. The empty glass shattered on the flagstones. Shards cut into Thorn's hands as he pushed up from his knees.

If Thorn's eyes had held the least shadow of respect then his father might have relented. If he had shown fear or lost his dignity and passed water like his younger brothers, then his father might have clapped him on the shoulder with mocking good humour and left him with one good clout. But Thorn's lips tightened and Robert stilled, a last lull before the full flood of rage.

Thorn had been wrenched from the floor, thrown hard against the wall and then dragged out into the steading. The sickly smell of animal waste hovered above the salt-ruined earth. Robert hoisted the boy from the ground and held him dangling.

Thorn saw his mother reaching out. The boy had been her delight, a consolation after a poor year.

Robert straightened his arms and pitched the boy over the dyke. Thorn grasped for handholds in the air, legs akimbo in the empty space. His body dropped out of sight, down onto a red nose of stone the size of a calf. Thorn's hip hit the hump of stone and twisted him around. He met the sand with a thud.

At first Thorn could not decipher the crowded signals of pain, then sharp and sickeningly clear he knew the worst injury by far was to his hip. The socket burned, lines of white pain radiated down his thigh. His body spasmed, doubling the pain, and he blacked out.

A bonxie perched on the dyke and turned its stony eyes on the discarded boy. On Robert's order, no one came.

7

Sleekit took up position by the green plastic cone, hind legs tucked, forelegs to attention, tail coiled. The remains of last night's chicken released rank odour in the protected nook. There were scratch marks in the earth where rats searched for the source of the smell.

Sleekit was alert to a new threat, the scent of a predator.

The thicket of rosa rugosa formed a vertical forest against which the cat detected the slightest horizontal movement. Bright butterflies of green leaves were beginning to appear against the grey stems. Deeper inside the thicket two boxes rested in the sparse spring foliage. One was the size of a large shoe box and made of black plastic, familiar around local domestic drains. The scent of dead rat still tickled the cat's nose.

The other box was wooden, sturdily built with an entrance on either side and grills through which is was possible to see the bait inside: an egg.

So far Stoat had remained untempted by the lure of the trap, noting its presence and passing by. She had instead found and killed a vole litter in a ground burrow.

Inside Erskine, Harriet searched for detergent, cleaning cloths and rubber gloves. She cursed the cat and herself, irritated at the thought that Anna would have both prevented the accident and cleaned more thoroughly.

~~~

The Wildlife Trust van trundled away, jogging Clem down the

lane to the smooth tarmac road. He patted his leg and smiled at bumping shoulders with Ernest. Him like a piece of jelly, and his uncle steady as a rock. Ernest was a miracle for being still.

The van drew up to the junction opposite Storrtang. A gouged-out track led to the shore where carts had once dragged burnt tang. It was disappearing under weeds and the old dyke's stones were being distributed by the tide. Steven Scarth had taken the better stones from the house and stacked then against the end of his barn where they still rested. Moss and grass grew in crevices until torn away by the wind and the walls facing the shore were strewn with whitening strips of bladderwrack and matted pink and green fibrous layers of dulse.

Clem thought it would be fine to wake inside the walls of Storrtang on a bonny morning and step barefoot to the rock pools. He liked thick walls, and the feeling of being safe they gave. His class had once gone on a trip to St Magnus church on Egilsay. He'd lost his sheet of questions, and told to sit on his own had been happy to stare up at the high white sky balanced above.

It was not like Balfour Rise. He easily put holes in those walls. He must lock his door. People on the scheme called him 'Half-mast' like at school. If Ernest heard the name Clem saw a look of disapproval. The same as when people called his uncle 'One-shoe' instead of Ernest.

It was a subtle look, never followed by a word.

Most often his uncle called him 'beuy', the same as everyone else.

Auntie Meg didn't like Balfour Rise or the nearby shop. He was not to go to the shop all the time. Not to buy things he did not need.

There was a stoat trap in the ditch by the side of the road. Clem sat up straight and pointed.

'No cheust noo, beuy,' said Ernest. 'Kieran's wanting tae gae tae Burray.'

Clem nodded and lowered his hand.

'Aye, well spotted though.'

Kieran glanced over and nodded.

'Demn pity, stoats got across these,' said Ernest, gesturing towards the first of the manmade causeways between Orkney's main island and the southern isles. Built by Italian prisoners of war to protect the British fleet in Scapa Flow during the Second World War, the Churchill Barriers were a wartime feat of engineering, and miserable hard work.

'Stoat's a good swimmer,' said Kieran. 'Three kilometres, I'd hazard.'

The words were delivered rapidly, vowels clipped to almost nothing.

'Problem with re-invasion on Secretary and Resolution back home,' said Kieran. 'Have to keep traps set and checked so population doesn't re-establish.' He paused at the junction and headed onto the first barrier. 'Only takes one pregnant female.'

The land flowed away behind them, a line of pasture low to the shore gradually rose to become the high cliffs of Rose Ness. A beacon stood against the horizon. They had set traps up there among the high pools, among the bog cotton and strong winds.

Kieran guided the van past the rails that separated the road from the concrete blocks and the water. The distinctive outline of Erskine's high roof was easy to spot, surrounded by a ruff of grey undergrowth.

Kieran's last words puzzled Clem. One female? Maybe he had not understood. Didn't you need a breeding pair? Ernest did not seem concerned. Clem stayed quiet and watched the Italian Chapel and airfield on Lamb Holm pass.

'Tides might be a problem,' said Kieran.

He squinted at the water.

'I bet you don't get too many things swimming between the islands.'

At this Clem turned and spoke.

'I can swim.'

'Good for you,' said Kieran.

'Not in the sea.'

'No?'

Ernest remembered telling Clem to never go beyond his waist in the sea. 'The muckle stoor worm'll takk a beuy oot o his depth.'

There had been plenty of taunts at his endeavour of teaching Clem to swim. The old pool had been poorly heated and steeply shelved; it would have been a different matter in the new sports centre. But then there would have been no diving board. It had been the boy's treat to take a turn on the board. He'd gone from fairly needing to be rescued from drowning to kicking himself to the surface and pawing through the water to the ladder.

Meg had not taken part except to clean and wash towels and trunks. But she had been waiting for them the day Clem finally got his deep-ender certificate. She'd given him a plastic pocket to keep it safe and had taken a photograph. It was pride of place on the mantlepiece.

Ernest's face grew pale at the happy memory.

'Ever do any diving?' said Kieran.

Ernest shook his head and Clem turned down of the corners of his mouth. People drowned diving, or took things from the sunken ships not to be touched.

The hillside rounded and the road passed a stretch of bright green windbreak stapled to the fence posts of a newly built house. As they came to the crest of the brae Kieran's phone broke the silence in the cab. The young man's hands tensed, the shortened index finger on his left hand curled as the ringtone repeated.

The tune took Kieran back to a shady verandah where a kowhai tree with vivid yellow flowers was in bloom and Mish was walking up to his parents' door for the first time, green-grey eyes under a dark fringe.

By the time the van stopped in a lay-by overlooking Scapa Flow the phone was silent. 'D'you mind?' said Kieran.

'Let's stretch wur legs and see aboot this sign,' said Ernest.

Ernest caught the door as it swung open in the wind and held it for his nephew.

Kieran watched the pair walk to the tourist notice, neither reading but focusing their attention on the stretch of water. Clem's thin hair caught the breeze, his top-heavy body seemed sunk halfway down to the knees of his blue overalls. Ernest was a foot shorter, lean as a fence post in comparison. The older man observed with close attention a new accommodation rig that had come in for shelter, a 'floatel' with great iron legs. At night, the tankers and rigs with their lights and the flare of Flotta's oil terminal stack were hard and bright in the dark.

Kieran turned away. His mother lost track of time differences and he didn't return her calls half the time, but it was past ten o'clock at night in New Zealand. A pulse grew behind his eyes as he waited for someone to answer.

8

Ten o'clock was late for his parents to even be awake. The flutter in Kieran's chest grew. 'K-P?'

His chest tightened.

'Mish?'

He tipped over the wheel, gaze fixed in the mid-distance picturing his ex-girlfriend.

'Why're you at Mum and Dad's? Where's Toni?'

'She's in Hong Kong. Anyway, your mum couldn't figure out if you'd be awake.'

Kieran interrupted.

'I thought you were in Timaru?'

A vision of the bright flat town with broad streets passed through his mind, flailing cabbage trees stood out like paper cutouts against a vast blue sky.

'It wasn't working out.'

Kieran took a short breath.

'You said couldn't stand Christchurch after the quake.'

'Listen,' she said. ' I've been trying to get through for an hour and it's late.'

'Signal's sketchy in Holm.'

'Ham?'

'It's spelt H-o-l-m.' Kieran sighed. 'It doesn't matter.'

The sound of a jug boiling in the background brought Kieran straight into his parents' kitchen. A line of wall cabinets and a melamine counter, an easy chair where the dog curled and a table that would have been folded since he'd left.

'I wanted to make sure your dad's okay.'

'What's the silly bugger done?'

'Got home with a gouge out of his head and face knocked up.'

He pictured her sardonic smile at other people's crises.

'He took Charlie to the park on Hamilton Drive. He was pretty confused when he got back. But he still had his wallet and Charlie on the lead. The paramedic said to go to the after-hours clinic and your mum called to ask if I could look after Charlie. Anyway, I drove them in.'

'What about the police?' said Kieran.

'No one attacked him. Must have walked into something. Your mum says the optician recommended months ago that he give up driving. She says they have a system and she tells him when to go at junctions.'

40

'She's always done that. Jesus, you do that.'

There was a short silence at the end of the line.

'I'm going to take Charlie for a few days. Give her a break.'

Kieran's lips twitched at the thought of Mish out jogging with the tiny Skye terrier skittering alongside.

'Can I speak to Mum?' said Kieran.

He waited as the phone was passed over the kitchen table.

'How are you getting on?'

After living in Singapore an ex-pat English way of speaking still lingered in his mother's voice.

'Fine, looking over Scapa Flow. How's Dad?'

'Can't remember anything, wouldn't go to hospital. I called Michelle. She's stayed until we could get hold of you. She didn't have to.'

Kieran could hear Charlie shaking his collar, imagined Mish fussing over the dog's ears. There was a slight pause.

'Did she tell you?' said Kieran.

'I knew you broke up. Why else would you take a job so far away? At least your father's embarrassed to be badly behaved in front of her. He's such a nuisance.'

'Dad or the dog?'

'Never takes doctors seriously if they're younger than him. I've told him I'm not getting in a car with him driving again. Michelle's got a nice place in Avonhead, big section, plenty of space. Have you found a flat yet? '

Outside, Ernest was pointing at one of the floatels and encouraging Clem to look down the length of his arm.

'Look Mum, it's starting to rain, and these blokes are waiting. Tell Dad I rang.'

'I don't think he's asleep. If you want a word.'

'Nah, it's ok.'

'How's your back?'

'Fine. I'll call tomorrow.'

'Take care. We miss you.'

9

The railed yards of the cottages facing the sea in St Mary's were obscured as grey rain flowed silently towards the southern isles and over Scapa Flow. Droplets began to tat on the side of the van.

Ernest had watched it come, hands in pockets, calm and still. Resigned. He'd hurried plenty of times to finish work for the electricity board before squalls arrived or darkness came. He should be a free man now. But, he had been so damned foolish.

Clem looked over to the van. He saw Kieran gesturing and nudged his uncle. He didn't mind a squall. Once he was wet he was wet.

'Come on then beuy,' said Ernest.

Clem wondered if the woman at Erskine had shut the door to keep out the rain. He wondered if he'd cracked the eggs he'd put in the van. Peedie strong things, eggs. Peedie fragile things, eggs.

~~~

At Erskine, Stoat paused by the trap and observed the egg. It glowed. She drew forward.

The area reeked of grease and rats, and the base of the green cone was soaked with spray. The sour smell of a male cat drew her attention. She stretched her polecat neck to sense the air, whiskers twitching.

The jill's bright eyes scanned the briars, paused and tuned into the tangled language of the wind and the sounds above her heartbeat. Sparrows were beginning to pair, emitting a tuneless and repetitive signalling.

She lowered back into the soft quiet of the thicket with the egg, snug in its wooden box. The shell was fleshy, hard and smooth, a thing of ineffable presence. An object of sacred stillness.

Stoat stayed by the egg as her hunger sharpened, a deep ache that drove her to hunt in preparation for the births to come.

A thrill rushed through her veins when she saw the cat. Unaware of being watched it sheltered in the hood of the byre. Stoat, nimble and quick, focused on her hunt. The black tip of her tail floated above the grass.

~~~

In the utility room, Harriet squeezed water from an intricate crochet blanket, one of Anna's projects during her final weeks of pregnancy with Eveline.

Outwardly, Harriet had admired her friend's attitude towards pregnancy. Anna had continued to work and travel, and stayed interested in the world outside her own body. Inwardly, Harriet's response had been more complicated.

When Anna's due date passed Harriet had finally made good on her promise to go and visit, prised away from Oxford to London during term time. The spacious flat near London Bridge had been bought when Anna was promoted to financial analyst. Martin moved in a month later. When Anna found out she was pregnant they married without telling anyone, and a week later held a party at The Ritz with Anna's bonus.

Harriet could never shake the feeling that the whole docks development was a film set, something knocked up for one of Martin's higher budget commercials. The windows of the apartments overlooked the Thames on one side and sunless warehouse alleyways on the other. A vegan cafe Addie favoured had trays of sprouting plants inside its windows and clusters of metal tables on the street.

Harriet had pressed the intercom.

'It's Harriet. Can I come up?'

'Well, I'm not coming down.'

Anna's laugh had cut off as the door released.

Harriet had stepped out of the lift on the fourth floor. The door of Anna's flat was ajar and she had felt for a moment like she was again in a film, a thriller. However, there was no corpse or evidence of violence inside, only furnishings in Scandinavian blue and orange, and floor-length windows that looked over the Britannic grey of the capital.

Anna was without make-up, dark hair pulled back into a ponytail, concentrating intently on a crochet hook and a length of ivory wool. The product of her industry rested on the mound of her belly. Anna should have sworn, thrown her crochet to one side and said she wasn't going to stand being under house arrest any longer. But Anna had held up a spiral of scalloped stitches and said, 'It's based on fractals. Can't you tell?'

'Oh,' said Harriet. 'Fractals. Very mathematical.'

They had stepped into new territory, an empty beach that stretched wide and flat with silent distant waves.

'There's a hyperbolic pseudosphere that would make a fun toy. You don't need a pattern once you understand the logic. '

'If you say so,' said Harriet.

The door to the bedroom had opened and Martin entered the room.

'Thank God, Harriet. There's a bloody balls-up. The short film guy, what's his name? Scottish? Who won the award.'

'Karim,' said Anna.

'Yes, him.' Martin pointed then ran his hand through his hair. 'Scottish and…very talented.'

'But?' said Harriet.

'Suffers from terrible motion sickness.'

'So?'

'The client happens to be…'

Martin repeated a familiar car advertising slogan.

'Oh dear,' said Harriet.

44

'It's a real mess. He won't get into anything that moves. I need to go and clear things up.'

'Rubber glove job?'

'Not funny, Harriet. Keep Anna here and in one piece until I get back. If you do leave the building on no account is she to walk more than fifty yards.'

'I promise,' said Harriet, holding up crossed fingers.

Harriet saw that dealing with a carsick, hungover, temperamental, award-winning director who in four years would probably be collecting a BAFTA had been a godsend for Martin. A ticket away from Anna's crochet.

~~~

Harriet shivered as rivulets of cold water travelled down her arms into the sink. In the centre of the lawn the strap-like leaves of a giant clump of flax bent violently backwards, exposing striped undersides, tips flickering like snake tongues.

She squeezed and rinsed, gradually removing the cat's urine from the blanket. Did Eveline still sleep with the blanket? When did children stop needing that sort of comfort?

She could not remember having anything of the sort, but maybe she had.

She had a flashback to childhood, the night Addie had moved into her own bedroom. Left alone, the room sounded different, the walls felt further apart, her own heart smaller, inadequate to the task of beating through the night on its own. Addie had skipped away in her red pyjamas, gleeful at the prospect of a first night alone. Harriet could not understand why it hurt so much, and why she must stop herself from wanting Addie back. And why she never once said anything about how she felt.

Three nights afterwards, just before dawn, Addie appeared back, drowsy and smelling of sleep.

'Can I come in?'

Harriet had shifted over, flinching away from her sister's

45

cold feet. They had slept knee to knee, breathing each other's spent air.

Harriet's throat tightened. The memory of childhood was replaced with memories of Art, and then of Martin, and numerous wrong things she had done. When Anna and her family departed she would be alone, left at Erskine with the breeze block-weighted bins and a lichen-covered wall.

She must work to save her career, compose erudite top-tier-articles, she must fulfil her obligations to the Leverhall Trust funding. She must think clearly, she must work hard and rescue what she could. She must put feelings away.

She had known the risk of being with Art, and had set it aside. Out of passion? Out of obsession? Out of weakness? Out of honesty?

She let her mind and body give way just a little more to her feelings long before anything happened. She persuaded herself that there was no risk in thinking about him when she was alone. Private thoughts did no damage.

So, when something finally occurred it had felt inevitable— and the risk insignificant.

10

Harriet hung the blanket to dry then stretched warmth back into her fingers. She returned to the kitchen to see Anna's hire car curl between the gate posts. It lost traction briefly then groped its way toward the house. Anna exited the driver's side, hair whisking upwards as she hurried around the bonnet to open the passenger door. She held it against the wind as Martin emerged, head bowed, a bloodstained handkerchief to his nose.

46

Once Martin was clear, Anna let the door slam and took her husband's arm and guided him through the horizontal rain.

Harriet was waiting at the open door.

'I warn you I'm not good with blood.'

Anna rolled her eyes, deposited Martin in the hall, then went back into the rain. He looked over the handkerchief and said something, then fumbled in his pocket. He drew out a folded tissue and gestured Harriet look inside.

An incisor, with its curved fresh pink root intact, tumbled to the edge of the tissue. Harriet flinched. The tooth fell, hit the floor with a ping and rolled out of sight.

'Jesus. Why didn't you say something?' said Harriet.

Martin groaned.

She went to hands and knees and scanned the wooden floor, wincing at the thought of contact with the errant tooth.

The door swung open again. Droplets of rain spat into the hallway. Anna had Oscar in her arms and Eveline under a coat,

'Stop! It's on the floor,' said Harriet. 'He gave it to me.'

'Martin, what were you thinking!' said Anna.

Harriet moved a pair of slippers and reached forward using the tissue to protect her fingers.

'Mulk,' said Martin.

'He means milk,' said Anna. 'You're meant to put it in milk. I've made an emergency appointment at Island Dental.'

Eveline stared at the tooth Harriet held up, eyes wide at the fluff-covered object that until very recently had been part of her father. Oscar squirmed free of Anna's arms, broke into a run and headed upstairs. Anna led the way through to the kitchen, poured milk into a jam jar and dropped the tooth into the fluid.

'Oh Harriet, you look like you need a brandy,' said Anna.

The patter of Oscar's feet reverberated through the ceiling, followed by a cry of, 'Mummy, s'all wet!'

'Someone needs to look before walking behind swings,' said

Anna.

She wagged her finger at her husband. Martin shifted side-ways.

'Eveline found it wedged between the safety mats. I thought he'd broken his nose as well, but I think it's been spared.'

Anna bent down and kissed her daughter and rearranged her wind-strewn hair.

The rattle of rain on the windows ceased as the shower passed and the sound of running could be heard more clearly above.

'Do you want something?' said Anna.

Eveline shook her head, her gaze turning to the stairs. There was a crack of something on a hard surface followed by a series of irregular, muffled bumps followed by a sharp cry.

Anna spun and strode towards the noise, Eveline skipping behind.

Harriet caught Martin's eye; they hesitated then followed. When they arrived Anna had Oscar was in her arms and was already determining what hurt most. Blond curls clung to the side of his face as he sobbed.

~~~

The boy reasoned that Harriet must have been playing with the toys. Harriet had to stay in their Orkney house after doing something 'a bit silly'. Silly could be funny and bad.

Naughty was just bad. Burying Eveline's inhaler in the sand-pit had been naughty. It had made white lines appear on his mother's nostrils.

He wriggled against his mother's embrace, tugging at the toes of his wet socks.

'Do you want to take them off?' said Harriet.

Oscar nodded.

'What done silly?' he asked Harriet.

Harriet's forehead wrinkled.

'I'm not sure what you mean?'

48

His mother smiled and answered.

'You're not silly, Oscar. You slipped. It was an accident.'

Harriet pinched and pulled. Oscar's exposed toes rippled in relief. A thumb travelled to his mouth and settled.

'I'll take Martin to the dentist,' said Harriet.

'Would you?' said Anna.

'I'd be a poor substitute here,' she said, looking down at him.

Anna glanced at Oscar busily lacing his fingers into her dark waves.

There was recovery, even from the very worst pain. It was a lesson Anna had learnt the day her father did not return from work, killed on impact in a head-on collision.

For hurt to heal did not mean love lessened. It had taken a long time to understand this.

After Harriet and Martin drove away Anna took out paper and pens. Oscar sat quietly mark-making, Eveline drew faces. The house kept the atmosphere of someone having cried, a ghost that accompanied the rest of the day. She would not want her children becoming fatherless; Martin had her there.

11

A shard of rainbow rested on Lamb Holm. Kieran passed the junction for Erskine, saw Harriet waiting for the van to pass, Martin at her side.

He turned briefly to take in the woman's appearance. The strong nose and tapering eyes had an unexpected sympathy, her soft lips were fleshy but not wide. Her poise communicated a trace of vanity, an awareness of her own allure.

There was no vanity with Mish, queen of the four minute

49

shower, she washed when dirty and kept her body in condition. She had been part of the camera trap team, and anything resembling the sweet fragrance of the kakapo had become associated with her in his mind. Each egg had been replaced with a decoy to be incubated in safety, away from the threat of predation, successful hatchlings later returned to the nest.

The team had celebrated the first hatchling return with swigs of Monteiths. It had been the first night he and Mish made love. Kieran's jaw tightened and he refocused on the road ahead.

'Gettin a piece noo,' said Ernest.

Ernest reached forward, pulled Clem's hand away from the radio buttons, guided it to his nephew's knee and laid it down firmly. Clem wanted something hot from the piece van. Aunt Meg said to never mind crumbs at the piece van, the gulls cleared it up. A bacon roll was good.

They turned out of St Mary's village and onto the open road. In the quiet, Ernest looked inwards, back in time. He felt shame, rolling like a wave, sucking like an undertow forcing him to speak when his habit before had been silence. His words tumbled rapidly, blending without their usual rise and fall.

'Dae you mak yir own weights?' said Ernest.

'Long as you know the increments anything'll do,' said Kieran. 'A stoat wants a hundred grams on the touchplate to trigger the kill bar.'

'Aye. Efter you've checked the neb,' said Ernest.

'Stoat's smarter than a rat, even for a fresh egg. Bloody hungry critters, not bloody stupid. Feeding them up sometimes just to kill them.'

Ernest nodded.

He wondered if he could drill the routine of setting a trap into Clem, same as learning to swim.

Clem watched Kieran's hands as he talked, going and stopping in the air and letting go of the wheel until Ernest shot a glance that said, 'Look awey, you're starin noo.'

Clem turned to the outside, straining to glimpse rigs in Scapa Flow, then staring into the passing fields. Half a dozen Highland cows stood planted in the grass, thick russet fringes blown across pink-rimmed eyes. The fields, bleached by winter, were edged by the skeletons of weeds that whisked past on either side.

The house for the peedie folk was coming up.

He squinted at the blank windows of the miniature house, a fanciful three foot high building, grand, styled like a country mansion. Clem imagined long tables inside, heaving with farmhouse cheese, bannocks and beer. The peedie folk would have a merry fire burning, one playing a fiddle as small as his thumb. Cosier than Balfour Rise.

Clem didn't like to put the heaters on anymore. He shuddered at the memory of fumes and melted cloth.

Kieran reached forward and switched up the fan.

'I know mate, you got wet through,' said Kieran.

There was a glance between Ernest and Kieran. A brief, silent communication that threw cold water on Ernest's hope that Clem could ever be trained to set a trap.

~~~

Harriet slipped into third gear and accelerated to overtake. A blind summit warning passed unnoticed.

If she had paid the landscape more attention she would have seen tiny tracks of green along the burns that roamed the knuckles of the land. She wanted to get Martin, and the tooth at the bottom of its milky sea, to their appointment as quickly as possible.

The road ahead looked clear as she pulled out to overtake The Wildlife Trust van. In her mind's eye there was an image of Art laughing. He was lifting his hand and motioning her to stop because he was laughing so much, long black eyelashes curling away from closed eyes, shoulders shaking, head bowed as if he couldn't stand to be so happy. What had she said to make him laugh so much? They had laughed all the time.

An oncoming car appeared, as if placed by an invisible hand.

Harriet turned hard, swerved onto the left hand carriageway and scraped the opposite verge.

In the van Kieran stamped the middle pedal. Clem lurched forward, his forehead crashing onto the dashboard.

'Jesus…' said Kieran.

Mrs Oddie was wide-eyed as she swung past, hands gripped on the wheel.

'Holy hell!'

Harriet absorbed the furious curse, it became part of her, sucked into her cannoning chest; drama come, drama gone.

'Gotta ask if it's worth it,' said Kieran releasing his breath.

Clem rubbed his forehead.

'You're aal right, beuy,' said Ernest, patting his shoulder.

The corner of Clem's lips pulled downwards, his eyes were wet.

'Mind, you're gettin a piece noo. Whit'll you have?'

'I dinna ken,' said Clem, looking sideways.

Ernest looked to the front and steadied his own breathing while Clem turned to see where Mrs Oddie had got to. She had been the school nurse. He'd had to stand in line, pulled out of class, even though Auntie Meg combed through his hair every Friday night. He had lice once or twice when he was living with his grandparents, but when they were dead Auntie Meg saw he never had it again.

A plastic comb and then a metal comb, a flashing row of pins, up behind his ears and down the back of his neck, until every snaggle was gone and his hair stood every which way.

Some children took the shame easy from Mrs Oddie and spat in the playground and shouted swears, others got the shame hard and went to a quiet place and cry.

Clem touched the grill that separated the cab from the back. He imagined a giant egg nestled there, shining secretly in the gloom, the shell perfectly smooth. He imagined the smell of straw and the good warm smell of hens. The stoats would line up for that egg. He forgot his head was sore and leaned on the wire.

'Turn aboot, beuy,' said Ernest.

Clem put his hands on his knees and fixed his gaze ahead. Poor stoats. He was glad they were not hung up on walls for all to see.

~~~

Gradually, Mrs Oddie composed her story to tell. Her heart settled. 'Whit if I hid swerved?' she'd say over the counter, taking a packet of square sausage. 'Good God, I thowt hid wis my time.'

There would be a satisfying commiseration and condemnation of the feckless individual who had not enough sense to value their own life.

12

Harriet was breathing hard.

'Doo awl right?'

Martin lowered the tissue from his nose.

She couldn't see anywhere to pull over and stop, so she kept going. Waves of sickness hitting. The fence posts went on and on, houses and driveways. Where could she stop? Someone might be watching. The van was gaining on her, the three men inside, all staring ahead. How could she have not seen what was ahead of her?

Martin reached out his hand and nudged the fabric of Harriet's coat aside, searching for the warmth of her knee. He thought about The Red Lion, her showering and redressing. He had been a father for six weeks, and was closing a funeral plan advert deal. He'd joked with Harriet about 'Cover & Care' when she insisted he wear a condom. In his experience, most seduction was actually persistence. There was an element of good fortune, and this was the recent departure of the tympanist from Harriet's life. Of course Harriet was missing Anna, motherhood was a big change, demanding. They were both missing her. He'd kissed Harriet and felt no resistance.

There are times, thought Martin, when I should stop. But I don't.

Did I walk behind the swing because I was bored to death of standing in a two-bit paint-peeling play park in the freezing wind, waiting for my son's urge for physical activity to be overtaken by my son's need for food? Or was it just to get attention from Anna?

He had actually been distracted by a passing herring gull, wings cocked, dart-headed into the wind. The constant movement of air wore on his nerves. The island might be a haven, but it was also desolate. The small desolations they were the worst, because there was no excuse for them. They could be described as weaknesses.

Anna had commanded the children to stand still and found tissues. It was all part of her solicitous provision and aftercare.

Martin's thoughts drifted. He pushed open Harriet's coat further. The cloth beneath was soft. His hand shifted towards the inside of Harriet's thigh.

He thought of his mother and her secret glasses of wine, standing hidden behind the door of the fridge gulping quickly and then bringing the bottle out and announcing it was time for her 'first.'

'Martin?' said Harriet. 'I best concentrate. Don't want to

lose any more teeth.'

She moved his hand aside firmly.

It was on his mind to say, 'Do you not feel desolate? You must. You of all people, Harriet, in that coat–just the right sort of avant-garde for Oxford, but here out of place, neither wind or waterproof.'

But he didn't.

'Dearly caught me owt doo, dhese dips,' was what he said.

A thin smile stretched on Harriet's lips. Addie would have been merciless about Martin's speech. Martin raised the handkerchief back to his lips unaware of Harriet's amusement.

A crescent of shortbread-coloured sand became visible as Scapa Bay opened to the west, a jagged-roofed distillery perched on the hillside opposite.

They passed another black-walled distillery at the entrance to Kirkwall and then came through the outskirts to a new roundabout by the hospital building. Saplings had been staked hopefully along the roadside. Martin's mind focused on the soft gap between his teeth, a hollow so deep that the tip of his tongue could not reach the bottom.

'I never explained to Anna,' said Harriet in an undertone, 'about the cat.'

She signed and turned the wheel. The divorced tooth rocked sideways in its milky sea.

13

Kirkwall, with its red cathedral, Norse-named streets and people, had always been Ernest's family's home. At the harbour, a rank of hotels and bars pressed together, the stonework eroded and stouter than more southern seafronts. Around the circular pond and Peedie Sea, knives of daffodil leaves pressed through the grass. Blossom trembled on the branches of a small copse by the roadside. The day length was increasing rapidly, but the sun had no warmth.

Over-abundance of electricity and what to do with it, was the new the challenge in Orkney. Electricity couldn't be preserved like fruit was on the industrial tables at the County Show. There was no prize for the best presentation of renewable energy arranged on a plate.

Ernest thought of Meg measuring out her lengths of yarn to make sure she was in limits for the scraps and oddments category, a playful competition entered with utmost seriousness. Her patterns matured in winter, needles tucked under her arms like a skier intent on a pernickety downhill slope, as she produced woollens for the craft shop near the cathedral.

Ernest cast his gaze in the direction of the cul-de-sac where Meg would be stitching the seams of a newly finished gansey. Bonny and bright, she called the pattern. Clem was no doubt thinking about the dilemma of pastry or potato-topped pie and already forgetting the pain in his head.

'What did you do before you retired?' said Kieran.

'Engineer fir the hydro,' said Ernest.

From Ernest's appearance Kieran would have said he was only knocking on the door of fifty and he wondered how Clem looked much the same age as his uncle, although there were times he acted much younger, his bulky body and grey hair out of place.

'Used to work in tourism,' said Kieran, 'taking groups tramping around The Catlins.'

'Aye. A fine wilderness the Sooth Island.'

Kieran's eyebrows rose.

'You've been?'

Ernest nodded.

It was a trip Meg enjoyed. New Zealand had reminded her of Orkney with its open landscape and farms, each a stone's throw from the next. The quality of light, the red horizon beneath a greening sky, and the hint of borealis curtaining the stars had also made him nostalgic for home.

The van came to the filling station roundabout and took the Hatston Industrial Estate exit. Kieran turned abruptly into a narrow car park on the sea front. Square stones as big as sofas created a ridge that stretched across to the marina.

Despite the patched blue overhead a grimy sea lapped the rocks. Strands of cat-gut seaweed looped and tangled. Toward Shapinsay, low on the north-east horizon, an inter-island ferry broke free of the land and headed towards Kirkwall Bay.

It was too early in the season for cruise ships mooring at Hatston, they could be seen from just about anywhere in the town, disgorging coach loads of visitors to Skara Brae. Mechanical clunks and rattles meandered from the harbour along the sea wall and the smell of diesel smoke drifted on the easterly breeze—as much part of a sea journey as the chop of water and the needling cries of gulls.

'Comin an goin,' said Clem, looking out the sky.

Ernest nodded.

A car pulled out from a space overlooking the water. Kieran took its place. Clem smiled to see his boss getting the hang of things.

Ernest sighed. He couldn't blame Meg for thinking less of him when he told her what had happened. Reputations were only as good as their wearers. He knew there was no choice except to tell her. In time.

Ernest cleared his thoughts and slipped back into his old self. He turned to Clem.

'Bacon roll?'

'I'll get these,' said Kieran.

'No. Clem'll want tae be in line tae choose, no doot.'

The flush on Clem's cheeks had faded by the time he was at the open hatch of the mobile catering van. Fluorescent stars of cardboard adorned the serving space. Ronnie understood folk needed to be prompted what to buy— and be reminded that sauce was twenty pence and not to be taken for free. Broad-chested and smiling, his apron was still decent and his manner improving as the line lengthened.

'Whit can I get you, One-shoe?' said Ronnie.

'Bacon roll an…whit's hid tae be, beuy?'

Clem looked over at the savouries beneath the heat lamps. He'd made up his mind on a bacon roll, but the starburst reminding him of hot sausage rolls had thrown him.

'Beuy?'

'I'll tak a pie.'

'Mince?' said Ronnie.

'Aye,' said Ernest, 'an wan coffee wi sugar, wan withoot, wi lids.'

Clem picked up a sachet of tomato sauce.

'Sauce as weel?' said Ronnie.

Ernest nodded and paid. He waited for Ronnie's daughter, a broom of a girl, to pass out the food and drinks.

'No a bad day,' said Ernest.

'Always warm in the van,' she said.

Kieran was next in line.

'Yeah, I'll have a bacon roll and…' He paused remembering the last coffee he'd had from the van. 'I'll try a cup of tea.'

'Try hid? You'll be buying hid, beuy. Hid's no a wine tasting.'

Ronnie smiled. The new stoat man didn't seem to ken what he was speaking about half the time, he passed a slip of paper to his daughter.

Kieran took his food and drink.

58

'Cheers.'

'No bother,' replied the thin girl. Her gaze followed Kieran as he walked away, a smile floating over her lips at the sight of his boots and bare knees.

They were laughing in the queue, holding someone up for fun. The sounds of the rapid, rhythmic speech of the snack van made Kieran suddenly melancholy.

14

The smell of fried meat reminded Kieran of barbecues in the back yard. He thought of his father. He'd not be a good patient and, before the day was out, he'd want the dog back. Kieran hadn't told his parents about the breakup with Mish because he couldn't face his father's stare. The exact same one he got after driving the ute into a chain across the Fresh 'n Go carpark exit.

Kieran's sister had been in the car, going for a ride to break up the monotony of a dull mid-winter day. They'd hung around the supermarket for a bit and he'd given her change for chocolate fish. Toni had squeezed herself into the toy car meant for little kids and made Kieran laugh till his ribs were sore.

The chain had pulled out of its brackets, buckling the bonnet and scratching the side panels when the links finally gave.

'How did you bloody miss it?'

'I didn't see it.'

'All you had to do was get a loaf and some tomato sauce.'

Kieran had been eighteen. To his shame tears had risen in his eyes.

'Did you have seatbelts on?'

'Yes, for Chrissake,' said Kieran.

Toni had been eleven years old and listening in the doorway, white as a sheet. She nodded.

The accident had felt like an adventure, but she'd known what would happen when they got home. 'No one uses that exit anymore. You can't see to pull out.'

'I'm sorry,' said Kieran.

'No one uses it. I've told you a dozen times.'

Kieran had looked down at his shoes just like he'd done as a kid and wished he could disappear.

Back in Orkney in the present he noticed a jandal stuck in the sea wall. It was striped with an orange thong. Kieran pushed away the ache from thinking about home, balanced his tea on the van roof, knelt down and fished it out. He looked up at a passing bird and picked out the spire of St Magnus Cathedral over the top of the mothballed power station as he strolled to the bin. He wondered why people called Ernest 'One-shoe'? He wondered if herring gull guts were as full of plastic as the albatross back on the Otago peninsula. Shearwaters were worst, feeding bottle tops to newly hatched young. Didn't discriminate.

He pushed the shoe into the bin so it couldn't be wheeled out by the gulls and sighed, appetite gone. He hadn't remembered Toni was going to Hong Kong. Mish had kept tabs on that sort of thing.

15

Harriet turned left towards the red pin indicating the dental clinic on her phone, and transgressed a no-entry sign.

Tam Berwick stepped aside stoically, noted the car hire sticker, its distinctive female driver and the male passenger's bleeding mouth. Victoria Street was a narrow, shared pedestrian and vehicular street. For locals the one-way rule was as obvious as they come.

Ten minutes later Martin was in the dentist's chair, sinking as Phoebe Shawcross lowered him to a comfortable working position. She noticed that a small sliver, approximately four millimetres long, had been struck from the enamel.

'There's a small chip.'

Martin's forehead wrinkled into a frown above his stretched open mouth.

'I'll apply paste to seal the wound before it's inserted. It'll need splinting while the ligament heals.' She repositioned the light on Martin's face and saw the periodontal ligament was well preserved and the root intact, but hypoxia and necrosis had set in as soon as the blood supply was cut off from the tooth. 'There's no need for any sutures, the lacerations on the gum are superficial.'

She nodded to the nurse, who carried over a tray of instruments then stepped back. Phoebe glanced at Martin's glossy face beneath the lamp. He had the sort of mannish look that was cast for military roles on television. He wasn't really her type at all.

'Thanks, Cherry. I'm going to irrigate the socket. It will be uncomfortable. But it'll reduce the chance of infection as the root heals. You'll need to contact your dentist for follow-up root canal and X-rays.'

Martin winced and tried to pull back. The pain intensified into a sickening sensation as cold fluid hit the exposed nerve.

The nurse's gaze fell on Martin's white knuckles. She repositioned the suction pipe and her mind wandered to the bank transfer home she'd just made to the Philippines.

Phoebe moved back fractionally and picked up the tooth with gloved fingers.

'Would you prefer to do it?'

'Wha?' said Martin.

'Push it in.'

Martin's eyes widened. He shook his head. His body tensed as Phoebe firmly plugged the tooth in place. He gave a convulsive twitch then slumped, sweating profusely.

'You should check your tetanus is up to date.'

Martin nodded faintly.

'Because of the swing,' she added.

'Was your son hurt?' said Cherry.

'Yesh,' said Martin. 'Tewible mump on the shairs.'

He mimed a lump coming out the side of his forehead.

Twenty minutes later, paperwork and payment were complete. Harriet pulled out and began to negotiate the winding street. The thought that she had been intimate with Martin added to her hormonal nausea.

'De wan-ned me do doo id,' said Martin, breathing awkwardly through his mouth.

Harriet nodded, but didn't reply. Martin turned and regarded narrowed eyes. Her concentration switched from side to side as pedestrians squeezed past throwing quizzical glances in their direction. The Wildlife Trust van was heading towards them.

'Shit. How do I get through?' said Harriet.

Rain flicked across the window. Harriet's hands left damp patches on the wheel and her abdomen clenched with menstrual cramps. She reached forward to wipe fog from the windscreen.

'Why doesn't he bloody get out the way?'

~~~

The cab of the van was calm. Clem was lifting the lid of his coffee, releasing steam, while Kieran and Ernest observed the woman from Erskine gesture with her hands.

Ernest checked his mirror, then put his hand on the door handle. Two cars whose drivers had seen the confusion waited opposite the bank at the top of the street.

'I'll see you back.'

'Cheers,' said Kieran.

Ernest stood behind the van and motioned with his hands.

Tam Berwick walked along keeping pace, 'Catchin many stoats, beuy?'

'Aye, twathree,' said Ernest.

'Seen a pair over Inganess Bay.'

'Takin over the coonty.'

Tam nodded and watched as the van sidled backwards into a parking space against the old butcher's shop. When Harriet came through Ernest signalled for her to open the window.

'Hid's wan wey,' he said.

'I didn't see any signs,' said Harriet.

Ernest sighed and lifted his hand and let her go on.

'What kind o body is she?' said Tam.

'Stayin at Erskine,' said Ernest. 'Gettin back on her feet.' He paused and added. 'You ken she's from Oxford.'

'That so?'

Tam walked away pondering the flagstones.

Ernest climbed back into the van for the remaining fifty yards to the office, a converted shop that had been an information centre for private tours, excursions by car, minibus, boat and light aircraft, complimentary tea and coffee provided. Unlike the neolithic monuments, tourist enterprises came and went.

The Wildlife Trust was expanding and had taken one of the largest commercial buildings in Victoria Street. In common with its neighbours it was made of grey stone taken from the shore, topped with slate, boasting a crow-stepped gable and small, deep-set windows. After months of negotiation the council agreed that a small sign saying 'Wildlife Trust Only' could be erected and an electric car charge point installed—the first in the Conservation Area.

'Do you know her?' said Kieran.

'Who?'

'The woman. Another writer? Place is full of them,' said Kieran.

Ernest shook his head.

'Scholar. From Oxford University, no doot.'

Kieran raised his eyebrows.

Ernest had nothing more to add. He felt for her, for anyone who was heading the wrong way. It was clear as day she was a fish out of water.

16

Kieran twisted, cracked his back then turned to the computer screen. There were two new stoat sightings and a message from Orkney Sales and Letting about a flat overlooking the harbour. His gaze lifted to the window and his mind drifted back to his mother's call. Ernest observed Kieran's preoccupation and decided it would be best to keep his nephew occupied.

In the back room Clem sat sipping his coffee. It was too early for him to go back to Balfour Rise and Ernest resolved to show him how to clean and set a trap again. Couldn't have Clem losing a finger. He'd lost him far too much already. And it wasn't going to be the retirement full of adventure he'd promised Meg.

Oh, it had started well, but now it was over. He remembered Meg smiling and touching the woven hangings on the market stalls in Bangkok where they stopped on the way back from New Zealand. Later, when the heat and jet-lag had caught up with her, Ernest had gone on his own among the young travellers, slim and shiny-skinned, smelling of tiger balm.

He had stood in front of a fifteen-metre reclining gold

Buddha in Wat Pho. He gazed at the smiling face and playful whorls on the giant toes as warm rain swept down in waves, breaking on a sea of umbrellas.

He had taken a boat ride along the Chao Phraya. The water, murky as pottery slap, hid giant carp from view. Their size as they broke the surface made him sit back in his seat, sucking mouths gulping air as they gobbled pellets thrown by tourists.

Ernest had retraced his steps back to the hotel, aware of doorways and passages, smooth walls and shadowy interiors.

'You wan Pad Thai?'

The hiss of batter frying turned his head.

What was he doing among these young people? With their half-grown beards, and their shoulders, hips and bellies exposed to the air. He was thirty years too late. A sense of disappointment had dogged his heels, not about the prospect of returning to Orkney, but the prospect of no longer having an occupation.

~~~

Kieran flicked open an old Department of Conservation template and began to cut and paste together a job description for a 'Wildlife Community Information Officer'. The new funding meant the operation could include outreach to schools and local groups. He glanced through to the back room. Ernest was midway through another demonstration for his nephew, pen and pencil in the top pocket of his blue boiler suit, a wire brush in his hand. He'd shown interest in the permanent paid position with a modest, 'I widna mind.'

Kieran liked Ernest's trimmed responses. He was sometimes more voluble at the piece van, taking part in the banter that went to and fro, with Clem listening eagerly. Ernest was key to local access and gathering meter readings had given him a manner that brought conversations to the point.

~~~

In Christchurch, the possum that had caused Charlie to pull over his father was venturing into Mr and Mrs MacKenzie's garden.

Later, as Harrison Mackenzie leaned on his garden fork and gazed on the reduced pile of bait his wife Rose came, tears welling as she passed on the news. John, their friend for thirty years, had passed away in the night.

'Do you think Kieran and Toni will get home? It's such a way,' she said.

'He's their father,' said Harrison.

'What about Jean?' she said. 'Poor Jean.'

'Think it took enough?'

He pointed to the bait.

'What?'

Harrison looked down at the crenelated outer leaves of the cabbages and the exposed pink veined edges chewed by the possum.

'I....I don't know. Will he come back from Scotland?'

'No two ways.'

'Jean had meant to go in and check on him,' said Rose. 'But she fell asleep. And when she went in this morning he was gone.'

Harrison's jaw tightened.

'They're a menace,' he said.

He shook his head, then gripped his fork handle more tightly and began to unearth the damaged crop.

17

'Hospital wouldn't have made a difference. Even if someone'd stayed up all night there's nothing they could've done.'

A rook croaked outside the office window, a stray from

Meadowbank. Kieran stared blankly, and tried to focus on the voice at the end of the telephone line.

'Kieran? You there?' said Mish.

He was remembering the ute, not the being yelled at, but how his father had shown him how to sand, coat and polish to get a deep finish. Kieran had paid every cent for the materials and he'd been proud of making good.

He remembered them driving over to Hamner Hot Springs when they were kids. Toni had dashed from one pool to the other, squealing from the cold.

Mish exhaled.

'I'm going to put your mum on.'

He wanted to say, 'No, please don't.' But said nothing.

He saw his mother as if she was before him, her chair with its back against the wall beneath the pride-of-place shelf, with its crystal clock and posies of china flowers. The noticeboard would have his postcard of the standing stones at Stenness, sky streaked mauve, fingers of stone breaking the landscape, and next to it a card with skyscrapers from Hong Kong.

There was a rustle as the receiver passed. He knew he should speak first, but nothing came.

'Kier..'

His mother's voice snagged on the first syllable of his name. Mish came back on the line.

'You'd better call back.'

Kieran punched himself hard on the leg, just to feel something. It released a brief burst of speech.

'How's she doing?'

Mish gave a sort of encouraging, sad chuckle then said, 'Putting one foot in front of the other.'

In the kitchen a shadow of a smile passed over Jean's face. She stood up from her chair and walked to the window. She stared at the coral pink and violet sweetpeas against the garden fence and saw seedpods were forming quickly. Summer was ending.

Beyond the fence on Hamilton Drive she could hear children's voices in the park, screams carrying in the bright air.

'Tell her I'll come. I want to…I'll…be there.'

The emotion in Kieran's voice released an ache in Mish's chest.

'Okay.' said Mish. 'I'm really sorry, Kieran.'

She waited until he hung up and then did the same.

'He's going to call back later,' said Mish, 'and find out about flights. You want me to call Toni?'

A bee floated over the scrambling flowers, it balanced on a welcoming keel and began to feed.

'No,' said Jean. 'I can do that one.'

18

It had been a day hard with hunger for Stoat. The vole litters were sparse after the cold winter and drought of early spring, the grain of harvest was a forgotten bounty.

All through the watchful day no one disturbed the thicket.

The egg was different in the afternoon. Its subtle roundness had a beguiling quality. The smell of men faded.

The noise and reek of cattle did not trouble Stoat. She was nimble and fly. Their reappearance into the fields when the land was greening and fecund held no anxiety for her.

The lifelong enemy was hunger, not predator or accident. The ditches were threaded with old trails, but nothing was enough to satisfy her needs.

And here was the egg, another egg, waiting in the wooden box that smelled of man and iron, and death.

Stoat was not blind to the fate of her forebears—all the stoats on the island were her forebears, it was a diaspora of kin.

Death and the egg waited. The allure played on Stoat's nerves and distracted her from the nearness of the cat.

19

Anna stood at the old door watching the rainbow fade. She'd laid out the fractals blanket found scrunched and dripping in the laundry and cleaned the carpet. Oscar was doing a rare thing, sleeping during the afternoon. He would have enjoyed the gaudy brightness that bridged St Mary's pier and Scarth's byre.

Sleekit yowled in the tangle of willow and dogrose and then shot into the open. Anna started then calmed as she watched the cat trot along the grass and disappear around the dyke. Inside Harriet's room her gaze lingered fondly on her friend's familiar possessions. She picked a silk nightdress from the floor, its fine threads caught in the ridges of her fingertips.

It would have been more economical to knock the croft flat and begin again, plasterboard would have been cheaper than repointing the stones, but it would have killed the place. She breathed deeply, searching for the scent of the old room. The original Erskine had never been smooth and watertight.

She remembered the high-backed hearth that had extended in a low wall, almost separating the original space in two. The flagstones had been soft with droppings and along with the sharp acidic smell there was the feeling of birds hidden and close. Collared doves had lifted as beams of light fell into the small secret space, her heart had beat faster and a chill had run down her spine when she had discovered the nook, the secret space hidden behind the wooden dresser.

'Is it listed?' she'd asked.

The young woman from the estate agents had shaken her head.

'This? No.'

'Could I change the original structure?'

Ellie nodded absentmindedly, thinking more about a pair of boots she had tried at lunchtime than the derelict croft.

'I want to make an offer,' said Anna.

Ellie had looked up from her shoes.

Anna corrected herself. 'Sorry, it's offers over here, isn't it. Is there a closing date?'

'I don't ken. Steven's had it on and off the market a peedie while.'

Ellie had paused and wondered if Mrs Chalmers knew what peedie meant. She better be professional if this was to turn into a sale, and keep quiet about what had happened. Even though it had been over a hundred years ago it felt as bad as lying. Steven Scarth would tell the new owner anyway. He talked to anyone who'd listen.

'You like it?' said Ellie.

'Yes.' Anna had said, 'I think it's what I need.'

A splatter of water had fallen between them, the drops whitening as they reflected the light in the broken space above. Ellie couldn't imagine life with an open lum. There was a farm museum in West Mainland where they'd preserved a house with its old hearth. She'd gone on a trip with her primary class. The twists of purple-blue peat smoke lifted and rose, coiling as if they were alive, up into the white square of the lum. A great flat fish hooked through the mouth had dangled in the path of the spirals, scales stiff and yellow. The sudden sight of the thing made her feel sick. By the end of day everyone had reeked of smoke and even though her cheeks had glowed from the fire, her feet had stayed frozen all day.

'I'm going to take some photographs,' said Anna.

Ellie shook away the memory and had watched Mrs Chalmers navigate the uneven surfaces in her high-heeled boots, soft leather with a gold zip at the back. Ellie wondered what you had to earn to buy boots like that, and to think nothing of tramping around a derelict croft full of bird shit.

'Do you want to see the garden?' said Ellie. 'It goes as far as the wall.'

Anna had tucked away her phone and they picked their way outside. She tilted her head skywards into the rain, searching.

The picture the estate agent had sent was a true representation, and yet it captured nothing of the level of dereliction, or the solar plexus thumping impact of the view out over the isles, a swept clean blue and green Eden.

Anna turned her back to the wind and tucked down the hair blowing across her face. Clean air. Those where the only two words she had given as a brief.

'I read there are skylarks here,' said Anna.

'In spring,' said Ellie. 'Hard to spot, but you ken they're up there.'

'Don't worry. I'm sold,' said Anna. In her mind's ear she heard the opening of The Lark Ascending by Vaughn Williams, sweet twisting notes that needed precise articulation, even as the sounds became undetectable, like colour dissolving into ultraviolet at the end of the day. She had smiled. 'It's just something I'd like to see, to hear, one day.'

~~~

When it had been explained that stoats were non-native and destructive to bird life Anna had become sympathetic to the New Zealander who'd called during the building work. He'd asked for permission to set traps as part of a pilot study. He assured her that the children could not get hurt and the stoats

71

died instantly. There would be regular monitoring and removal of carcasses.

'The green cones are a magnet,' he'd told her, nodding at the newly installed bins. 'Not for stoats so much, but attracting prey.'

She had made progress understanding Ernest's turn of phrase. His nephew Clem spoke rarely in her presence yet she hoped this would change over time.

Anna looked through the long windows at the narrow cleft in the hillside that ran from Erskine to Storrtang, the ruined croft by the shore. The builders complained about rats following the burn and The Wildlife Trust had provided rat traps as a sweetener to participating in the stoat study.

Last spring, when she had taken possession of the house, the burn had been thick with yellow flag iris and lurid green whips of willow. Sage green tips of daffodils were emerging and the cold air was sweetening again.

Anna turned away. A black cat sat cleaning its ears in the centre of the floor.

'How do you always find a way in?'

She lifted Sleekit into her arms. Thank God Eveline was not allergic to cats, at least not so far.

She went to sit with her daughter, stroking the cat with one hand and checking for return flights to London on her phone with the other.

She wondered if Martin had walked behind the swing deliberately. The only time she had seen him display physical courage was playing rugby in college. A series of black eyes resulted in him missing the chance to assist with child development research—he was unpresentable to parents and young children. At the time she patched his character weaknesses with the excuse of immaturity.

The cost of next-day tickets for flying back over the Pentland Firth made her sigh and pull the cat closer. She wondered how many locals could afford to fly.

'Mummy?'

'Yes.'

'Why did Daddy walk out behind the swing?'

Anna turned from her phone, raising an eyebrow.

'I don't know.' She glanced at her daughter's picture. 'That's a pretty scene.'

Eveline looked down at her paper and thought. How was it possible to draw a rainbow when they didn't really exist? You couldn't touch them, and Ernest told her last time that if you stood on the wrong side rainbows were invisible.

Ernest would be a good dad, Eveline thought. Even though he was old and hard to understand, and killed stoats for his job. You could tell by the way his hands managed things.

Her father's hands were soft, and didn't manage so well—he couldn't get Oscar off her tummy when he bounced up and down, and he couldn't find her inhaler, and he couldn't cut up apples so they had to eat them like cricket balls. He *could* give out chocolate when they were quiet and he was busy on the phone.

The rain moved and Eveline picked up a grey pencil and began to scribble over the multi-coloured arc.

'You're spoiling it,' said Anna.

'It's clouds,' said Eveline.

'Leave it.'

'No.'

Anna reached over, but Eveline pulled the paper away then screwed the sheet into a tight ball.

'I'm rubbish at drawing.'

It was a 'terrible' thing to say, but she said it anyway.

'Didn't I say it was pretty?'

'You're only saying that because you have to. It doesn't even look like here.'

Eveline pointed out of the window, light fanned over a paradise of fields mottled by clouds above.

'Well, it's not a photograph,' said Anna. 'It's your drawing.'

But Anna understood exactly what she meant—the more time she spent in Orkney, the less she felt able to relay what it was really like to anyone.

At six o'clock that morning, she'd been reading *The Tiger That Came To Tea* with Oscar and had watched the dawn break. It grew from a slash of deep amber, spreading and changing tone to luminous pink then streaking the belly of the clouds. Vapour trails from east to west deepened and flushed as the sky changed through pink to tangerine and finally mauve. After half an hour the colour withdrew, exhausted, and there was nothing left except tinted grey. Her memory balked at the truth of its brilliance.

How was Eveline to capture such paradox?

'Draw it as you like it.'

'I don't like it. I can't.'

Eveline felt her chest tighten. How was she ever meant to do things right? Why didn't the cat ever come to her when she loved it so much? Why did it go to her mother?

She stalked over to the kitchen bin, flipped the pedal and threw the screwed picture inside. Now there was no way for anyone to get it back. She felt her mother's gaze and the tide of breathlessness rising.

'Darling, do you need your puffer?'

20

In the much deeper past, the cold tide roused Thorn from his torpor. Its frothy kiss fell on his fingers and rolled onto his chest. He dragged himself a few metres out of its reach then lay exhausted in the hollows at the base of the cliff.

Dusk advanced. The water lapped, quietened and withdrew. The wind dropped and the sea became flat, the horizon two tight lips of grey. Thorn's younger brother found him, bringing a piece of bannock and a warning to not come home.

Thorn pictured his mother in the farmyard, hesitating and then sending Issac rather than coming herself. He wished he could cut himself loose from all of them, from Storrtang and the island that held him fast like filings to a magnet. He'd seen it at school—school he no longer attended because his father needed labour. He buried his face in his arms and wept, stiffening with cold, filled with bitter pain.

A month later when the offer came for Thorn to leave Storrtang he had sensed the peril it represented, but he did not refuse.

~~~

When Thorn arrived at Erskine Gudrun waited at the door. She had tilted aside to let her husband pass before inspecting the teenage boy. The rips in Thorn's clothes exposed his skin and showed purple and grey bruises. She noted the delicacy of his features, and wondered at his origin. She had heard the rumour that the lairds at Kingsgarth, dark-eyed and handsome in their youth, had a hand in more than making their rightful heirs.

Gudrun saw nothing of her husband in his nephew.

Time passed. The wind turned to the north and soon carried the sound of migrating geese. With an old man's determination the sea continued to chew the land around Storrtang, and the dunes curled and collapsed into the hungry tide. Thorn spoke little for the first month, addressing James if the three of them were together, preferring silence or communicating by gesture if he was alone with his aunt.

It gave Gudrun pleasure to hear Thorn speak fondly to the

cat. The boy had a habit of placing one hand behind its ears while the other played in the fur on the soft underside of its belly. Gudrun paused preparing fish for salting and had addressed her nephew, 'Friends are you now?'

Thorn nodded.

Gudrun had come to where the boy sat on a stool. She reached down and touched the cat beneath the chin, she rubbed its bristles and held out a scrap of fish. Thorn noticed how her eyes gathered the light filtering through the lum and became brilliant as pearls.

'He'll never sit when your uncle is inside.'

Thorn began to say something, but instead of speaking aloud he stopped, and now also saw how the line from his aunt's ear to her chin was like a fine crescent moon. He swallowed his words and moved his hand deeper into the soft belly fur of the cat. A memory of being held by his mother came back to him. He imagined himself homesick.

At the same time, Gudrun imagined the pelt caressed by the boy's fingertips, and imagined her feelings were maternal.

'The sheep are to go out th' day,' she said moving closer.

Thorn stood up abruptly. He put the cat into her arms quickly then stepped away.

'Aye. I'll be going.'

In the past, he had spent little time alone with his uncle's wife, although they'd seen each other at the peat bank and cutting fleece. Living together as they did now, with his aunt and uncle sleeping in the alcove and him on a cot set down by the embers, was a different way of knowing people. He overheard to the movement of his uncle's passion at night, his aunt's occasional sighs.

He tried to concentrate on outside sounds, but he always returned to listening. Only when his uncle and aunt were silent did he finally close his eyes. It affected him in a way he'd never experienced when his parent's couplings disturbed the croft.

At Erskine life was gentler. Thorn was not goaded into rebellion. He became less guarded, and new ideas grew in his mind, surfacing at night in the restless tunnels of dreams. The tense, hollow curves of Thorn's body filled-out and grew stronger.

He lay in his cot at night, eyes open in the great dimness of the croft. The black cat comfortable on his belly, needling his flesh while he stared at the silhouettes in the moonlight over the lum. His gaze roamed the chain Gudrun worked, moving the kettle up and down from the hearth, links flexing and chiming together.

One evening the three of them had sat around the fire and Gudrun cast a new garment onto her needles, the wool moved smoothly through her fingers. A pattern of brown and white grew from the needles. She had already amply clothed her husband, and made blankets and covers to furnish the croft.

His uncle removed his pipe, tapped it on his shoe and raised his eyebrows at his wife.

'No needin a gansey.'

'It's for Thorn,' Gudrun replied. 'No one else is going to make for him.'

'Aye,' said James.

After a period of thoughtful silence, James leaned forward and poked around in a nook on the wall and pulled loose a small item. After glancing at Thorn he filled the recovered pipe with tobacco. He lit the dried weed with an ember and pulled through the smoke and then handed the lit pipe to his nephew.

After a brief spell of coughing Thorn settled to smoking and staring into the fire like his uncle, watching the blue smoke rise into the updraft of the lum.

In the weeks that followed, if the cottage was empty, Thorn ran his hand over the half-finished knitted garment. The musky smell of lanolin lingered on his fingers. One night before Gudrun retired to bed she held it up to him, pressing it against his back with her hand.

'You're growing apace.'

She held it steady, and adjusted the work around his hips. Later, Thorn looked hard into the eyes of the cat on his belly, trying to displace the ideas that came to him as he recalled her touch. The cat tensed, pupils glowing flat in the darkness like an animal from a dream. There was a hidden movement in the dark and the animal sprang away.

Uncle James was a man of patience, could avoid someone's eye if it held something he didn't like in a way his own father was never able to. At Erskine they didn't mock his limp, and he worked harder to make up for the deficiency of his damaged hip. Thorn had no wish to be returned to Storrtang. He shivered and pulled his blanket higher and again resolved to sleep.

Still the memory of Gudrun's touch lingered.

21

'I thought we might as well eat with the children,' said Anna.

Harriet looked up from her laptop.

Anna was in an apron, the belt wrapped twice around so it looked like an eccentric piece of holiday clothing—an essential for the Scottish Island capsule wardrobe. The image of Oscar working food from plate to mouth passed through Harriet's mind. She pursed her lips.

'Oh, it won't be that bad,' said Anna.

A black shadow flew past Anna's ankles, followed by a red-cheeked Oscar wielding a banana.

'I said no more bananas! And not in here.' She plucked the

banana from the boy's hand and ushered him out of the room. '…and don't chase the cat.'

The sound of voices bled through the open door into Harriet's room.

'Hit's dot even our cat,' said Martin. 'He can chase id ash much ash he likes ash far ash I'm concerned.'

'It's the cat I care about,' said Anna.

How very little Martin really understood Anna, thought Harriet. No matter what, Anna always invested in relationships—feral cats included. At college she had taken tea with the chaplain, discussed politics with the hacks, supported linguists in essay crises, sympathised with chain-smoking aesthetes as they suffered bouts of bronchitis. Bundles of scrawled messages were constantly clipped to Anna's door, a form of communication that had since disappeared from college.

Harriet remembered a dewy morning in early May, orange day lilies were opening in the college flowerbeds. They had been heading to the porter's lodge.

A man with high cheekbones, smoking a roll-up, had greeted Anna in the main quadrangle.

'Who was that?' said Harriet.

'Father Gerome,' said Anna.

Harriet had raised her eyebrows.

'He doesn't look like a priest,' said Harriet. 'What's he doing here? And how do you know him?'

'Visiting his brother probably.'

An overweight young man with a tuft of black hair jostled into her side.

'Sorry, I'm late again.'

'Morning, David,' said Anna.

David was a mathematician known for his plentiful stock of Scottish spirit and over-enthusiasm for small talk.

'Either of you coming to choir later?'

'Maybe,' said Harriet.

Harriet looked over his shoulder. Of course he wanted to stop and talk, but he really couldn't after saying he was late.

'I don't sing,' said Anna.

'Everyone can sing,' he said.

'She's playing Bach's Partita in D minor,' said Harriet. 'Not many people can do that.'

He looked from Harriet to Anna, nodded, then scurried away towards the lodge, feet hastening without extending their stride.

'Thank you,' said Anna once they were alone again.

'It's not like you to lie.'

'But I don't sing. I haven't sung that I can remember, since my father died. '

'What about at school?' said Harriet.

'I played accompaniment,' said Anna. 'Oh, Harriet. Don't look so disappointed.'

'You'd sing well. That's all.'

'Not as well as you.'

They entered the mouth of the lodge.

'What do you think of Martin?' said Anna.

'Who?' said Harriet.

'From the party, you left early because of Addie.'

'He might be interesting.'

'Do you think so?' said Anna.

'Why?'

Anna disappeared to check her pigeon hole. Harriet listened as she exchanged greetings with the porters on duty, even persevering with Ancient Harold whose habitual opening phrase was, 'I'm a little deaf in one ear.' The truth was that he was practically deaf in both ears. Harriet found it more efficient to write queries in block capitals on scraps of paper rather than communicate verbally.

She stepped out into the warmth outside the main entrance.

The sun had turned the sandstone to gold, throwing the shadows inside the college fortress into deeper relief.

Her appearance on the street coincided with a young man walking past. Martin was sporting a black eye. He nodded in acknowledgement, but kept moving.

Harriet kept her eyes on him until she sensed a shadow in the broad archway behind her.

'You must do something with your hair. Don't you have a clip?' said Anna.

'No.'

Anna began rearranging Harriet's blond locks. Her fingertips grazed the nape of Harriet's neck as she coiled a thick twist into place.

'It can look so nice.'

Harriet shrugged. She didn't care. It bored her that her hair drew attention. Who wanted to be known for being 'blonde'? Anna was never so simply described, especially when her friend's hair was often recovering from a trainee's bungled shortening of her dark curls.

They turned their steps towards the science area.

Ahead of them, Martin continued towards the Zoology and Psychology Department, a concrete structure with the ghostly air of a hospital. He had seen Harriet at the party on Iffley Road—he remembered how she had taken one brief look in the door, sized up everyone in the room and left.

The image remained suspended in his mind as he entered the department. He had no desire to be involved in research or clinical work, or for that matter any of the diseases of the mind that he was being lectured on. A chance meeting later in the term when the brother of his flatmate would enlighten Martin about the opportunities 'going begging' in advertising and had given him direction

Two streets away, Harriet had also been also considering

her future. It was her final year and Professor Paracchini had indicated a studentship for a PhD could be hers. He'd been vague and expansive rather than making any concrete offer. Thoughts about the future had stalked her as she browsed the museum collection with her sister the day before.

'Shrunken heads first?'

'No, last,' said Addie. 'It will give me patience.'

Her sister was still half asleep on a makeshift bed in Harriet's study bedroom. They had gone out to Kismet and returned late. The bar served flat breads with olives and dukkah, and had an affordable cocktail menu.

Addie's demeanour had been understated at the outset, but when Harriet returned from showing her face at the party she had found her sister at the bar, a cocktail in her hand and a young man at either side. It was hard to imagine that after half term she would be back in school uniform.

A ripple of laughter escaped when Addie saw her sister return to the bar.

'Harriet, you should try this one,' she said and had held up a fluorescent blue drink.

It had been in the early hours when they returned to college, swiping in at the small rear gate. Arm in arm, they had breathed the falling scent of the wisteria, and walked under the long sinuous shadows of its foliage.

A fortnight later Addie had returned from an overnight stay at a friend's house with the word Kismet tattooed on her forearm. Harriet had a phone call from her mother.

'She says it means "fate",' said Julia. 'Apparently, it's the name of a bar she went to in Oxford. Not that I blame you.'

'No,' said Harriet.

For the next ten minutes, her mother continued to not 'blame her'.

After the call Harriet had gone directly to see Professor

Paracchini and told him she wanted to stay in Oxford, to apply for the studentship and pursue an academic career.

Over a decade later she was in the same department, taxed with writing grant applications and teaching duties, her life occasionally coloured by brief rendezvous with musicians. The year repeated in a predictable fashion.

One of her new undergraduates she was teaching, Art Rivers, was living in the same rooms she had once stayed in. The coincidence was amusing at first, and she smiled at the thought of him returning there when he left tutorials.

22

A gull's screech drew Harriet out of her reverie. The flagstones beneath the desk leached the warmth of her feet, and she was faintly hungry. She rose and went to find where the cat had sought refuge. In a small recess by the old front door a long mirror reflected her image. She looked taller from being thinner, her skin pallid, as if she had aged a decade between Oxford and Orkney.

Her mother was right, highlights had spoiled the natural glow of her hair.

What had Art seen in her? She shivered slightly and turned away from the mirror.

Another rainbow was forming, garish against the slate-grey sky. Either they were uncommon in Oxford or Harriet had simply failed to notice their presence. What she remembered were layers of mist rising from the water meadows, and empty cold that persisted day and night. There were days when the sandstone shone and the spires with gothic embellishments rose like bright carvings into the blue sky. But the horizon remained a figment compared with the long, low lines of the islands.

The rainbow strengthened, red and orange, marmalade, glowing yellow and green and finally to the bright violet of periwinkle. The arc fluoresced as it plunged into the grey water.

Harriet's throat tightened. Her eyes lost focus, her arms hung limp. She had shed tears after making love with Art. He had held her long after other lovers would have turned away and slept. She thought he had been oblivious, but maybe, maybe he had known, and been extraordinarily kind.

Harriet turned from the rainbow.

The cat was curled up on the Orkney chair. Anna had it specially commissioned to complete the renovations. It had an elaborate woven straw hood and two drawers beneath its seat; one for whisky, the other for a Bible. It was just like Anna to put the expensive chair out of sight by the back door just because it was ineffably right.

The animal opened its eyes and gave Harriet an insouciant look. She caught Sleekit up into her arms. She pressed her face into his neck and breathed the heavy, rich smell of cat. Sleekit twisted away.

'Go then,' she said and put him on the floor. 'Go.'

The cat sat where she put him, tail moving deliberately across the flagstones. Harriet sighed. The smell of boiled mince had invaded her room and she reluctantly headed towards the kitchen. Sleekit watched her leave then regained his position on the woven chair.

~~~

The air in the kitchen was heavy with a sweet meaty aroma that turned Harriet's stomach.

'Harriet, you look awfully grey,' said Anna. 'Come and have something.'

'I'm not hungry.'

84

Oscar and Eveline looked up from their plates. A spoon of mince hung in limbo by Oscar's mouth. He wondered what his mother would do next. He'd seen her take a knife and scrape the food from his father's plate back into the serving dish when he had not come home. Would she scrape her friend's portion back into the pan?

Eveline sat at her brother's side. She saw Harriet was thin, not small with a dainty way of moving like her mother. Thin.

Martin had his back turned and lifted another forkful to his lips.

'Delishioush,' he said. 'Why don't dou do dhish more offen? You like id, don't you children?'

Oscar dug up a large scoop of mashed potato then poked it into his mouth. Eveline nodded, less certain.

Harriet sat.

'You see. You can be a good girl,' said Anna.

She laughed and poured a glass of wine. Harriet started to laugh too.

Eveline didn't understand what was so funny. The laughter didn't sound right either. She saw that Harriet's eyes were tired like Ugly Owl, a present from her grandmother. When she hadn't said thank you her father had called her ungrateful and grandmother had snorted and told him to fix her a drink, and then for some reason they had argued about how early in the afternoon it was to have a drink.

Eveline observed that even if she wasn't hungry, her mother's friend Harriet was very thirsty. It wouldn't fill her up, though. It wouldn't make her less thin.

Oscar swallowed his mashed potato, feeling it sink in a warm trail down his throat. He wondered why it didn't squeeze upwards when he swallowed. Oscar swung his legs and hummed. He wondered if his father's tooth was now removable like the mouth for Mr Potato Head, and if he got a good grip on his own front tooth and pulled hard enough would it come out or did it need to be knocked by something first?

At the end of the meal the children and Martin settled before the television. Oscar climbed on Martin's knee and Eveline leaned against his shoulder. Anna's gaze rested for a moment on Eveline's fair hair, the same shade Martin's had been when they met at college. In Orkney fresh air flooded energy into the children. In London it was safer to keep windows closed.

Martin spoke over the sound of the cartoon.

'Have you dold her yet?'

Anna shook her head.

Martin tentatively moved his hand to his lips. The replaced tooth provoked him in the same way Harriet's knee had done in the car. He moved the back of his knuckle as close as he dared to the splinted incisor. He remembered its brief goneness in the pit of his stomach and moved his hand away.

Harriet picked up Oscar's fork from the table and grimaced, the underside was smeared with a mixture of mashed potato and gravy.

'Oh, let me do it,' said Anna. 'We've found a dental surgeon.'

'Shpeshialish in tooth avulshion,' said Martin.

'Avulsion?' said Harriet.

'Root canal treatment too,' said Anna.

'I wash lucky to get an appoinmen,' said Martin.

'I've managed to get flights for tomorrow. The car's booked until the end of the week, so have it. Harriet?' said Anna. 'Will you be okay?'

'I don't need looking after.'

'No?'

'I have work to do. "The insularity of traditional tribes people and the multiple disadvantages of ethnic grouping following displacement to the UK".'

She picked up Oscar's plate and frowned.

86

'Oh, just put it in the sink,' said Anna. 'I think you might get on better without us here.'

Really, it was only gravy, thought Anna. There were far worse things to clear up.

'I'm sorry about the blanket,' said Harriet.

'It's only used for teddies now,' said Anna with a shrug, her voice suddenly flat.

Harriet saw Anna pause and stare at the back of Martin's head. For all her brilliance and virtue, Harriet understood her friend was cornered too.

23

Decades ago, on the rare days when the air was still and the sea sluggish and dead, the sound of trickling water could be heard at Erskine. The burn provided fresh water for all their needs on the hill and by the shore.

The thought of revenge had brought a smile to Thorn's lips as he walked away from the door of his new dwelling. For a time he had pissed in the burn each morning and sent a curse downstream to his father at Storrtang, only afterwards remembering the water was used by the whole family.

He grew tired of revenge, and as the months passed Thorn grew negligent of the fondness for his siblings; he did not let himself dwell on memories of their high jinks in the dunes or the lost look in his sister's eyes when the bargain was struck for Thorn to leave.

His father's treatment polluted his affections. Even though he knew his mother loved him above all the rest, she had agreed to send him away. The confusion of emotions warped into a tangled knot of homesickness, anger and unfamiliar desires.

Sometimes a terror of being alone came on him at night, overtaking his wandering thoughts. His stomach tightened and sweat rose on his brow. He lay perfectly still, fearing to breathe, fearing life and wanting death, fearing his heart would stop in his chest if he moved in the slightest, and fearing he would never be held in anyone's warm embrace again.

24

Harriet scraped the slops from her plate onto a crumpled ball of paper with a picture of a rainbow. Garish music blared from the television.

'The broadband might be better once we're gone,' said Anna.

Yes, thought Harriet. It would be better if the house was empty. She could work. She would drink less. It was a timely sabbatical that could advance her career.

'It's all about more publications,' said Harriet.

'I know. And you will.'

Anna unravelled the ties of her apron and found fresh glasses.

'I picked up some local gins.'

'Gins?'

'There's a boom.'

Without thinking Harriet said, 'Art couldn't stand the stuff.'

Anna looked away.

A sinew tightened between Harriet's temple and jaw. She became aware of a deep, warm ache, as if he were beside her. It was absurd the way Anna froze. God knows how many people were talking about them, yet it was taboo for her to even say his name.

'I said, Art couldn't stand the stuff.'

Anna turned to face her. The corners of her mouth lifted a fraction.

'It's an acquired taste.'

'What do you mean by that?'

'Nothing. I mean nothing. Calm down, Harriet.'

Neither moved. Harriet pictured the scene from the outside, watched herself break eye contact and stare sulkily at the table waiting to be poured a drink. Anna's mouth stretched tight in annoyance. Then she was back inside herself again, drinking thirstily and remembering how much she'd hated Martin's hand touching her in the car. Hated Martin for Anna's sake.

Her sister Addie's deep dislike for Martin had hardened after an encounter in Oxford on May morning. Harriet had lost track of Addie somewhere around dawn and when they were reunited on Magdalen Bridge all she had wanted to do was leave.

'You don't want to see people jumping off?' Harriet had said.

Addie had shaken her head.

'Or hear the choir?'

'No. Give me your keys. All I want is shower and sleep.'

Harriet had turned to look for Anna. There was a group of students in ballgowns and black tie, and others in fancy dress, but no sign of her friend in the crowd.

'I'll come with you.'

'Stay,' said Addie. 'You want to watch.' She had smiled weakly, her eyes innocent beneath the mascara. 'I'm done.'

She had taken the keys and had pushed through the crowd. It hadn't been like Addie at all. Addie who was always last to admit the fun was finished. Harriet wondered again what happened that night, and why its discussion had become off limits.

Addie had returned home to London, and for a period she had actually applied herself to her sixth form studies, enough to gain entry to the City and Guilds School of Art. Her piece in the final degree show was titled *The Garden of Eden*. Harriet had gasped when Addie had first shown it to her. It was a self-portrait, Addie as a serpent, and as the figures of Adam and Eve, a resplendent gender definition-defying representation of humanity. It had sold to a collector and established Addie's reputation. She had never painted with the same intensity again.

Addie's presence was salty, an acquired taste, and something Harriet found she craved now they were far apart.

25

Professor Paracchini's position at the Pitt Rivers museum was as iconic as the Star House totem pole; his office excited as much curiosity as the public galleries.

When Harriet had explained her relationship with Art the Italian professor had shaken his head and sat in silence. Harriet was unsure if he hadn't understood or did not see an affair as a problem.

'You understand how it can happen.'

'I see,' he had said. 'If you must be away, then go. Anyway, it is impossible to write seriously here.' He glanced at a figurine of a woman's head on his desk. 'Yes, good.'

'It's not because I want to,' said Harriet. 'The guidelines demand it. The handbook.'

She glanced around at the cabinets filled with books, gold edges glinted like diadems in the gloom.

'The new post-doc can do your teaching,' he said, referring to a doctoral candidate. 'Always we teach and learn.' A light came into his eyes. 'I have always wanted to visit Scotland. Cool breezes. Space for breathing.'

'The dean says I can return in Michaelmas, and also during the long vacation when the undergraduates are away,' said Harriet.

'Come any time if you want. I will send you dissertations for marking.'

'I don't think I can.'

'Why not?' said Professor Paracchini.

'I can't mark his paper.'

'Ah, but this is only one.'

There had been a short silence. Professor Paracchini inhaled, his nostrils flared seeking an old fragrance. Smoking had been banned everywhere in the museum, and the professor's office, which had been famous for its Milanese atmosphere, was one of the few places where the odour of tobacco remained.

He lifted the figurine on his desk and inspected the features.

It was a Baule woman, tall as his hand and made of dark red wood, once the possession of a trance diviner. The object had the heft of a weapon and was stained darkly from libations, yet there was delicacy in the interlaced hands. Its poise was one of repose. It was the sort of thing that might be featured in one of the crime stories set in the university.

'Professor?'

He looked over the figurine to Harriet. He had hardly seen her lately; she looked tired. Sometimes he thought she might be terribly unhappy.

'They are from Bergen.'

'And will mark with your supervision.'

'Hmm?' The professor looked up. 'Yes, of course. I will supervise.'

Harriet rested her head on the chair back. Her eyelids felt heavy. She wanted to be cared for like the figurine, like an object in one of the cabinets. She wanted to see nothing but random shapes in the inkblot picture above the fireplace. But it wasn't so.

She had risen, said farewell and left the office.

When the door closed behind, she had rested, steadying her self on the rail of the upper gallery of the Pitt Rivers Museum. The recent achievement of displaying ten per cent of the etiolated collection of three and a half thousand spears had delighted Paracchini, as had the rearrangement of shields with their lush swatches of human hair from the Molusca Islands and neat geometric patterns from Australia.

He had a parents' regard for the hundreds of thousands of artefacts possessed by the museum, and an inexhaustible encyclopaedic knowledge, yet Harriet could not shake her doubt that it was impossible to know them all, never mind care for them.

She had stared into the patterns of dots until they bled together and her eyes watered.

Why had she done it? Why should she not do it? Why did it matter where Art was from, or how old he was?

Harriet had turned her gaze to a black and white photograph. A man with a broad moustache stood behind a woman in Edwardian white. Her hands held an indiscernible but precious object, the bleached-out focal point of the portrait. What did any of it matter over time?

She had imagined a vast warehouse, filled with wooden drawers marked with identifying reference numbers. She was simply a card in one of the drawers. Did she, like the museum founders, express the history and culture of her time just as much as the objects? Was her life simply a story that expressed the community where she belonged?

She had felt her limbs become endlessly heavy. The end of the end was coming. She had heard footsteps approaching, and she knew she must leave, hide her tears.

~~~

In his office, Professor Paracchini had run a yellowed fingertip over the figurine. He sensed its power. Yes, Doctor Wolf was right to get away.

Behind the door the collection clamoured, the upper levels echoing with the heat of conflict, weapons yearning to become glorious again. In the lacquered cabinets instruments desired to be played. Yet, in the silence of the museum there was grief.

Where was the heart? The soul? He could teach the difference between Nuar ceremonial, sacrificial and warrior spears, their purpose and design, but could he teach anyone how exquisitely fashioned each had been to its purpose by the hands of the maker?

'Always in the hands of the maker there is belief, there is knowledge.'

This is what he wanted to convey to students who came to Banbury House. What possessed the hands of the maker, when he, Paracchini, was created? What informed that moment?

Was belief similar to an atom travelling under the kinetic forces of the universe? Position or energy could be known, but never both. To know one, is to alter the other. To know belief's logical tenets was to strip the essential extension of the imagination.

He had placed the sculpture back on the desk next to a photograph. It was of himself as a young man. He had stopped to swim in Bagni di Lucca and was standing next to his Vespa, white helmet in hand. Three friends gathered around him, one bending to inspect the machine.

What a coincidence it had been to find one just like it at a motorcycle gathering in the middle of the English countryside.

He sighed.

Where had the young man in the picture gone? The thatch of dark hair was now grey, the jaw line soft, the vigour that remained known only to himself. Was he becoming absorbed little by little into half a million objects?

Professor Paracchini had rested his chin on his chest and

stared at the figurine. He did not believe himself to be a maker, that had always been clear.

Paracchini sifted through his memories. The volumes of anthropology journals soldiered the bookcases, and the conch shell dozed beneath its bell jar, and the elephant leg umbrella stand waited. He had kept his eyes on the photograph of the small moped from his youth, and recalled again the chance comment he had made to José Blanco about the surprise of seeing Harriet and her student at the motorcycle meeting.

His thoughts had been interrupted by a tentative knock. The door opened and Art entered.

'Did we arrange this?' said Professor Paracchini.

'I need to speak to you. I would like to change topic for my dissertation.'

'Good, good. Change means you are interested in something new.'

'It's not too late?' said Art.

'No.'

The young man's gaze travelled to the inkblot that adorned the chimney breast. The invaginated emerald edges gave the impression of rapid, repetitive movement, such as a bird in flight. The colours deepened in its centre and were tinted with layers of crimson that intensified into a black heart.

Art blushed and looked away.

'Can belief and knowledge coexist without conflict?'

'Pardon?'

Paracchini tapped twice on the desk with the index finger of his right hand.

After a minute Art had offered, 'Do you want the new title?'

'That is a starting point.'

Art raised his eyebrows.

'So, I can change.'

Professor Paracchini had nodded.

'Most likely there will be a form to fill. Do it at the department,' he said. 'I have seen you. You attend my so-called lectures. Few bother. Why do you?'

Paracchini had held eye-contact, he saw the reflection of himself in the young man's dark eyes.

'It was a recommendation,' said Art.

'Yes, and it puzzles you. Remember, we are all puzzles.'

Paracchini had risen and slowly paced to the astragaled window. He saw Doctor Wolf walking with her head down into the rain and wished she had waited and taken shelter.

'And in a sense, we are all solutions.'

The silence of an empty church fell in the study, the book-lined walls drew back into the crepuscular dimness of the saturated afternoon.

'Can I go?' said Art.

'Yes, go. Go as well,' he said.

Professor Paracchini had held his hands behind his back. More rain, he thought. More rain has come. More rain will come.

26

Art had descended into the crowded belly of the museum. He imagined it as the inside of Professor Parachinni's head, cluttered with novelties from tennis ball-sized shrunken heads to beaded moccasins. A museum where once-plentiful, perishable items became valuable. The cost of preservation for a repurposed tin can was far more than its original value. The collection was a history of constructing history.

He thought about the criss-cross of identities in Mauritius, and his parents insistence he always speak French rather than creole with Nounou. Their aspiration had always been that he should leave. His mother would have little patience for the museum, she would call it brocante, bric-a-brac.

He passed through the double door, a portal into the glass-roofed chamber of the natural history galleries.

A small girl with fair hair had been peering at a life-sized raptor. Her eyes wide, worn-down thumb momentarily withdrawn. She looked from the dinosaur to the baby parked her side, replaced her thumb wistfully and skipped on to the salt-water crocodile.

The flow of glass cases chaperoned Art to the gift counter and then outside.

He had exhaled deeply and loosened his shoulders.

Keith Marden, his new sociology tutor, was expecting an essay. Rational choice theory was more prescient for business dealings than understanding gift exchange relationships. His parents would approve of the change in direction.

The tutorials were pedestrian compared to Harriet's. She had never hesitated to point out the lacuna in his reading.

'I haven't read Evans Pritchard.'

'No?' said Harriet. 'Why not?'

'It wasn't on the list.'

'Read something because it's important, not because it's on a list.'

'How am I meant to know what's important?' said Art.

She had smiled. Despite his outward enthusiasm he'd never really been curious about what she offered until he sensed a shift in her own curiosity in him.

He began to realise that the woman who sat on Governing Body and sang in the college choir wasn't who they thought she was.

The rain had moved on, leaving wet stains on the bark of

the coppiced hazel trees. By the entrance to Rhodes House, he had seen Harriet speaking into her phone. She was making the effort to smile as she spoke, even though the person on the other end of the line could not see her face.

'It'd be perfect. No, I don't care. I want to go. I'm amazed you've got it finished.'

Her voice had faded away when she saw him. There were tears in her eyes.

'Harriet?'

'Oh…I'm sorry, he's actually here. I've got to go.'

Her face had been discomposed for a moment and then she was herself again, her gaze drawing him in as it had done from the start.

'It was Anna,' she'd said.

He'd smiled, remembering an occasion of past amorous persistence even as Harriet spoke on the phone to her friend. A flush rose on her cheeks.

'It's always Anna.'

'She has a place, in Orkney,' said Harriet.

'Orkney, Scotland?'

'I'm going to visit. I have to leave.'

They had walked together in the steady parade between the centre of town and the outer colleges and faculties. He had supposed it didn't matter any more if they were seen together.

A young woman with red hair had drawn near from the opposite direction. She'd looked from Art to Harriet then crossed the road, hair roaming free in the breeze.

'Was it required by the dean?' said Art.

'He didn't specify Scotland, but you know I'm to take a sabbatical.'

The certainty of Harriet leaving being a fact had not yet sunk in, and a temporary heroic feeling had risen inside him.

'We didn't do anything wrong,' he'd said. 'Nothing illegal.'

'No.'

They'd reached a tall pair of wrought iron gates that framed a hard-edged rectangle of lawn. At the far end there was a high wall and an arched doorway which led to a private Fellows' Garden. Art had slowed his pace and reached for her elbow.

She glanced up and down the street.

'We can't stop here,' said Harriet.

'Let's go somewhere,' said Art.

'No.'

Her voice had been firm. Art had felt his desire stall, then strengthen. 'I want you.'

'Why?' said Harriet.

She was going to say more, but had stopped.

They had left the iron gates and moved towards the corner of Broad Street. The synchronicity of their strides broken. Art had moved slightly ahead.

'They're following the statutes,' she'd said.

'But you know it's rubbish. It's an excuse.'

Harriet shook her head.

'What if I come forward now?' said Art.

They'd come to a halt, blocking the pavement.

'Let's say goodbye,' she'd said.

Art had stepped forward, grasped Harriet's hand and pulled her closer. How could he no longer see her, no longer borrow and return her books, no longer be the one to hold her.

'For the moment,' he said. 'Not forever.'

She'd interlaced her fingers with his. Art could not hold her gaze. He looked blankly into the street. The rift was coming— and it would be final.

A girl cycled past. Art had known he would remember the image forever; a stranger associated with that moment of goodbye.

27

Without any appetite or company, Art spent the early evening in the college music room. It was rarely booked until dinner in Hall was over. College was quiet. Lonely. He locked himself in, preventing all interruption except for memories triggered by a trickle of notes. The minutes slid by, his hands moving over the keys.

In his mind's eye he saw the night sky framed by his childhood bedroom window, black-green and shimmering with the organic particles. Only at dawn did the sky turn mineral grey, briefly matching the northern latitudes where he now lived.

Art allowed his eyelids to close and memory slide into focus.

His mother's steps were retiring to her room as he lay on his bed listening to the hum of insects, enjoying the sensation of illicit rum cocktails. It was well after midnight and most of the guests had gone. Curiosity flashed over the whereabouts of his friends, buzzing on scooters around Port au Prince. His eyes had closed.

A sound had disturbed him, the sky had become purple-black and a murmuring breeze was disturbing the undergrowth. There was the rumble of male voices. Shoes tapping on the floor. A woman's laugh echoed through the house. How long had he dozed?

Art had risen for water, his throat dry. He crossed the upper landing without a light and saw it was dark under his parent's door. The evening gala had been gay, voices loud, laughs long. His mother's eyes had twinkled darkly and his father had appeared and disappeared, always with a new guest on his arm.

A stripe of light licked the polished wooden floor of the spacious entrance to the villa. It did not come from the reception room where their guests had been entertained, where hands had been shaken and congratulations given after success at the races, but instead from the drawing room. The image of the hallway stuck sharply in Art's memory, gold mirrored edges, scalloped tables, the reflected world of polished wood.

He had been curious, lured downwards to the sound of piano, an arpeggio of F major, a decision was being made about a song. He could have stayed on the stairs and listened, or returned to his room. Yet it had been impossible to do anything except draw closer once he heard the sweet, imperfect voice begin. The sound shot him with a deep sensual pleasure and the hairs on his neck stood on end,

'All of me. Why not take all of me…'

Art forgot his thirst. He had to see the woman who was singing.

'Rita, Rita. No one plays like Rita.'

His father had spoken with the local tone and inflection in a way Art had never heard before. Art froze.

'You teaching Art any of this?'

'Non, cherie. This isn't for boys.'

Who was the woman with the voice that sizzled like butter in a pan?

Three steps had taken him to the crack of the door. The room was laid out before him. The alabaster lamps were lit, a gift from the Italian priest who came when the hibiscus flowered. The green velvet sofas taken from grand plantation salon were arranged to face the piano. He could see the backgammon table Nounou refused to dust, she did not mess with any gambling game, even to dust.

The decanters of liquids on the buffet were open, their contents usually stationary for months had bolted in one night.

An inch further to the right and he would have been able to see the piano fully, a Boston Steinway, bought after the sensational win at the races by his uncle. It had unwisely been used as security in a card game soon after. After a debt had been paid by his father, the instrument had been moved to the colonial villa.

There was a run of notes, this time B flat major.

'You can call me Miss Brown.'

'Lovable huggable?' His father's voice again.

Art had put his eye closer, the deep damson brown of his iris lit up, elusive flecks of violet reflected in the beam of light.

It was her, but not her. His piano teacher–Madam Marguerite Ramdin, née Tremaine. Her high heeled shoes were discarded, showing their red insides, her sequinned dress scrolled up revealing slim calves that stretched down to the pedals. She played in stockings, hands shifting like swallows on telegraph wires. Her hair, a shade lighter than her skin, hung loose to her waist.

Art ran his tongue over his lips, adjusted his position, unwilling to lose sight of her, but needing to see who else was watching.

There were three men and a woman. His father, bowtie removed and shoelaces open had a glass tilted on his knee, a laconic hand on his forehead, eyes fixed on Madam Ramdin's bare shoulders. Uncle Faustin, was leaning forward, elbows on knees, a broad smile on his face, empty glass on the floor. The third man was unknown, he had rheumy eyes and a worn out air, but was no older than the two other men. The woman had her head laid on his shoulder, eyes three-quarter closed.

'Rita Ramdin. It sounds a stage name,' said Uncle Faustin.

'A certain type of stage,' she replied.

She had paused playing and took her drink from the piano. Her gaze had flitted briefly to his father, then rested like a bird on the other men without taking perch on the woman.

'She's gotta go,' said Rita.

'Tellin me,' said the rheumy man.

'We all gotta go at some point.'

'Not yet,' his father had said. 'Rita, not stopping are you?'

'Not yet.'

Her gaze had moved towards the door and for a microsecond her expression shifted, she was again Madame Marguerite Ramdin née Tremaine. She raised an eyebrow in Art's direction.

'No. It's early yet for you children to go to bed.'

Uncle Faustin slapped his thigh and laughed out loud. His father tilted his head sideways, a bittersweet light in his eyes.

'One more, and one more after that.'

Rita had begun to sing.

'A tinkling piano in the next apartment…'

Art felt the sting of tears. Why? What was happening? Why did he feel this way?

His knees were giving way, he needed to leave or they would be pulling him up from the floor and he'd have to explain everything. And he wouldn't be able to—they would think he was drunk. They wouldn't understand.

She had stayed forever in his memory like she was that night. There was no getting rid of it. Not in his bed in the dark, not at dawn, not at school, not in the afternoon drinking iced tea in the kitchen, not in the formality of their lessons, not ever.

He had wondered if anyone would ever feel that way about him that for a short intense period he had felt about Madame Ramdin? The question spurred both elation and despair.

He'd sworn that he'd suffer anything rather than not know.

Art opened his eyes. In the shadows of the music room nothing stirred. He loosened his shoulders, stretched his fingers and began to play the jazz he had begged her to teach him.

There was as knock on the door soon after the college bell rang for eight o'clock. Forever onwards, he knew it would never be Harriet who found him, or waited for him, or loved him.

28

Harriet accepted a refreshed glass from Martin. His cheeks were flushed from painkillers and alcohol. A raft of lemon slices floated in a cloud of bubbles. The children had finally gone up to bed

'How's the tooth?' said Harriet.

'Improving.' Martin picked up a bottle of gin and sat down close to her. 'Lammas Gin, infused with local herbs. What the hell's a Lammas?'

'Why do you keep adding lemon,' said Anna. 'It's not a fruit salad.'

Martin looked over to the opposite sofa. Anna's hair was loosely piled and a shawl wrapped around her shoulders. He remembered Peter saying, 'Anna looks elegant in anything.' Another time he'd remarked, 'You have a really beautiful family.' Peter had looked Martin directly in the eye. and had become silent, as if waiting for something—Martin still had no idea what it was.

Long-suffering suited some people, he thought. Peter had dealt with Danny Mason, the Best Boy on the shoot for Pet Fresh. It had been challenging because of the drugs element, but Peter had made it all go away. Martin had sworn it was only once, sworn it was consensual, and sworn it would never happen again. Peter swallowed it all down because he needed to believe. Danny had been paid and found alternative employment.

Martin glanced at his phone. There was no signal, so he read back an old message from Peter. He was currently distracting himself with alterations to the flat, but wanted to see Martin as soon as he returned. Martin flipped the phone over and turned his attention back to the two women in the room.

Harriet was watching the bubbles escaping her drink; she

leaned back and let out a sigh.

'Do you keep in touch with Art?' said Anna.

Harriet looked up sharply.

'What? How?'

'Did you, though?' repeated Anna. 'Before a terrible friend offered you a signal-free island hermitage with intermittent broadband.'

'I told him my flight details,' said Harriet.

It was rare that Anna let her curiosity get the better of her, thought Martin. They were too old to rehash relationships, like they had done in the past.

'He made me laugh,' said Harriet. 'Really laugh and...'

She lifted her hand to her heart as if in pain. Martin felt her shoulders shaking against him.

'...and he was young...'

'Stop,' said Anna.

'Stop what?'

Harriet started to giggle.

'You'll regret it.'

The smile faded from Harriet's face. Her eyes darkened. The shifting shadows brought out the contours of her nose and heightened her cheekbones. She had grown more beautiful over time, thought Martin. She was still prickly, but a disapproving smile had its attractions.

'I can shee why he did it,' said Martin.

'Martin,' said Anna.

'Doesn't she look great. God knowsh why you cut your hair, but I bet he ishn't the only student who fancied...'

The wind rumbled against the windows.

'Wrap it up there, darling,' said Anna. 'He doesn't mean to be offensive. He just can't help it.'

Harriet threw back her head and laughed.

'What's sho funny?' said Martin.

'Nothing you'd understand,' said Anna. 'Go to bed.'

The tooth weighed on Martin's mind. He wanted to look in a mirror and touch the numb places. He pushed his glass onto the table and moved from Harriet's side. He wanted to slide his hand somewhere warm. His wife's thighs if she would let him.

The room swam as he stood.

'Careful brushing, darling,' said Anna.

'Aren't you comin?'

She shook her head.

Martin padded from the room, lifting his hand in a wave that knocked into the doorframe. He took a moment to get his balance, glanced at his wife and wondered what proof she was waiting for, then mounted the stairs, bending forwards as if against a headwind.

Once he had gone Anna leaned forward and took Harriet's glass.

'Another?'

'Skip the tonic,' said Harriet.

There were muffled footsteps above as Anna discarded the old slices of lemon.

'Martin's such a bore.'

Harriet joined her at the kitchen counter.

'Did you love him?' said Anna.

'You mean, do I?'

Anna shrugged.

'Well? Did you? Do you?'

'I couldn't think of anything else when I was with him. He wanted me and…' said Harriet. Memories of their first intimate encounter, their awkwardness and then togetherness. She began to give him pleasure for no return. He didn't refuse.

Anna raised an eyebrow.

'It hasn't happened often,' said Harriet. 'There's not many people who… who I genuinely want to please.'

Anna cut her off.

'Is that your best excuse?'

'It's not an excuse.'

Anna shot her friend a sharp gaze.

'You knew what would happen,' said Anna.

'Do you know what I've noticed?' said Harriet, her tone sharpening as she poured herself another measure of gin. 'Happiness makes people uncomfortable. Unhappiness, well, that's different,' said Harriet. 'Everybody wants to get involved with unhappiness. A crooked picture frame gets noticed more than one that's perfectly straight.' She gestured towards a mirror on the wall.

Anna sipped her gin, lips pulling tight from the tang of the raw spirit.

'Well, it'd annoy me. After a while.'

Martin's irregular footsteps crossed the ceiling again.

'God, what a mess he is,' said Anna.

'Have you ever put a tooth back?' said Harriet.

'No. And I never want to. He can't stand the thought of not seeing a cosmetic expert. There's a lot of vanity in his line. It rubs off.'

'From him or on him?'

Anna shrugged and smiled.

Harriet recollected Martin's campaign for gingivitis mouthwash. Never had a woman with gum disease appeared so healthy, youthful and sinless. Her delicate, shocked response at the sight of blood in the sink was the epitome of the unjustly blighted. She was the perfect opposite of anyone needing oral hygiene intervention.

'Remember the mouthwash virgin,' said Harriet.

'Apparently not when off camera,' said Anna.

Martin had won the People's Choice Award for Dental Advertorial at the annual industry gala. Anna had since boycotted attending all advertising industry events.

'I'm going to check-in for the flights,' said Anna. Then we will have tea and Tunnock's.'

'Tunnock's?'

'Caramel wafers—holiday food.'

She reached for her laptop,

'I'll put the kettle…'

Harriet stood, then sagged at the waist and held onto her chair.

'Actually, I think I need some air.'

Anna looked up to the black reflection of the room as it shifted from the pressure outside.

'It's from the south. Go to the old door.'

Harriet steadied herself.

'You know I love you,' said Anna.

'Yes,' said Harriet. 'And you know not to take any notice of me. I'm all wrong.'

She moved to Anna's chair, ran her fingers through a coil of dark hair and kissed Anna lightly on the top of the head. Anna's voice followed Harriet into the old part of the house, 'I'll try and keep Oscar out in the morning.'

Harriet raised a hand in acknowledgement.

Cold flagstones greeted her feet and the bed tempted her to lie down and enjoy the numbness of her limbs, to think of Art and find her own pleasure. But she walked on, passing Sleekit asleep on the woven chair.

The door latch slid and Harriet stepped outside. A cool sheet of night air draped over her body.

The urgent wind passed by the nook of the doorway. Above, the sky was blind.

There must be some life in the darkness, she thought, some glimmer. She waited. But there was nothing, no connection, no sense of significance in anything, as if even the darkness had turned its back.

~~~

The opening door drew Stoat's attention. The woman breathed with a choked, soft, urgent sound. Stoat understood it signalled pain. Staying with the egg was leading to physical exhaustion, her meagre fat reserves were being stolen by the growing embryos in her womb.

Stoat's whiskers twitched. Deep in the thorns the scent of man was clear and present, but there was another odour coming from the woman, the faint fragrance of blood.

Soon there would be no other option but to give way to the egg's allure; compulsion would override fear and the risk would be worth taking. How could she stay and resist?

29

In the century before, when the fields sounded with song at harvest time, it was late September and the summer days were waning. Ripples of change spread northwards. On the Isle of Wight, the monarch of two generations died. Queen Victoria passed away in her bed, the name of her husband on her lips. Edward had taken her throne, and her grand houses, and set about enjoying finally being King.

In Orkney, the tides carved new forms from the land.

Thorn's duties with his uncle's animals and at the peat bank were soon to be interrupted by harvest. The barley was greying, losing the rich golden sheen of false ripeness, the cleft grains were swollen and heavy. Stooks already peppered the fields in the west, harvested by sickle and individually bound, so ownership was not in doubt should the wind rise and disperse the gathered crop.

A final inspection was carried out with Thorn's father. The men rubbed the ears of barley to loosen the grains. After observing his neighbours and the weather James Poke decided they would begin cutting once the night dampness lifted the next day.

'Losing sweetness,' said Robert.

'Aye.'

James crushed a few grains between his teeth, tasting the nutty grain and picturing the pregnant sacks. The chaff blew from his palm.

Over to the east, a sliver of moon tipped on its back, above in the darker blue a single orange star revealed itself to the islands.

In the outhouse, Thorn shut away the hens. He cast his gaze sideways at the ewes coming back into season now a young ram had been introduced. The tupp was inexperienced and teetered on their backs, unsure of welcome. He listed this way and that like a ship in a swell, before juddering briefly and then descending to firmer footing.

When Thorn returned, Gudrun was at the back door. Depression had fallen heavily on her that afternoon. With one swift cramp her monthly blood had begun, rich and heavy, and determined to drop to the earth. Her muscles ached from walking away her grief on the clifftops, her whole body heavy and empty from passing childlessness off as contentment. She wiped away tears briskly as her nephew approached.

'What do you think of this?' she said, gesturing around the croft.

Thorn examined her face to discern her meaning. Her skin was no longer smooth like a girl's, but its lustre remained unblighted with the weary determination of his mother.

'It's better than my father's land,' said Thorn. 'You showed patience with my grandparents.'

Gudrun's gaze searched the horizon, picking out the spot where she knew the sun would soon set. Thorn noticed his aunt's cheek-bones seemed less haughty than when he had met her as a boy.

'It's nothing,' she said, 'if I am barren. I still hope for a child, even if your uncle does not.'

'You are not yet old,' said Thorn.

A glimmer appeared in his aunt's eyes, bright and blue as a lochan at dusk. Thorn watched as they half-closed and she withdrew into a private world. He felt the desire to offer her comfort. Little by little it had grown, just as the moon waxes unnoticed then suddenly becomes full circle.

'The land is good,' he said, more warmly. 'And…you are generous to me.' He indicated the garment he kept on despite the mild evening. 'Without your kindness I've less than a byre cat.'

Mention of the cat, which now always slept on Thorn's bed, lightened the tone of their conversation.

'That black cat has sired far and wide,' said Gudrun.

She paused as if to say more, but instead drew back into the doorway. Thorn passed inside, and in that moment of closeness breathed deeply to catch the musky sweetness of his aunt's body.

Later, the sliver of tilted moon rose high, and the fire, bright with last season's dry peat, burned warmly. James announced the day to harvest had arrived and noted that Robert had kittens in his peat stack.

'All black as the devil.'

Gudrun caught Thorn's eye.

'Will he keep them?' she said.

'No need,' said James. 'Nor do we.'

He turned to Thorn and observed how his nephew had changed since he'd arrived. The gansey Gudrun knitted had been a good sort of joke when it was far too large, but now it fitted snugly around the young man's grown shoulders.

'No room in your bed for another cat,' said James.

Thorn's cheeks flushed hearing his uncle chuckle.

'Barely room for me,' said Thorn. He laughed to keep his uncle company. Gudrun took up her hand spinning, a smile caught back before it spread over her lips. It was true. When Thorn lay down to sleep his heels were over the end of his mattress and his shoulders reached either side of the wooden frame.

That night when his aunt and uncle retired, he closed his eyes in the warm peat scented air and imagined Gudrun stepping aside from the doorway in the dusk. Her eyes bright, like the lasses dancing at the bonfires to celebrate the king's coronation. They had huddled together, throwing glances sharp as the sparks drifting up into the dark, daring him to follow but moving away when he approached.

Did he imagine that his aunt had a look that he should follow?

The thought had a curious effect on his body, as it had when she held her ground earlier in the day. He lifted the cat away turned on his side, and hearing his uncle breathing steadily and thinking his aunt asleep, dealt with the matter in his customary way.

30

Clem's struggle between wanting to be part of the exciting, mysterious dark and the need for sleep frequently went on deep into the night. The sound of cars slipping through their gears on The Braes infected his imagination. He pictured himself cruising past The Kirkwall Hotel at the wheel of a powerful machine; electric-blue, Japanese, with a winged spoiler. There was a machine parked by the end wall just the same. It shone in the grey, dribbling damp.

He would feel like a king with a machine like that. He could cut a swagger. He spoke about spoilers if he ever there was a conversation about cars, said alloy wheels were only for show. A spoiler glued the car to the road.

He mustn't touch a thing if it didn't belong to him. Even a car on the street. Aunt Meg taught him that when he was a boy. It was terrible for her to punish him when he took a thing from a shop. He didn't like to look at her afterwards for the shame of the sorrow on her face.

Clem wondered how much the car cost. The owner took what he wanted from the shop, written on a pad of paper without the bother of counting coins. None of that for Clem.

More than once Clem had been swindled out of change. Dounby show had been the worst. He'd been pleased because he'd rooted up one of the people Auntie Meg had warned him about—someone out to take advantage because he, 'wasna queek oot the blocks'.

Clem had grabbed the skinny man who was running the darts game by the shirt and lifted him right up off the ground.

'Gae me hid!'

A crowd had gathered to watch, the man flailing his arms around, face going from red to pink to grey, his body dangling. Far better than catching a sea trout, catching a man, watching him flapping and sucking in air.

When Ernest arrived, Clem had smiled and held out the man. Ignoring the jibes and jokes. 'Set him doon. You're chokin the beuy.'

His uncle had spoken softly in Clem's ear so the crowd could not hear.

Instead of a dart board there had been individual numbers inside wire rings set on a large rectangular piece of wood. The price of the game, the conditions and prizes had been clearly displayed. 'Score over eight to win. Three darts for two pounds, five darts for three pounds.' The numbers inside the rings had been zero, one, two and three.

The man's face was radish-pink, topped by threads of white hair. Clem had gradually loosened his grip. Ernest spoke quickly before full recovery took place. He'd apologised for Clem's behaviour and blamed himself for being strict with his nephew spending money.

'He's muckle strong in the body, but no in the heed,' said Ernest.

The man had rasped back.

'I telt him the deal. Held the money oot before he took another shot.'

Clem had felt the victory slipping from him.

'Hid wis a twenty,' said Clem . 'A twenty!'

'You've spent hid beuy,' said Ernest. 'Every demn penny.'

'I wis tae get a prize,' said Clem.

'No buey, there's no prize.'

Ernest took out his wallet, nodded to the stall holder and had held out a pair of notes.

'He didna mean harm.'

The money had been taken quickly, and a high, bony back turned.

As soon as the scene ended people move on. Clem and Ernest had walked away past the stalls, plastic sheets pinned to protect the furry toys and packs of guns and arrows from the rain.

'Stay away fae the games,' said Ernest.

Clem had looked miserably at the faces of the lasses on the Heartbreaker, their hair going up and sideways as they spun around.

'Come an see the kye.'

'I'm watchin the lasses.'

113

Ernest sighed and had said, 'Hid wis a poor game, but there's no need tae kill the man.'

Clem didn't respond, too busy watching the cars, blurry and bright. The faint feeling of having recently shed tears remained, and a funny sort of emptiness he mistook for hunger. He knew Ernest should be going around the handwork tables with Aunt Meg, but he had stood with him instead. Both were frowned on for getting so wet and missing the awards.

No touching was a rule for a lot of things.

He mustn't touch stoat traps because they take off fingers. He mustn't lay rat poison. He mustn't take the handbrake off the van. He mustn't fiddle with the radio.

Ernest had told him that even if Kieran didn't say it was annoying he was still finding it annoying. Ernest was deadly serious about keeping in with Kieran.

Clem could feel his uncle's sadness, even eating a morning piece at their favourite spot and watching the Shapinsay boat come into the harbour. Sad and serious, no matter what words he was saying.

It was because of the lost money. The money they could not talk about in front of Aunt Meg. He mustn't say anything about going into the bank to prove who he was, or say anything about the money being transferred.

'Hid'll niver come back,' Ernest had said.

His uncle's mouth had corners down, his eyes like he could do a dreadful thing. Clem wondered if it had been enough money to buy the car with golden wheels, one to sit in, eat a piece and watch the water.

The idea of the car eased him into sleep. When the throbbing engine echoed at two o'clock in the morning Clem was deep in a distant dream. He did not hear the tick-tick of an engine cooling, or the querulous voice and the start of yet another tit-for-tat fight.

31

Before the phone call three weeks ago Ernest is many things. He is an active member of the community with regular duties refurbishing furniture for charity and a part-time volunteer at The Wildlife Trust. His talent is to understand the workings of mechanical objects. He is a husband, an uncle, a friend. A man.

~~~

This is how it changes.

~~~

Ernest sits with a cup of tea and a caramel wafer on the desk, reading through a fortnight of emails on the computer. Meg is absent. It is Tuesday and she has gone to the library to return her book and attend the knitters and cross-stitch group. She is mid-way through helping Christine Burgess edge a shawl.

The smell of high-gloss paint lingers in the spare room even though it is months since Clem left and Ernest redecorated. Meg said Clem must have independence, whatever they felt themselves. He must go to live in Balfour Rise.

Ernest clicks on an email from the bank.

The phone rings— Ernest answers. After a short delay a female voice speaks, the accent is from the south, like a St Magnus Festival goer.

'Good morning, I'm calling on behalf of your bank. Thank you for responding to the email you received. Unfortunately this was a scam e-mail and contained a malware virus that means your computer is now vulnerable to hacking by online fraudsters.

Ernest stifles his Orcadian accent and speaks in a flat respectful tone.

'It looked like it was from you.'

'Unfortunately, scammers are getting better and better at mimicking official communications.' She pauses. 'We are pursuing the origin of the false emails, but anyone who is duped into clicking the link is at risk. The best thing you can do in the future is to report the email to our official phishing helpline. It is in our terms and conditions that customers must never click on links in unsolicited emails.

'Now you have clicked the link we must go through the recovery process as quickly as possible and move your money into a safe account that I set up for you now. If I could just take you through your security questions.'

Ernest's gaze goes to the plug socket in the wall.

'What if I just unplug the computer?'

There is a short laugh at the other end of the line.

'If only it was that simple, but if someone has accessed your personal information all they need to access your account is a remote server, regardless of whether your computer is switched on or not.'

'God's sake.'

'We really need to get your money into a safe account as soon as possible, Mr Manse. I have your account details here, but I need to verify your identity through your usual security protocol.'

Ernest's confidence falls, he forgets to moderate his Orcadian.

'I canna gae tae the bank an dae hid?'

'The sooner we get a safe account set up the sooner your money will be safe. There have been delays with payment transfers and some customers have ended up being defrauded of thousands of pounds of savings in a matter of hours.'

'Hid's just…'

Ernest remembers something he heard on the radio. While the woman speaks he double checks the number on the telephone with the helpline number on the bank's website. The number is the same.

'Once the scammers have the information on your computer they can access all your online purchasing accounts, your direct debits for utility companies, TV license, car insurance. They'll be able to use your identity and not only spend the money in your accounts, but leave you in debt.'

Ernest imagines his details up on a screen somewhere, every transaction visible, and his bank balance sliding down to zero. A premonition, of sorts.

'Our advice is to act immediately to make sure your money is safe.'

Ernest reaches for a box file and opens the first page. He checks the bank statement and sees the Thai Orchid hotel payment. He remembers the energy-sapping humidity of Bankok, he remembers the lost and empty feeling as he walked the energetic streets. He desires to travel to other, cooler, places with Meg. He needs to keep the money safe. He takes down a second folder with the statements for Clem's saving account.

'The bank will not refund defrauded money unless you follow our advice to move it into a protected, safe account.'

'Aye.'

'There is a designated fraud department who will pursue the scammers, but you will be held responsible for clicking the link and knowingly leaving your security details at risk, which constitutes gross negligence.'

Ernest fingers the paper in the binder. There is enough saved for Clem to get a car, or soon afford a place better than Balfour Rise.

'If I could take you through your security questions?'

'Aye.'

'What is the name of your first house?'

'Windbrek.'

'The name of your first school?'

'Glaitness.'

'Can you confirm your date of birth?'

Ernest confirms his date of birth.

The scammer looks over to her colleague. They sit shoulder to shoulder in the small room, all wearing headsets. The air is fusty and the bubble of adroit voices is at odds with the windowless office on the outskirts of Luton. The operatives only receive a modest percentage of what they extract. An automatic dial system links to the click bait email triggered by Ernest.

The scammer senses that Ernest's anxiety at losing money is turning into trust and positive action. The tide of the call is turning, suspicion is on hold.

'Okay, we now have the new account set up for you. If you would like to log on to your home banking I can give you the sort code and account number, so you can make a direct payment.'

'Noo?'

'Yes, now. Go to the adhoc payment menu on the righthand side and click new person. For reference use the words 'Safe Account.'

The scammer feeds Ernest the sort code and new account number.

'It's safest to transfer the money in a series of payments. If you enter a figure of five thousand pounds into the amount box, and click the date for today. Do you have your mobile phone there?'

'Aye.'

'The bank will send you a One Time Payment code which you must enter to authorise the transaction.'

'It's come through. Five, eight…'

'Stop.' The scammer's voice is sharp. 'You must never share this code to anyone. No one should ever ask for this code. Simply fill it in on the screen to authorise the transaction.'

The scammer smiles. She can see exactly what Ernest is doing on her screen. The malware virus that was genuinely inside the email displays in real time all the activity on his screen. She sees the transaction authorised. She also sees every detail of Ernest's account, including the five-figure balance.

'I can confirm that has been successful. We need to make another three payments today so all your money is protected.'

The procedure is repeated until twenty-eight thousand pounds has been transferred, leaving only one hundred and fifty three pounds remaining.

By the end of the call Ernest has been on the telephone for over an hour. His headaches and he needs the bathroom. Meg is finishing a row of purl stitches at the library.

'Any accounts that have been accessed on this computer are also vulnerable.'

Ernest believes everything now.

'I hiv a savin accoont fir wur nephew.'

'Is it in your name?'

'Aye.'

'To save setting up another safe account we can temporarily move the money into the same account. If you log on as before, I can support you through the process of transferring the money again.'

A sweat breaks over Ernest's brow, his fingers hit the wrong keys. His mouth is dry.

'Hid'll take a peedie minute tae get in.'

'Our fraud office will telephone you to confirm the closure of the compromised accounts. The funds in the safe account will be allocated to new savings accounts. I have all the details here. Enter the safe account number and sort code as before then enter five hundred pounds for the first payment. Remember, you must never reveal the One Time Payment number to anyone.'

A number buzzes through on Ernest's phone and he enters it carefully. He moves the mouse and clicks, 'Complete'.

'That's the first payment made,' says the scammer. 'Nearly there now. Just a couple more transactions.'

'Aye,' says Ernest.

He can't take his eyes off the screen. The black numbers in grey boxes don't seem to mean very much. It's like doing a subtraction sum at school, with the aim of getting down to zero in four steps.

The scammer has a brief feeling of success, like a win at the dogs. Something about the process used to trouble her, not breaking the rules, she always found that a thrill. It was the feeling of everything being rigged in her favour.

It doesn't trouble her anymore.

'Thank you for being so co-operative this morning, Mr Manse. The bank acts swiftly when it becomes aware of new scams. Someone from the fraud office will phone you after I hang up to advise you about removing the malware from your computer and take you through additional security measures to keep your financial details secure.'

The call ends, Ernest sits back in the swivel chair and tries to take a deep breath.

~~~

Ernest looks from the computer to the phone, to the phone wire and the plug socket in the wall.

Ten minutes pass.

Nobody calls.

Ten more minutes pass.

Ernest stands, his legs buckle. He doubles over and presses his hands on the desk as if receiving a punch to the gut.

His skin shrinks, tightening, and pressing on every nerve, until he feels nothing, it's as if the floor drops away and he falls and falls and falls. He leans against the desk, weakness running through him like water, and stares at the computer screen.

It's all gone.

The realisation is a moment of bereavement.

In one minute he grows older than he ever imagined possible. His past self is erased from every happy moment. Gone. The useful. The wanted. The needed. Gone. The man. Gone. All taken away.

Worse. It is given away. Ernest becomes a ghost.

It is worse than when he lost his brother at sea; there is not even an ocean grave.

Ernest picks up the phone and calls the fraud department of his bank. He is put on hold for a short while. He tells them about the email and they thank him for reporting the problem and tell him he was right to be suspicious. He is about to tell them what happened next when the woman goes on to tell him that they will never contact him by email or ask for his security details. Her voice has the same accent and tone as the scammer. Ernest hesitates. He cannot bring himself to say what he has done. He cannot even speak. He doesn't know who to trust. He hangs up, believing it is too late. He has given everything away, his security details, and then he sent the money away. He has been gullible beyond belief. The nephew he loves has had the rug pulled out from under his future.

A sound comes from somewhere. It means nothing at first and then Ernest understands. Meg is coming through the front door.

Sweating and unsteady he staggers to the bathroom and locks himself inside. His face is ashen in the mirror, he looks like a different person all together. The good deed he had been doing for Clem that was secret and safe has been erased. Everything is tainted and lost.

Ernest knows now what it meant to be happy.

There are footsteps outside the door. He knows that he must come out, and soon he does. He passes through the routine of evening, of eating and complimenting the tatties, of washing

121

the car and polishing the paintwork. Dusk falls and the circles of his cloth shrink until his hand becomes still. All he can do is stand and stare into the red paint, unable to move from one spot to another. Night falls heavy on his shoulders.

When at last he comes inside Meg is there, smiling over her needles.

Later, a man in the mirror brushes his teeth. The grey colour has lifted, but Ernest isn't really there. He lies down without hope of rest, lets an hour pass then abandons the bed and leaves Meg alone.

He stands at the window in the living room and stares into the shadows. The rows of low houses on the other side of the street invisible to his eyes.

Over and over again, he teeters on the edge of sleep only to touch his forehead on the cold glass and be propelled into wakefulness. He sways and rests his hand on Meg's chair to drive away the giddiness. He feels the guilt and humiliation afresh.

The room is full of photographs. Why are they smiling? He isn't that person anymore. His face should be scratched out from every photograph on the mantlepiece.

He's a damn fool.

~~~

The next morning, Ernest sits at the table in overalls ready for a day of stoat trapping. Meg has cleared the breakfast, soon she will be on her way to buy buttons. She is looking at him.

Her man is pale.

'Dae you good tae be oot.'

'Aye,' says Ernest, 'Clem can come too.'

'Keep an eye oot. He canna alwis be trusted,' said Meg.

Neither can I, thinks Ernest

32

A small aeroplane rises over the dovetailing waves of the Pentland Firth. It heads south to Aberdeen. After Aberdeen Kieran will connect to London, from there to longer flights: Dubai to Sydney, connecting to Christchurch.

Kieran hopes that Ernest will be able to understand his hurried note. He'd planned to send an email to explain, but remembered Ernest had said his email wasn't working. What the hell could he write when two words said it all? Dad gone.

A memory from the summer before he left to join The Wildlife Trust came back to him. He had been standing at the barbecue with his father.

'Gonna get one of those gas models next summer.'

Kieran had idly stirred the smoking charcoal with a poker, revealing curls of white-hot undersides.

'Let them settle.'

Kieran swigged his beer and prodded harder.

'Leave it alone will you. Bloody go and talk to your mother. '

He had taken the poker, then nodded a curt dismissal. Kieran stayed where he was, scalp itching with irritation. His father couldn't be more considerate to people he hardly knew, he'd checked to see if any neighbours had washing out before lighting the coals, but he was bloody hard to live with.

Mish had called from the back door. She had an eye for deciphering his slanting hand, and had been interpreting his battered black notebook now they had returned from fieldwork.

'K-P? Your mum says stop fighting with your dad and get some salad from the MacKenzies.'

'I wasn't…'

Mish cut him off.

'If they've a cucumber she'll take it as well, but no tomatoes.

She's got plenty.'

'Pass on my regards,' said his father. 'And take Charlie. He's not had walkies today.'

Mish had held out a colander as Kieran came to the steps. She was still wearing the Department of Conservation shirt and shorts she'd worn the last forty-eight hours. The previous night they had been in a cabin in Kaituna Valley on Banks Peninsula. No one else had been there. The southern sky had been embroidered with stars. They had slept on a wooden platform outside and now and then the bright glow of a meteor streaked overhead. Dew-laden air settled, cooling their bodies.

They had woken at dawn and listened to the birds.

'You want me to name them?'

Mish had nodded sleepily.

'Bellbird, that one's easy, tui...'

Her hand had moved onto his chest, then over his ribs tracing the landscape of his muscles, placing her palm in the arch where his heart pulsed. His awareness drifted from the birds to the presence of the woman beside him.

'Your heart's speeding up.'

He had glimpsed the white of teeth as her lips parted. She gave him the same smile at his parents' back door. He'd rested his hand on her hip, accepted the colander from her hand. She was good for him—that's what he had been thinking as he walked to the Mackenzie's.

'Will this do? Or shall I pick you some more?' said Mrs Mackenzie.

'Nah, that's plenty,' said Kieran.

'We said it'd be John firing up the coals.'

Mr Mackenzie had nodded.

'Can't give you any cabbage, I'm afraid,' she said.

'No?'

'Possum,' said Mr Mackenzie.

'I don't like him putting the poison down,' said Mrs Mackenzie. 'Isn't it bad for the environment? You're into all that?'

'Doing the world a favour,' said Kieran, taking back the colander. He pulled the dog away from where it was sniffing the chewed-out cabbages.

~~~

The scent of fresh-grown tomatoes hit Kieran with homesickness like nothing else, even the sight of the green spider tops hunched over the shiny red fruit in the supermarket could bring it on. He'd discovered a poly-tunnel full of them when he'd taken a trip to see Dr Corston over at Widewall, confirming a stoat sighting.

'Dinna ken whit they were, chasing each other over the road. No a rat, more like a squirrel you ken. Then I saw the piece in the paper an the pictures.'

Walt talked as Kieran set up the trap, pausing to raise his hand to every person who drove past. He wore a coat tied round with a belt that had once been blue, and retained only a vestige of colour in its deepest creases.

'Cheust gutter,' he said, pointing towards the edge of the road. 'These monster machines that come up an doon.'

He had shaken his head, raised his hand again to a tractor spewing out clods of earth from its treads. He followed Kieran to place another trap to the rear of the property where a land drainage pipe emerged.

'Is hid a good pelt?' said Walt.

Kieran paused in setting the kill bar on the neb.

'Not worth anything,' he said. 'Ermine if they're white, but not here.'

'Aye,' said Walt.

He nodded, the light squinting off his spectacles. Kieran was invited into the poly-tunnel. Darker clouds had come across from the north-west and the shelter from the wind was welcome.

The light was bright and diffuse through the double layers of polythene and the scent of tomatoes spicy and intense. Kieran's gaze followed the snaking vines, forgetting where he was.

'Here you are, beuy.'

Walt handed Kieran an empty plastic bag.

'Tak as many as you like. Go on, twa-three pounds need picked.'

Walt observed the young man as he pulled the fruit loose. He knew plenty of men who rapidly overheated working outdoors and wore shorts. What interested him was the way the young man bent awkwardly as he picked. After a few minutes he had said, 'Hiv a problem wi yir spine, beuy? Scoliosis?'

Kieran placed a hand at the small of his back and stood upright.

'How'd you guess?'

'Dae you hiv a brace?'

'For a while. Hated the thing.'

'Dinna ken anyone who liked them.'

'My mother said I couldn't have the surgery.'

'No?'

'She worried about it. Anyway, I get on okay.'

Kieran held up his bag. Walt sighed at the sight of so little gathered.

'I sell some, but thir's no many folk gaan past to buy any.'

'I'll be back in two weeks to check the trap.'

Kieran held out a leaflet about the extermination project.

'Use this number if you want to get hold of me.'

'I'm alweys aboot hands. Come back and tak as meny as you want.'

He gestured to the plants.

Walt watched Kieran walking away. He had always seen through to the bones, even as a boy. He'd seen skin as a tent rather than any sort of truth. It was fated for him to be a doctor.

He'd known his mother's stomach complaint would take her life. He'd known his father's tendency to lean was nothing to do with his legs, but a heart grieving the loss of his wife. Walt turned away from the retreating van and back to the house. He could see the young man's spine was curved, but not so much as to give such pain. There was something else out of whack. Why else was he on the other side of the world?

33

The Pentland Firth grew wide and the islands became scraps of green cloth floating in a petrol-blue sea. Kieran tried to marshal his thoughts and review the months since he had left New Zealand. His gaze returned blankly to the sea. The goneness of his father heaved inside him. His mind shifted and settled in new places where it had not been before.

He remembered his mother's favourite photograph, one of his father with a bushy moustache, sporting a pair of stubbies, hand-knitted jumper and walking boots. His feet were planted in the shingle of a riverbed. Toni on one side, in a pink cowgirl hat, and Kieran on the other. He had pudding-bowl hair and for some reason was holding a stick like a twirling baton under his arm.

They were apart but together. Separate but inseparable; that was his family. There hadn't been much of a farewell at the airport when he had left. His father, now with a grey moustache, had been more focused on how long he could park in the drop-off zone without getting a ticket. Kieran had moved forward for an embrace, but both had stopped short of a hug and shaken hands. Kieran looked into the blurred propeller.

Grief squeezed his throat, running through his whole body, into every last cell. His stomach felt like a stone; he had to hold his breath just to stay in one piece. When his vision began to blur he finally released, the damned-up tears began to spill.

~~~

In the next seat, Martin leafed through the inflight magazine. He noticed a bar he knew in Barcelona was being reviewed as one of the five best tapas places in the city. He smiled and thought of pointing it out to Anna, then remembered he'd been with Peter. It was the first night they'd spent together. Peter had been grieving the loss of his mother; the wound had been the door to persuasion.

Martin raised his hand to his mouth. The reinserted tooth felt like a foreign visitor. Touching it caused tangible pain, yet it was easier to bear than the constant, vague, metallic nerve pain.

Eveline, in a single seat on the other side of the gangway, was proud to be sitting on her own even if the smell of the plane was making her feel sick.

'Okay, Eveline?' said Anna, lifting her voice over the drone. 'Not wheezy?'

Eveline shook her head.

Anna glanced at the seatback pocket for paper bags. She could still taste gin at the back of her throat. Enduring Martin's smirks during check-in had made the hangover doubly annoying.

'What's that one?' lisped Oscar.

He pointed at an island scattered with crumbling steadings that drifted through the indigo water.

'Swona or Soma or something. It has wild cows.'

Oscar looked back keenly. A vision of predatory cows entered his head. It would be messy, he thought, cows eating meat. He pictured their sideways chewing jaws grinding meat. He wondered if wild cows were true, or if this was another story.

He looked back at his mother. One hand was rested on her upper lip partially covering her mouth. She didn't look right.

The island moved away beneath them, white-ringed with froth as if dragged along in the water, taking its imprisoned cows away.

On the other side of the aisle, Eveline watched the giant step of the Caithness coast approaching, rising out of the sea. She thought back to Harriet saying goodbye.

She had felt a bit sorry for Harriet being left behind on her own, especially because she didn't know how to be in the countryside or get along with the people. But waiting by the security line she had grown bored of Harriet and her mother talking and letting everyone past. She hadn't even been allowed to look at the silver necklaces in the cabinet.

'The oil tank's getting refilled,' said Anna. 'They've the code and it's paid in advance. The shop is open from ten until four, Saturdays until three.'

'I can drive into town,' said Harriet.

'And bins go out on Monday. Put them with Steven's, it saves the lawn being destroyed.'

'I'll remember.'

'And they'll come to check the traps.'

'I've decided.'

'What?'

'I'm going to call my sister,' said Harriet.

'Call Addie?'

There had been a pause.

'She'll love it here,' said Harriet.

'For a minute she will and then…' said Anna. 'Oh well, have as many visitors as you like. If you need them.'

Oscar had stood on his mother's feet and began pushing the two women apart.

'Don't do that, you're too heavy. Oh, hello…off on a trip?'

Kieran had joined the queue for security. His face was grey, but he spoke in his usual friendly tone.

'Going home for a blink.'

'A break from the project?'

Anna had bent down and removed Oscar from balancing on her feet. Kieran and Harriet had made eye-contact.

'Harriet, this is Kieran. Oh listen, they want us to go through. I don't suppose you'll see each other much now.'

'I won't be gone long,' said Kieran.

'No?'

'Couple of weeks max. My dad died.'

Eveline had become suddenly alert to the conversation above her head. Oscar had actually become still.

'Recently?' said Harriet. 'Sorry, that was thoughtless.'

'Last night, well, yesterday morning,' said Kieran.

His jaw had tightened. There had been a moment of silence.

'Will someone else come?' said Harriet.

'Yeah. The boys'll drop round.'

'I've told her not to go near the trap,' said Anna.

'It'll have your finger off,' he said.

Kieran lifted his hand and her eyes had widened.

'I thought you were joking,' said Harriet.

Oscar had peered forward to get a better look at the finger stump, his mouth open. Kieran had let the boy get a look, then fished around in his pocket and retrieved a card.

'Call if there's a problem. Ernest will get back to you.'

'Give Harriet a kiss,' said Anna.

Kieran had looked confused for a split second, then Anna swung Oscar forward, lips pursed.

'Please, you go first,' said Anna.

Kieran stepped past. Martin had folded his newspaper and pecked Harriet by the ear. Eveline noticed that she had drawn back quickly.

Anna had run her hand up her friend's lapel, unconsciously going though the motions of straightening and smoothing the long blonde hair that was no longer there.

'Look after yourself,' said Anna.

Harriet nodded. Anna had kissed Harriet's cheek, both bowed forward for a moment and then Harriet was all smiles and had said in a too-cheerful voice, 'Goodbye, Oscar. Goodbye, Eveline. Look after Mummy.'

~~~

When they were out of sight Harriet felt smaller, lost, the warmth fading from her body, like heat from an abandoned bed.

She remembered her first arrival at Erskine, sensing a past more deeply rooted in time and place than anywhere in Oxford. A place with a history she knew nothing about, foreign.

The sensation of aloneness grew the further she drove away from the airport. She had been given instructions on how to survive, yet in her heart she didn't know how to follow them. The road's grey sinew held tight between the fields and drew her along. The low hills had so few landmarks she could be heading in the wrong direction. The chest muscles around her ribs tightened.

After passing three wind turbines stood in a row she gained confidence in her position. The low heathland gave way to a view of Scapa Flow. There was no reliable phone signal at Erskine so she pulled over at the dilapidated croft by the shore.

The building, broken-slated and pounded by storms, was diminished with each tide. The dark rocks were littered with tangles of seaweed and alive with the hatchlings of flies. The sulphurous air pinched at her nose as she wandered amongst the waning salt pools. How could they endure never reaching equilibrium? How were they full of life?

Her breath became short and shallow. She searched the hill-side for Erskine, for somewhere she knew, a fixed point. There it was, she saw the extension standing out rudely, uncertain whether it belonged. She wiped her cheeks and steadied her breath. She had trusted Anna and come north.

Now what was she to do? Call Addie?

Flow

1

'Addie?'

'Harriet…Jesus, I'm running late.'

Muffled engine noise filtered over Addie's hurried speech.

'What's the quickest way from Soho to Piccadilly?'

Harriet looked over the layers of stone tilted towards a sky at the base of the cliff. Orkney's curves of green and grey receded and became Regency terraces, tawdry shop fronts, red buses and traffic lights. The images settled and became a street where Addie had taken her to a tapas bar with open windows. It was next to a shop that sold 'I love London' on everything from bibs to baseball caps.

'No idea,' said Harriet.

'Not you, him. Where's the nearest tube station?'

Harriet heard a male voice and her sister laughing. The imaginary city paused suspended over the sea. A shiver passed through her as a tight menstrual cramp returned then faded.

'I think I need a taxi.'

'I can call back,' said Harriet.

'Don't. We can talk. What is it? Mum says Anna has kidnapped you.'

'I'm in Orkney.'

'Where?' said Addie.

'Off the north of Scotland. Anna's bothy. They were here.'

'God I'm so blind…it's right over the street.'

Addie laughed again.

In her mind's eye Harriet's saw her younger sister, fair hair reaching the hem of a mini-skirt, hurrying past shop windows, like a piece of paper caught in the breeze, twisting and shifting through the crowds of pedestrians. Christened Adelle, but always called Addie. Harriet's mother Julia never used to her sister's given name even during their fiercest arguments.

'Will you come?' said Harriet.

'The installation has hit the fan. Gregor and Leo can't agree on how the pieces relate organically to each other. I'm picking up the last vase at twelve. Well, I'm meant to be. How's Anna?'

'Her usual self. Martin broke a tooth.'

'He would.'

'So?' said Harriet.

'And how are you? Oops…cyclist. Sorry, I've too much going on. Bleak islands not top of the list. Why don't you ask Dad?'

With that Addie hung up.

The red buses faded into the murmuring waves.

She should have known Addie would not do anything as simple as accept an invitation.

Harriet became conscious of the pungent reek from the mangle of fishing nets and creels piled by the walls of Storrtang. The squat structure's windows were crying seaweed. It was absurd to have built anything so close to the shore. They must have known ruin would come.

~~~

Inside Erskine, quiet melancholy encroached like haar. She found a framed photograph placed by her bed. It was graduation day, she was grinning, clutching Anna, long hair escaping beneath a mortarboard, covered in streamers, grinning.

Harriet burst into tears. Their release brought unsought memories of Art, and a bittersweet feeling of emptiness after having been satisfied.

The first night alone in Erskine echoed the abandonment she'd seen at the shore. Feelings emerged that pulled up memories of childhood. One was connected to the time her mother had decided to convert the attic into a new suite and given the master bedroom to Addie. For weeks there had been dust and mess, tradesmen coming and going, but looking back it seemed

135

that Addie suddenly disappeared from the bed opposite her own, as if abducted.

Addie carried away her clothes, hidden trinkets and their bedroom mirror. Harriet had lain in bed, eyes fixed on the empty space, oppressed by the burden of solitary survival. A hollow space had grown inside here, pushing against the limits of her skin, becoming vast and fathomless yet somehow straining within her. She had tried to call out, 'Help….help me I'm drowning.' But her voice came out as a whisper. No one heard and no one came. There was no one to breathe with her through the night. She lay in the dark staring and staring until she sunk beneath a bleak, internal sea. It was not sleep, but numbness that eventually came.

Afterwards she understood separation was an inevitable part of her future.

The same had happened the next night, and the next, and the next until exhaustion drove her body into more familiar rest. Then, just when she thought she might survive being alone, Addie had appeared. She stood by the side of Harriet's bed, her hair a halo of silver.

'Can I get in?'

Harriet shifted position. She felt the cold tips of Addie's toes and the warmth of breath falling on her cheek. They had woken knee to knee. The morning was bright and fresh. It had been like waking into reality from a long, troubling dream.

Harriet had left Addie sleeping, hungry for breakfast. There in front of her rising from the landing were new wooden stairs. The sight confused her for a second and then she remembered. In the future she was to sleep alone. Addie would come and go as she wanted. They would grow up and everything would change.

Harriet thought, Addie's company might be exactly what she needed, even if it was just for a little while. Or it might not.

2

Thorn's great-grandfather, Stuart Poke, had built Storrtang from stones hauled up from the shore. It had been in the heyday of kelp processing, but the benefit of proximity to the shore had eroded with time, just like the land. The laird's mania for collecting and burning kelp to make lye had brought in much needed income and Stuart Poke had inserted himself into the position of middleman. He was an all-round opportunist and when Cooper Flett drowned, leaving a widow at Erskine, he urged his son Alexander to marry and secure the adjoining land. They subsequently had two sons: Sydney, who took possession of Erskine, and Samuel, who moved down to the once-profitable Storrtang.

Samuel was suited to the relentless tug of war between the sea and the land. He lived for a decade with a woman from Orphir without marrying. Thin as a rake, and thought incapable of having a child, the parish tolerated the arrangement. Yet one spring it became obvious she was with child, although she would not admit to the fact or call for a howdie wife when the birth began. In all events the child was stillborn, and the woman died within hours. Two thin bodies lay unresponsive on a crimson sea.

Samuel was found wandering the dunes, his senses slipped. He lapsed into trances lasting hours at a time, mumbling and rocking his head to and fro on the back of his chair. The hearth at Storrtang became more dead than alive. The fields were invaded by reeds and great pools of seawater sat undrained on the land.

~~~

Sydney had married Margaret Grind from Deerness and she bore him a boy, James, and a girl, Janet.

Janet had been thirteen the summer she met Robert at the county show. They both stayed with relatives in Kirkwall and when they parted it was with enough warm memories to tide them over before they contrived to meet again the following year.

They had been married before Janet turned seventeen. Robert, the fourth of six brothers, was heartily sick of the duties of home and no more content living with his in-laws at Erskine.

One afternoon around this time, the new laird had felt the ancestral burden of a shortage of funds and had taken an interest in the dereliction of the fields around Storrtang. He had ridden out and surveyed the ruined croft, forming a resolution he dismounted and entered the place to speak with old Samuel. The mumbling lips and saucer-wide eyes that lurked in the corner of the hovel sent a chill through the laird's spine. When Samuel rose with outstretched arms the laird had inflicted his riding crop.

Samuel acted before thought intervened and felled the laird with a single blow, leaving the landowner unconscious. Coming to his senses he had fled to Stromness for the first boat he could find.

Robert had heard the news of the happenings at Storrtang with an interested ear and began scheming how to escape his in-laws' hearth. Janet was engaged in a plan and agreed she should accidentally meet the laird while he fished at Kingsgarth loch and present a convincing case that Robert would be a model tenant. Her skin glowed in the rosy dawn as she presented her winsome face to their potential benefactor. They had thought there no danger her acting in a friendly way.

Janet reported nothing of the encounter to her husband except to say afterwards that she had ensured the croft was secured. When Robert carried their few possessions down to Storrtang Janet's belly had been as round as a melon. Erskine had been her childhood home, but Janet had no desire to be nursing parents and a child.

Thorfinn had been born in a hard winter followed by a dire spring and a dour summer. The baby fed like nobody had ever known. Robert had laughed at first to see his son's puckered and angry face as he was taken from the breast and admonished.

James had continued to bide with his parents.

Gudrun came annually from Burray to Holm during shearing time with members of her family after finishing their own small flock. After the season she became sixteen James had taken a bottle of Scarth whisky by boat to her father and shared a dram. The men had agreed marriage was desirable for young Gudrun and James had married her after a swift, silent courtship the following shearing season.

The next Michaelmas James's father Sydney had suffered a paralysing stroke. He lived on, cared for by his wife Margaret and daughter-in-law Gudrun, until pneumonia took him in the spring gales. Margaret took permanently to her bed the following week and the responsibility of the hearth passed to Gudrun.

The old woman showed no signs of ill health except that she no longer rose. As Gudrun served soup into Margaret's bowl she would raise her eyes to the engraving of the monarch on the croft wall and say, 'Pass that to Janet when I'm gone. James'll not care for it.' Margaret's every need had been cared for by Gudrun, and then after a year, as if finally well rested, she followed her husband to the kirkyard.

Gudrun had liked the old woman well enough and the burden of her care had been sweetened by the prospect of Erskine's fine dark earth. She watched James thinning the neeps with methodical strokes and planned how she would like the house rearranged when a bairn arrived.

The red clay wore away beneath the marram grass, the dunes rolled and sank, and the spring and autumn floods eroded the land. The kelp was no longer profitable and Robert had become dependent on open-land grazing. He begged a share of his brother-in-law's fields for raising crops to feed his family.

Years passed and the tides re-birthed the shore.

~~~

Since Thorn had left for Erskine, Robert felt the storms to be harsher and more frequent. In late spring, an easterly blow lasted three days and nights. Balls of ice scuttled under Storrtang's door and boulders the size of a man's head spewed up from the shore with the force of cannonballs.

The violence had relented enough to allow crude repairs and the children were released outside. Thorn's sister had returned weeping. A dozen seal pups, their heads wedged in the sand, soft bodies lying in the direction of the ebb, were dead on the beach. Her brothers Issac and John had taken their knives and tried their hand at removing the pelts of the drowned animals. Patches of bloody ruin marred the sand with nothing of worth to show for their butchery.

Janet had no interest processing seals or whales washed up on the shore, but decent pelts could be swapped for a bottle of whisky with Malcolm Scarth. He was a notoriously slothful man with a gift of determination only when it came to the distillation of spirits and the preservation of skins.

'Let Thorn have them,' Janet had said.

Robert spat on the sand and walked away. Thorn had always been knacky-handed with a knife, with the patience and stomach to see the process through for a return. Issac and John made a pile of the most intact carcasses, returning smeared with sand and blood.

Janet had gone up the hill to Erskine. Her progress up the brae was easily visible and she was surprised that Gudrun was not waiting at the door.

The farmyard, swept by the broom of the wind, was even

neater than usual and the sweet smell of freshly spread hay contrasted with the iron tang of the shore. There were winter neeps lined waiting in the ground and four fat ewes penned ready for lambing.

Janet paused before the door; it was a queer, yet she felt she could not enter as was the usual custom. She shifted from foot to foot, half turned and looked back down towards the shore, regretting having come herself when she could have easily sent one of the girls or let the boys do as they please with the cubs. Finally, she raised her hand and knocked.

Cautiously, as if expecting a stranger, Gudrun opened the door.

'Why, Janet,' said Gudrun. 'Have you finally come to fetch Thorn back? I'm afeared we've kept him a long time.'

Janet laughed at the joke, her voice a pitch above normal, high as an oystercatcher whistle.

'No. You'd best keep him still. Robert's none the gentler,' said Janet. 'He's hellish hard on the boys when his temper's up.'

Gudrun cast her eyes behind Janet into the yard.

'I came to say there's twa-three seals collected on the beach. Thorn can take the pelts if he wants them.'

The sun-silvered door creaked again and Thorn stepped out from the shadows of the house.

'Mother?'

'Thorn? Are you not gone with the sheep today?'

Thorn shook his head.

'Uncle James wanted air after being cooped up by the storm.'

Janet glanced from her son to her sister-in-law and noticed Thorn was the taller now, half a foot taller than his aunt. The sun broke free from the scudding clouds and set a glow on their faces.

'Well, Gudrun can tell you, but I'll say it again. There's seals on the beach if you will get to them afore your brothers are tempted to make a worse mess of them.'

Thorn nodded.

'I'll get my knife,' he said to Gudrun.

'Scarth will take them from you,' said Janet.

'We'll make sure to get something for Robert,' said Gudrun.

Janet's gaze followed Thorn's movements inside the gloom of Erskine and her heart grew tender towards her son when he returned.

'See how well you are taken care of here,' said Janet. 'Although we miss you.'

Thorn gestured the knife was found, nodded farewell to his aunt and went to his mother's side. Gudrun smiled to her nephew and nodded to her sister-in-law as they left together.

She watched them walking away. Goosepimples rose on her breasts as she noticed Thorn's shadow mingling with the windswept grass. He would return smelling of the sea, and the processing would keep him at home.

It was her preference to have him bide with her.

James rarely saw any reason to balk against her small wishes. Thorn wasn't a child anymore either, he must be accommodated in decision-making.

Gudrun brought her butter churn to the window and trained her eyes on where Thorn would appear when he returned. It was plain the sea would ruin Storrtang before long, no matter how much her brother-in-law Robert cursed or how often he rebuilt his dykes.

3

Harriet stood on the cliff edge. Was farewell to Art a farewell to life? Was this depression? Was she altogether lost?

Time alone was relentless.

More and more time alone, more and more questions. Floods of melancholy passed from her feet to her knees then groin, sucking the heat from her core, rising up her neck and into the cavities of her nostrils, filling her with cold, astringent shame.

Salt water. Time. Alone.

Sometimes her mind blanked. She grappled to cross voids where nothing she had done, or did, made sense. Over and over again she saw a world that would not notice if she were gone. It might be better. The world might be better had she not been born, like her aborted half-sister.

She began to collect stones.

It was a small act, keeping one in her pocket at all times, one she could grip to survive the lapses in her thoughts. They varied in colour from pumice grey to red sandstone; she chose ones no bigger than a quails egg. Some were deep blue-grey, like the skin of a whale, others striped with quartz, like layers of sin compressed under the weight of time. Some stones were dark as graphite, a reminder of how she was blacklisted. Sometimes a stone would be smaller, the size of a chestnut, and jangle in the cage of her fingers trying to escape while she pushed against the wind.

The land slid down like a green wave, tired clay overhanging the shore washed by saltwater, curling under Harriet's feet. She concentrated; she did not want to fall by accident into the waves.

Only when she chose did she receive any communication. And she chose to do this rarely. The possibility of communication made her hands shake and yet she must call somebody eventually.

One day in the future someone might contact her and want her story. Stones might be thrown at her. Whoever had already betrayed her once might do it again. She imagined herself the focus of the student 'It Happens Here' campaign that circulated around the campus.

Time took on the idiosyncrasy of memory, slow time recalled the hours she'd waited for her mother to return from collecting Addie from the school. She had boasted how she loved having the house all to herself—but it was a lie.

There was a certain upright post she walked to, bigger than the other stock posts, around six feet tall, wide and round as a telegraph pole. It looked constructed by some sort of insect colony pushing rounded pinnacles skyward from an inside labyrinth. She felt the entry holes worn by the wind and stroked the pale blue tongues of lichen that curled away from the surface. They withstood the most brutal storms, yet yielded under the brush of her fingertips.

Reach the turning post, objective one. Find a stone, objective two. Carry the stone safely back to Erskine, objective three.

It was not guaranteed. She might not fall landwards when the bullets of memory hit. Find, turn, carry. Bring it back. That is it. The last remaining acts.

Some days the turning post is out of reach, when the black wave is rolling and rolling and never breaking. The edge of what is real and imagined blur and confuse. Harriet lies in bed until the rectangle of light above calls her to try again, to claw her way back.

Stone by stone. The place she gathers them is Erskine. When she returns, head hung low, straining under the burden of a small stone, she places it in a line. The lengthening line is real, proof of her presence.

4

Steven Scarth's bin was yet to appear at the end of the farm driveway, but Harriet was sure it was the right day. Her phone buzzed as she dragged the wheelie bin against the wind.

'Harriet? This is Addie…of course you know who this is. I'm coming.' There was a pause. 'Oh, yes put it there and then we'll change the lighting. I'll sort it with front of house…don't tell Gregor. Listen, I'm at work. Have to go. See you in May, or start of June. I can't remember which. I booked a ticket. No, no. Not there. Here. Bye.'

The message didn't guarantee anything. Addie's trip might be abandoned at short notice for just about anything else.

Harriet went around the house, collected a breeze-block and returned down the drive to secure the bin lid. She looked over to Scarth's yard; a new blue tractor gleamed among its rusted forebears. The organisation and reorganisation of Scarth's machinery and provisions remained unfathomable to Harriet—as did much of Steven's speech. Steven's son, Iain, was holding up his phone trying to find signal. He nodded when he saw her, then turned away.

She laid her hand on one of the weathered pyramids that topped the columns guarding the entrance to Erskine. The surface was soft, smothered with lichen. The splotches did not visibly altar, but they were alive. She ran her fingers over the crenelated ridge of a mustard-coloured colony, disturbing the velvet surface. Her gaze ran over the line of stones on the ledge beneath. She really would like it if Addie came.

The night was sober and quiet, the wind inexplicably absent.

Sleekit, curled up at the end of her bed, slept soundly, but the silence kept Harriet awake. She listened to the beating of her heart, to the click of her eyelids as they opened and closed in the

145

dark. Her awareness travelled to the shore, the vast emptiness of the low tide haunted her.

That day she had walked further than ever, at first following the orange bin collection vehicle and then away from the roads around the nose of land towards Rose Ness. Thistles barred her way, reaching out under the skirts of marram grass. She had been forced onto the shelves of flagstone and mess of weed and stones. The ground shifted beneath her boots and her arms had flailed outwards for balance. Several times she lost her footing. She had smiled wryly at the distant sea as she picked herself up. Why hadn't she simply walked on the sand rather than sticking to the path on land?

She had picked up a stone to add to her collection. It was red ochre, cut through with strips of grey and white marbling.

On her return, after finding fresh clothes, she meant to work. The idea was to walk and work. Yet the laptop was rarely opened, notes remained half-finished and correspondence with the Nepali community in Aldershot trickled to nothing. What had once felt important was slipping away. She pictured the shelves in her study, felt the guilt of abandoned books.

Sometimes the space her body occupied felt unjustified, an unwelcome encroachment on Erskine. Other times ,when she had walked and eaten, and spoken to Ernest or the woman in the shop, she felt some sort of balance had been achieved, only to be caught in a sudden fear that she had forgotten everything she knew. She would sit up through the night writing and rewriting. The next day she could not face reading back a single word, certain it was worthless.

Exhausted, she would take the fractals blanket, curl up on the sofa and watch the grasses in the fields waving in the wind, until she was lost in hypnotic waves of green. Her sense of frustration slipped away, until she was present nowhere, either inside or outside, absent and at rest.

~~~

The fields broke into glowing fragments of green, a haphazard mosaic of shifting shades split by freshly ploughed strips of blackish-mauve. Harriet stood and watched the progress of Steven Scarth's tractor as it slit the winter-snaggled grass to reveal the soil. Gulls of all sizes followed in the wake of the plough, an angular white crowd fighting for grubs and worms.

The earth bleached and dried, and the furrows were broken into a russet crumb ready for seed. After sowing, collared doves pecked the sprouting grains. Pale coral-pink and grey, with delicate black chokers and inquisitive blinking eyes, the birds reminded Harriet of her mother.

The number of stones on the pillar grew. She fell less often. She chose to sit, stay, and then consciously return.

5

In June, Addie finally came.

On their first walk down to the shore she flagged down Steven Scarth and introduced herself saying, 'You wouldn't think it, but we're sisters.'

'I like him,' she said afterwards. 'He couldn't be anything but a farmer. Is that an awful to say? What do you think he thinks of me? I expect he doesn't,' she said, answering her own question.

'Doesn't?' said Harriet.

'Think about me, head full of ploughing. Or should that be heed?'

Addie was already practising the lilting rhythm of Orcadian speech, scattering staccato stops and vocal lilts into her conversation as they walked on the shore. The local dialect still fell foreign on Harriet's ears; but after a day Addie was able to throw the sounds around as if they were her own.

'Everyone will know you're here by the way,' said Harriet.

'You told them?'

'No. We'll have been seen at the airport, and in the car, and taking this walk. They'll know you're not Anna. We're close in age, and if my hair was still long we might look alike.'

'You and I? What is it Mum says? "Not peas from the same pod." What does that even mean?'

'No idea. There's even less privacy here than Oxford,' said Harriet. 'And that's saying something.'

'No one really knows who you are.' Addie's eyes picked up reflections of blue from the sky at the thought. 'I think you could bring Art here. And no one would know who he was.'

'Bring?' said Harriet, coming to a stop. 'How exactly? He's got finals.'

'Everyone's so brilliant at Oxford—aren't they just a boring chore?' Addie drew a deep breath about to make another pronouncement, but her nose wrinkled and she covered her mouth. 'What's that smell?'

Harriet barely noticed the tang of the rotting seaweed anymore; unrepulsed by the freshly hatched flies that rose from the lines of kelp. A cloud stretched its arm across the sun, and the blue-grey of the two hills unevenly split by a valley in the distance deepened and drew closer.

'What does it look like to you?' said Addie, recovering herself.

'What?' said Harriet.

'Those hills.'

'It's Hoy.'

'It's two elephants. Do you think I could get some paints?' said Addie.

'In Kirkwall I suppose.'

Harriet wondered if she was utterly without imagination

148

never to see anything except hills. Addie stepped forward and shook her arms away from the sides of her body, then crouched on the rocky beach. Her gaze roamed over the bladderwrack, watching the olive-green flies rise and settle.

To have had an affair with her student indicated passion, thought Addie. At least Art wasn't a man already obsessed with something else. Her sister didn't need another virtuoso musician, or financial consultant, or academic where she was second place from the start. It was a relief to know her sister was capable of such a thing.

Addie cast her gaze over the beach.

The patches of vivid seaweeds in fluorescent pink, deep orange and fresh green were all tempered by layers of grey and brown. Addie mused that the colours would make a fine scheme for the house in Pimlico their mother was redesigning. It was for a new client, an older bachelor who entertained. Nothing had been done to alter the property since the death of his mother.

Their mother, Julia, said the key to unearthing a client's taste was identifying a possession that illuminated a hidden corner of their life. She had invited Addie to see the curiosities the house contained.

'He wants something with a totally different feel,' Julia had said. 'That's the brief.'

Addie had picked up a ceramic dog, one of a pair of jade green Staffordshire pugs that sat in a generous bay window overlooking the street.

'I'm not surprised,' said Addie, touching the creature's nose. She placed it down about-faced, showing its back to its mate.

'I know they're awful, but leaving them like that is even worse.'

'I don't have taste, mother,' said Addie. 'I'm an artist.'

'You're not an artist, darling,' Julia had said. 'You market gallery openings and occasionally daub a canvas when the feeling takes you at the weekends.'

Addie had been only half-listening, her attention taken up by a cabinet of antique thimbles, each embellished in floral designs and edged in gold; the proletarian thimble transformed to expensive aesthetic trinket.

'They're valuable,' Julia had said. 'To a collector.'

'Hideous,' said Addie. 'Worse than the pugs.'

Julia had taken a photograph of the cabinet, then moved on to explore the upstairs study. Clients valued the stories behind her designs, even if the overall look was precise and plain. She was planning to explain to Peter that the pictures in the hallway had been the key when something else caught her eye. The sketchbook had been open on the desk, and impossible to ignore.

Julia turned the pages carefully, examining the impulsive sketches of male torsos and the carefully controlled line drawings of the trees outside. It was an insight into her client, but not one she could claim for her design. As she stood to walk away Julia had noticed a photograph propped on the antique inkwell stand. It was of a middle-aged man with a sort of military look, unkempt as if demobbed and in need of discipline again. She had recognised him from somewhere, a gathering for one of her daughters. Not Addie, so it must have been Harriet.

Julia had held the photograph up and scrutinised it more carefully, then remembered: she had met this man at Harriet's thirtieth birthday at The Red Lion. It was Anna's husband, Martin, the advertising man who had accosted her with diverting stories.

Of all people.

When Julia returned downstairs she became more attentive to the framed pictures in the hallway. Her client had a fine sense of line and proportion that reminded her of *The Yellow Book* and Beardsley, but they had none of the simmering energy of the book upstairs.

'I think they're wonderful,' Julia had said, gesturing to the framed pictures.

Addie had paused and looked critically.

'I suggested to the client that they might be worth something.'

'And?'

'He laughed, and said I could have one as commission.'

Addie's gaze lingered on an androgynous figure disappearing between the wands of trees, then she had followed her mother back upstairs. Julia had taken her to the desk in the study.

Kneeling on the beach in Orkney, Addie remembered the occasion, and what she had resolved to do next time she had an opportunity.

'Is Anna coming back? Addie half-turned then stopped. 'Oh, Harriet. What is it?'

Harriet shook her head and wiped her eyes.

'Why? Why would you say that about Art coming here? Whatever you think, he will have to study and after finals he's expected to go back to London. And it's over. You know it's over.'

Harriet's hands dropped to her side.

Addie rose. She put her arm around Harriet's waist and they stood together facing into the wind, the breeze streaking her tears. In the mid-distance a seal bobbed in the water then lowered out of sight. The soft grey of the returning tide rolled forward, the edge foamed and split as it reached the shore leaving traces of bubbles, then drew back, sighed and prepared to come again.

The waves cast their calming hypnotic spell.

'I'm hungry,' said Addie. 'Let's go back now.'

She linked arms with Harriet and leaned into her side as they headed towards the remains of Storrtang. Seeds lodged between the knuckles of stones were germinating, blue-green foliage hunkered beneath the balls of pink flowers. Addie unhooked her arm, took out her phone and began to take photographs. Built without mortar, the irregular stones were losing their grip and the structure listed towards the sea.

Harriet's gaze lingered on the curl the lapping water. It came steadily, filling hidden spaces in the sand, flowing beneath upturned shells and into every secret void. Harriet crouched down, her fingers rambling over the stones, and pocketed a pebble. She began to collect wild flowers.

'Done,' said Addie sliding away her phone.

Harriet held out a posy of thrift flowers.

'For you.'

Addie accepted the gift, smelled the bright pink heads and they walked on.

The Wildlife Trust van was leaving Scarth's farmyard as they passed. Addie perched on the bank to protect her brogues and waved. Behind the wheel, Ernest passed a small nod to Harriet as the vehicle turned towards the Erskine. Clem's head bent towards Addie in curiosity.

'It's the stoat men,' said Harriet. 'There's a trap in the garden.'

'In your garden?' said Addie.

'Anna's garden. They're a menace to the native birds, and Orkney voles.'

'Orkney voles?'

'Yes,' said Harriet.

Stepping down from the bank Addie looked like someone from a tourism brochure, in her mustard-coloured tunic, white shirt, wide teal scarf and knitted socks.

Harriet remembered her mother saying, 'She's always known how to put herself together,' when they were shopping in Oxford. 'What Addie wears should look like a dog's dinner. But it works. You couldn't get away with it, not just because you're older. And anyway you have a position.'

The comment had made Harriet return a camel-coloured

sweater to the sales rack. It was cashmere, luxurious to touch, and not at all a garment a young woman would wear.

'What about this?' said Harriet.

She held up an electric-blue slash neck top.

'Vulgar,' said her mother. 'You should have sleeves, and the colour is too harsh for you.'

Julia picked out a mannish white cotton shirt.

'For me?' said Harriet.

'No. For me.'

Harriet had glanced in one of the shop mirrors, there were dark patches beneath her eyes, high colour in her cheeks. She wondered if Art compared what she wore with anyone else.

A few minutes later her mother had said, 'Well, what do you like?'

Harriet had faltered. She stretched out a hand and pulled out a blouse at random.

'This.'

Julia cast her eye over the fabric, navy blue silk embellished with a scatter of pink.

'It has flamingoes on it,' said Julia.

Harriet had looked again.

'It's fun,' she said.

'It's hideous.'

Julia had sighed and turned to a fresh rail. Harriet held up the shirt in the mirror. She had purchased the flamingo blouse while Julia took the white shirt. Before setting off for Orkney Addie had picked it out of her mother's wardrobe.

'I'll borrow it and leave it behind.'

'She's not lecturing is she? She doesn't need to look a part. I suppose it's her choice to wear it or not. Send her my love,' Julia had said, 'and tell her she will move on.'

Addie delivered the message as they stepped down from the verge into the lane and given her sister an approximate translation of its meaning.

'Mum says you've to get over him. She's missing tea at The Randolph.'

Harriet wondered what she could possibly say in return. Suddenly, all she could think of were the tiny secret spaces between the sand, nobody knowing or seeing they were filled, until they were totally engulfed.

6

The Wildlife Trust van came to a halt on the run-off by the dyke.

'Where's the trap?' said Addie.

'At the back. Come and meet Ernest.'

Addie looked over to where Clem was meandering around the house.

'Later.'

Harriet watched her sister take off over the wet grass, but did not follow. She diverted her steps to where Ernest was opening the back door of the van. A jar of peanut butter and a fresh punnet of eggs lined up with his cleaning materials.

'Everything all right, Ernest?'

'Aye. Clem's checkin the trap,' said Ernest.

Harriet watched Ernest's hands as they gathered everything to clean and reset the trap. She felt apologetic about Addie's visit; she had brought another complication onto the island.

'How long's yir sister stayin?'

'A week,' said Harriet.

'Hid's company fir you.'

Harriet nodded.

Ernest was solemn, his eyes empty of laughter. They were

sea-grey, and held their colour regardless of the season. In contrast, Clem's eyes were brilliant blue on a fair day, but changed rapidly depending on the surroundings. She wondered if he were a nephew by marriage, because there was little physical resemblance between the men. Not that it made any difference; Ernest treated Clem like a son.

As the weeks passed it had become a relief to see Ernest arrive and climb out of the van—she had a strange fear that one week he might not come, and then never return, an irrational thought she could not shake.

'Is Kieran back now?'

'Gettin a new vehicle,' said Ernest. 'Electric.'

~~~

Around the back of the house Addie strode towards the mass of rosa rugosa. The cerise flowers with yellow hearts drew her attention and there was a hint of fragrance in the air. A few feet from the compost cone Clem appeared suddenly up out of the thicket. Her heart jumped.

'God, you gave me a fright,' said Addie.

Clem's face brightened, clouded, then brightened again. He dropped his arms to his side and pressed his lips together.

'Sounds like you've caught one,' said Addie.

Addie came closer and bent to look. A lock of her hair brushed against Clem's hand. He stood immobile and mute, staring at her back.

'How does it work then?'

Only when Addie hunkered down and began to explore how to lift the lid of the trap did Clem intervene.

'Hid'll brak yir finger,' he said, reaching across to her shoulder and sending her sprawling backwards into the thorny rugosa. A groan escaped his lips.

'I'm sorry. I didna ken you wis so light. I'm muckle clumsy.'

Addie began to laugh. Her eyes creased in the corners, and

Clem saw they looked like crescent-moons.

'No harm done. We've got to get it out though,' she said.

Clem looked back to the house and gripped the penknife in his pocket.

'We shouldna. She'll bite.'

'I'll be careful,' said Addie.

Addie examined the wooden box, her fingers moving over its lid. Clem drew out his knife and opened out a tool then gestured she should move back. He bent over and began unscrewing the trap's lid. Addie stayed crouched, smiling encouragement as Clem deposited the screws into his top pocket like Ernest had shown him. He laid a hand on top of the lid to weigh it down.

'Hid can kill an animal ten times hid's size.'

He slowly lifted the lid.

The egg had been smashed. The box scored by claw marks and flecked with yolk and blood. The jill stoat was caught by her rear paw; it was nearly severed, held on by strands of sinew and fur.

~~~

She could not forget the egg even as she had pursued other prey—it was a constant in her mind, a thing desired. The glow of the egg, rude and rosy. Waiting to be possessed. Waiting to be hers.

There was hesitation where there had been none before. Birth had changed her. She was not to kill all. Not to kill. Not to kill the small selves she had created. They must be fed. And the egg waited. A hunt with no chase. It would nourish her and the small selves.

It was a hard, anti-instinct, not to kill. Drip, drip, dripping in her blood, like milk. And still the egg waited. And she went to the egg. Her patient idol. Its tapering sides had drawn her away from her brood. Her reward when she gave into temptation was blood. Pain.

The kill-or-be-killed Stoat was born again. A creature of pain, of thrumming blood and teeth, of tearing at her own flesh to be

156

~~~

Yaps and screeches burst from Stoat's throat. The animal jerked convulsively. Her black eyes stared up at Clem and Addie, dull from exhaustion, yet still pin-pricked with stars of fury.

'Can you get her out?' said Addie.

Clem shook his head.

Blood had clotted around the metal kill-bar. The wound was livid but no longer bleeding. Stoat's claws gripped the exposed edge of the box as she twisted her body and bared her teeth.

'You must be able to help. How d'you lift the bar?'

Clem pulled away.

'Your knife,' said Addie. She pointed to Stoat's foot. 'You do it.'

Clem looked back to the house again and shifted his balance to lean away.

'You can do it.' Addie reached out and guided his hand.

Clem's breath caught in his throat.

Addie lowered and steadied her voice. 'I'll wrap it in my scarf and I'll take it away. I'll hide her.'

His hand followed hers back to the trap. It dawned on her that the slowness of her communication with Clem was not simply because of a shyness, or difference in accent. Perhaps, she thought fleetingly, she was taking advantage of him. People might see it like that, even if it wasn't true.

Clem looked down at his knife.

Addie whispered, 'I won't tell anyone. It could have just escaped.'

Stoat hunkered down among the pieces of shell. The sun cast pale yellow light through the trap's grill. The high-barking sounds subsided and the smell of fresh spray rose from Stoat's haunches.

Addie unhooked her scarf and caught it deftly around the animal's body, wrapping it firmly. A half-formed laugh in her throat as she watched Clem stoop and hold forward the knife.

There was a flash as the blade moved inside the box. Three passes and the foot was severed, the animal freed. Addie held the bundle tightly, feeling the animal writhe against her chest. Her father would approve—merciful whatever the cause.

Clem smiled up at Addie. Framed by the sky, her hair was a halo as she stooped and kissed him on the cheek. She stood up, looked right and left then crossed to the old croft door. Addie felt Clem wishing to follow, and again a laugh rose in her throat.

A few minutes later Ernest came around the house to see what was taking so long. Clem had put his knife away, but the trap lid was still open.

'Hid got away,' said Clem.

He pointed at Stoat's ragged foot. There was blood on his fingers.

'Hiv you hurt yourself?'

'Peedie scratch,' said Clem.

He tucked his hand into the armpit of his blue overalls.

Ernest raised an eyebrow. He'd taught Clem how to clean and sharpen a knife as a boy and he had put cuts all over his thumb from prising the knife open and pushing it away. Ernest had washed the boy's hands and taken the knife. After a week it was returned. It was a slow, painful way to learn.

'I'll get the peedie weights an we can test the kill bar.'

Clem nodded. He looked over at the door of the house where Addie had gone and he wanted to follow.

'You biding or gaan tae the van?'

'I'll bide,' said Clem.

He would get in trouble if Ernest found out, then Ernest would get in trouble with Kieran. It was their duty was to kill and record, whatever they felt about it, and Ernest had said he badly needed a paying job. There were no savings anymore.

7

Harriet shrugged off her new coat off and hung it on the back of a chair then set to making a fire. The storms during May had forced her into purchasing a more island-practical garment, navy, wind and waterproof, the only one her size in the shops.

Ernest passed the window, head dropped forward, without a glance at the landscape. Harriet wondered if eradicating the stoats lay on his conscience. No. She sensed it was something more personal, more complicated than life and death.

The Wildlife Trust team would make an interesting anthropological paper: 'The technical expertise and belief systems of Northern Isles eradication experts.' She thought briefly of the slaughter of the poisoned animals around Chernobyl, and the competitions to kill non-native species in New Zealand. She wondered if her thinking was becoming unclear, leaping from one place to the next without facts or research, or was her mind becoming more gregarious and astute? In any case, she needed to redraft her paper for *Anthropological Quarterly*: a third reminder had been sent.

She heard the back door open and shut.

'Addie? Do you want coffee?'

'Quick, come through.'

Harriet moved towards her sister's voice. Addie moved agitatedly away from the bathroom door.

'What is it? What are you doing in here?'

Streaks of blood blotted her sister's clothes.

'God, what have you done? Where's it coming from? Did you fall?'

'It's not me,' said Addie.

'What? Who then?'

Harriet turned to the window. Clem stood at the green cone

looking at his feet and talking with Ernest.

'Clem?'

'No. Not him.'

Addie took hold of the bathroom door handle.

'Well, there's no way I can keep her secret,' she said.

She threw the door open. Stoat's sleek head peered over the edge of the bathtub, her black eyes fixed and hard.

'I saved her,' said Addie.

'Jesus.'

'She's injured,' said Addie. 'Clem had to cut her foot free. Well, he cut it off.'

'No, not here.'

'There's no way she'll survive in the wild.'

'It's not supposed to be surviving in the wild,' said Harriet. 'That's why they're getting rid of them.'

The animal began to chatter rapidly and emit small, high-pitch barks. It slid back from standing upright into a braced attack position. Harriet stepped backwards. Blood was smeared around the sides of the tub and Addie's scarf lay rumpled in one corner.

'She's nipped me already,' said Addie. 'Maybe she'll calm down if we feed her.'

'I'll tell Ernest.'

'Who?'

'To get rid of it,' said Harriet.

'What'll he do?' said Addie.

'Wring its neck, I expect.'

Addie gestured out of the window.

'But he helped me.'

'Who?' said Harriet.

'In the overalls.'

'Clem?' said Harriet.

'You don't want to cause him trouble. Come on, Harriet,'

said Addie.

'It's got to go straight away. The bath cost a thousand pounds.'

'More if Anna bought it,' said Addie. 'But she won't care.'

'It's not funny,' said Harriet.

Addie turned to the animal. Its pelt captured the light and became translucent and silvery, the black tip of its tail stood out against the whiteness of the bath. A bib of snow-white fur stretched under its belly.

Harriet sighed.

'She is beautiful.'

The animal glared at Addie, shivered backwards and turned a tight circle in the confines of the bath.

'What she needs is a vet,' said Addie.

'Addie, you are not…'

A knock at the front door echoed through the house.

'Don't say anything,' said Addie.

Harriet shook her head and walked away. Ernest was waiting at the door holding a screwdriver.

'The kill bar's missed hid's mark.'

'Oh?'

'Ah'll calibrate the trap and bring hid back in the morn. Don't want animals suffering.'

'No problem,' said Harriet.

Inside the house there was a sound of a door hurriedly closing and Ernest glanced over Harriet's shoulder into the interior.

'Anything else?' said Harriet.

'Have a good visit,' he said.

'She'll keep me busy,' said Harriet.

Ernest nodded and walked to the van. Clem wandered after him, turning once to look back sharply and nearly losing his balance in a rut on the drive. He waved his arms to avoid falling, then trotted over to the waiting van.

~~~

As Erskine grew small in the rearview mirror Ernest remembered its story. It haunted his thoughts all along the coast road. What worthless creatures men were. They injured each other until there was no hope.

There was no way out for him either, no hiding. The one thing worth anything that he had he couldn't sell. He couldn't use the Merkit Place webpage to sell the motorbike; everyone would ken. If he borrowed a trailer to go off island and sell the bike folk would see him coming and going, everyone would still ken.

Such a damn fool, everyone would ken one way or another.

In the passenger seat, Clem bunched his hands into fists and tried hard to be still. He thought of the mauve-white inside of the wound and the nub of foot left behind. He minded Auntie Meg separating chicken pieces, wriggling the knife into the joint to free the pink-purple portions of meat.

'You didna meddle wi the trap?' said Ernest.

'I didna mean to,' said Clem.

Clem reached forward to the radio and Ernest slapped his hand away from the dial.

'Whit's wrong wi you beuy? Can you no bide?'

The slap stung.

'Can we go tae the piece van?'

Ernest sighed and shook his head.

Dirty grey clouds heavy with hail bulged overhead. Clem looked past the flaking facade of the peedie folk's house, thoughts too busy to take notice of its dark-windows, too busy thinking about Addie's soft hands and hair. He wouldn't have minded getting bitten to help her. She wouldn't slap him away.

He lifted his hand and ran his fingers over where she had kissed him then looked sideways and saw a black look on his uncle's face. Clem lowered his hands, held them together on his knee and fixed his eyes on the road ahead.

8

Kieran had returned to Orkney six weeks ago. He was still catching up on sightings, finding it hard to concentrate, and spending half his time scrolling through pictures of home. The funeral had been the first time he'd ever seen Mish in skirt and tights.

He found a picture of her crouched by the stump of a macrocarpa tree. Her smile was candid, open. The stumps were monuments to the determination of the early settlers. Clearing forest and introducing new species were how settlers made wilderness home. It wasn't long before whole hillsides had rippled with rabbits. Competitions made sport of necessary culls. Grainy photographs showed young ladies in full skirts holding uncocked guns and long rows of corpses.

There was an exhibition in Arrowtown they had been taken to as children. It was in a converted villa that smelled of wood smoke and paraffin oil with real filigree ironwork on the eves rather than the plastic fake stuff people put up now.

His father had said, 'Must have got sick of rabbit stew.' And Toni had got weepy seeing the photographs. She had a pet rabbit called Blackberry that roamed the garden.

Kieran wanted to call Toni, but he should call his mother first, and since he couldn't bring himself to do that he didn't do anything. So he waited for Ernest and Clem and kept swiping from picture to picture. There was one of his parents' house near Christmas time, bristly red flowers covered the pohutakawa tree, the sky stretched tight over the orange roof.

One summer, when he was eleven, they'd stayed at the Mackenzie's bach in Tekapo. Kieran had loved being in the water, free from pain, swimming out with Toni into the cooler, deeper reaches. His mother had sat on the deck, making cards celebrating the sacraments to sell at church. His father sat at the end of the jetty and fished.

It had been the summer before he was fitted for the back brace that he would wear for the next two years. It had been the summer Blackberry went missing.

His mother had been up in the attic above the hall when his sister came in, bottom lip trembling. A norwester was blowing outside and Toni's shorts were grey with dust.

'He can't have gone.'

Jean swung down a tan leather case, dusty from sitting unused. 'He is gone,' Toni had insisted.

Jean had shook her head.

'Well, I shut him in last night.'

'He left all the carrots.'

'Maybe he got sick of them,' Kieran said.

They had checked the fence for escape holes and their mother spent the hot afternoon between searching and packing.

Kieran had been sent to crawl under the house, an activity usually forbidden because of the unstable pilings and the threat of quakes. Toni sat on the verandah picking at the old paint, red-cheeked and hollow-eyed as if she had a fever.

'Quit doing that, Toni. Look for Blackberry.'

'I've looked everywhere,' said Toni.

'Well, look again,' said Jean. 'Your brother's going to get squashed to death and you're sitting like a wet weekend.'

She had wiped a hand over her forehead and stared up into the yellow-grey sky. The clouds had drawn lower, clothes were sticky with sweat and dirt.

Toni sloped to her feet just as Kieran crawled out, filthy from dragging through the narrow space.

'Did you see him, K-P?'

'I found a hole.'

Toni's eyes had brightened.

'Blackberry wouldn't have fit. Must be rats.'

'What if she eats p-poison?'

Kieran had looked at his mother and shrugged. She wiped her hand across her top lip to clear the sweat. 'Why don't you go to Mrs Mackenzie and get some fresh carrots to put round? I can't search anymore, there's still packing to do.' '

His mother's hand dropped onto Toni's shoulder, then she carried on inside.

'Sorry,' he said.

Toni had looked him in the eye and he felt himself pegged down in her estimation.

'Kieran, put out the trash,' called his mother.

He had traipsed inside and taken the bag. It twisted and knocked against his leg, something scratched his skin. He pulled the lid off the metal can releasing a thick, shitty-cabbage smell and swung the bag over. As it landed he glanced the sack. He lurched backwards, disturbing a cloud of flies.

He could swear it was a paw, poking through a tear in the sack.

He remembered the day before his father saying, 'It's once in a blue moon I get three weeks off. I'm not cancelling because we can't get a bloody rabbit sitter.'

'Everyone's going away,' said his mother.

A sick feeling had risen inside him. The bluebottles settled and Kieran reached forward and pushed down the lid on the can. Later, he'd watched Toni put out vegetables from Mrs Mackenzie.

'He's probably gone on holiday,' Kieran said.

Toni had nodded, concentrating on arranging the cabbage and carrots. She had looked up and had given him a half-smile.

'But he doesn't like holidays,' she said.

The rain had finally come at dinner time and the temperature began to fall. By bedtime they needed blankets. They never saw Blackberry again.

~~~

Kieran came back to the present, a dull ache of grief in his limbs, a stone in his gut. The happier the memory, the more it hurt. He swiped the phone again and pressed Mish's number. Immediately his thumb went to cancel, but the video feed came on. The handset glow was the only light in the room.

'It's midnight,' said Mish, pushing back the covers. 'What do you want?'

The screen went dark. She reappeared a few seconds later in an unfamiliar kitchen.

'How's Mum?'

'I didn't see her today.'

Mish yawned, glanced out of the window and tucked her T-shirt around her legs.

'She was going with Anne Mackenzie to the cemetery. Why don't you call her?'

'It's never the right time.'

'She's worried,' said Mish.

'Tell her I'm fine.'

'Tell her yourself. Did you call Toni?'

'She's got Eric.'

'You're her brother.'

Mish pushed back the hair from her face .

'You did okay at the funeral,' said Mish. 'But you need to be there for her even when there's nothing to arrange or talk over.'

Kieran's throat tightened.

'You could have stayed longer.'

'What was there to stay for?'

He drummed his knuckles on the desk and tried to find a way of saying all the things he wanted to say. The door into the street popped opened, paper flapped and shifted around him. The moment was gone.

'Put hid in the corner,' said Ernest.

166

'Look, I've gotta get back to work.'

'So now you're busy. Jesus, Kieran. You're the one who woke me up.'

The screen went blank.

Kieran tapped the phone against his forehead then threw it down on the desk.

'Clem fund a foot up at Erskine.'

'In the trap?' said Kieran.

Ernest nodded.

'The animal wis awey.'

'Won't last long injured,' said Kieran.

Kieran pushed back from the desk then rose to his feet.

'Needin the weight caddy,' said Ernest.

'I'm going to get eggs,' said Kieran.

'Clem can do that.'

'If he wants a job he can clean the van.'

'How's the vehicle?'

'Like driving a bumper car. Hardimans are going to fix up a charge point.'

'What cabling they using?'

'No idea mate.' He turned to Clem. 'You can have a sit this afternoon. The new car.'

Clem smiled and nodded. Kieran headed past him out of the door.

9

Since Kieran's return he'd noticed the small differences again. The portions of butter and cheese looked small, Orkney milk tasted different. What stayed the same was meeting someone you knew every time you were out.

Harriet was contemplating the cartons of eggs.

'G'day.'

'Picking up a few things,' said Harriet. She hesitated. 'My sister's staying. She's vegan.'

'So you're getting eggs?'

'No…I need eggs.'

Kieran began checking the use-by dates on packets.

'For the traps?' said Harriet.

'Yup.'

Harriet took a box next to one he had selected.

'What else do stoats eat?'

'Anything they can get their teeth into, bite the back of the neck and hold.' He mimed the action, bringing together his fingers like teeth. 'Adaptable buggers'

Harriet glanced at the packet of chicken fillets in her basket. Kieran caught her eye.

'How long's your sister here?'

'I don't know. Long as she likes it, it was meant to be a week.'

Kieran was going to say his mum and dad were going to visit and then remembered. He looked away down the aisle. Two old men were moving towards them from the tinned soup.

Walt held out his hand.

'Heard aboot yir loss beuy. Hid wis a long way fir you tae get hame.'

Kieran returned Walt's handshake.

'Caught a muckle male last week. Been in the trap twa-thee days, stunk to high-heaven.'

The doctor's basket held a bag of frozen peas, a pie in a tin can and a box of tea.

'Hid's bleeding the toon dry,' he said, waving at the shelves, 'but hid's cheaper than anywhar else.'

Harriet nodded farewell and walked away to the check out.

Addie must see they could not save the stoat. Why was she buying food? The conveyor began to drag away her packages.

A message flashed up on her phone, 'Get steri-strips for wound.'

She texted back, 'No.'

She tucked away her phone and watched someone tickling a child in a trolley. She felt half-disconnected, half-engaged. Underneath everything there was some sort of connection. Did she deserve any part in it? The question triggered a notion inside, a value passed on from their father, a man who'd abandoned his own career to develop better euthanasia protocols for laboratory animals. He would prevent suffering if he could.

'Actually, I've just forgotten something.'

Harriet found the pharmacy section and picked up two boxes of plasters and a roll of bandage, then returned. The cashier processed the items without comment. When everything had been scanned the woman nodded towards the carpark. The light was changing from blue to grey.

'Wish it'd make up hid's mind,' she said holding out the payment keypad. 'Do you hiv a reward caird?'

~~~

Eventually, the sky gave way and rain began to fall. Harriet followed the row of traffic along the Holm straight and headed east. The car had no capacity to move quickly and she had lost the desire to overtake. Ernest had found her the vehicle and he handed it over saying, 'Hid'll last a year no doot. Go easy mind.'

She took him at his word. Apart from Addie the stoat men were the closest she had to friends for hundreds of miles. The thought brought a wave of emptiness. She wished she could vanish, absorbed into something useful like the tarmac, something that could at least be walked on and driven over. Life carrying on was absurd.

She was absurd. It was ridiculous–she still wanted Art. It

was ridiculous—tears rose at the thought of being with him.

She remembered standing in the Oxford University Museum of Natural History. Art had stood at her side. To an observer they would have looked like visitors casually coming together—her in professional wool coat and high-boots, he a student browsing the collection. They had stood before the *Homo habilis* skull, the link species between bipedal australopithecines and the hominids that would go on to become Homo sapiens. There had been a mock-up impression of the physical appearance of the changing species. Art's forehead had drawn into a frown.

'Does he look Ethiopian to you?'

'I don't know,' she had said.

He had persisted.

'Look at him. Does he?'

'I am looking.'

Art's delicate lips had drawn into a tight, thin line.

She had wanted to say, 'We've only a short time, don't be distracted by this. Don't be angry at things like this.' Even though she knew she should be angry for him, with him, but they had hardly seen each other all week.

'Perhaps they just don't know,' was what she had said.

Art had turned to her, his gaze hard beneath long black lashes. He'd never looked at her like that before. He had stepped away from her, shoulders hunched as if walking into rain.

In tutorials he was always quick, smiling when she corrected Gregory's misquotations. When they were alone together his gaze moved more slowly, languid as his hand on her skin.

She had followed him cautiously, pausing to look down at a cabinet of ammonites. She saw her reflection on the glass. This is what Art would see when she was above him. She turned away quickly, cheeks burning.

Art's attention had become intent on the primate display and the pose of a taxidermy chimp. His hand had rested on the glass, forehead almost touching. The animal had white hairs on its chin, its fingers gripping the branch. The skin of the animal was putty-coloured beneath the coarse hair, lips speckled with sunspots.

She had reached out and touched the back of Art's hand.

'I'm sorry,' she had said.

'What for?'

'Let's go somewhere else, get out of town again.'

Art had closed his fingers around hers. The light filtered down through the sky-lights above the ribs of the building, sturdy like those of the great whales harpooned or driven to the shore. The diffuse glow brought out the bronze depths of Art's skin, his irises grew deeper and darker. He had lifted her hand and brushed it with his lips.

'No,' he said. 'I have an essay. And a meeting about the play, the set isn't finished, the flyers need designing.'

She'd sighed.

'Can't it wait? Can't they do anything without you?'

'It has waited.'

Harriet flushed.

'After the performance?'

'It will be late,' he said. 'We're having drinks.'

Art had walked away, shoes clipping the stone floor. He averted his gaze as he passed the dodo , trapped in its case, once a native of the island where he was born. He was fastening his coat, anticipating the cold, petrol-laced air. She knew he would stroll along Manor Road to the Sociology Library and disappear into the shoal of students. Students rehearsing plays, students discovering and re-inventing themselves, students walking in the dark, walking in the rain, anonymous as paint.

Harriet had waited by the display case for her sense of loss dissipate. It was mid-afternoon, yet she could not face going back to her office or the college. Walking up the Banbury Road to her flat she had felt easy prey. A dodo.

10

Stoat drank from the saucer of water until exhausted. With a slow, hobbling motion she went to the hole criss-crossed with metal and applied her claws. Her escape barred, she rolled onto her back and settled to her wound, tending the raw fringes with teeth and tongue.

Addie was keeping half an eye on Stoat, balancing a laptop on her knee and trying to connect to an online meeting for the gallery. In a brief moment of connection, a call came though diverted from Harriet's phone. It gave her an opportunity to explain the newly developed situation.

The connection was temperamental. At times Anna looked like a twitching mannequin on fast forward.

'You don't mind about the stoat, do you?' said Addie. 'She's very sweet.'

'Could you keep it in a hutch?' said Anna.

'I don't know if she's going to make it,' said Addie. 'And it's your house, Anna, of course you can come.'

'Tell Harriet I'll hire a car at the airport.'

The sound stuttered, sped up and slowed down. Addie smiled, remembering Harriet's description of Anna as a student: 'Kind, funny and smart. It's impossible to be her friend.'

'Nonsense. Harriet will pick you up.'

'All of us?' said Anna. 'Will the car manage?'

Addie laughed.

'Is Martin coming? I never know why you keep him hanging on.'

'He is the father of my children,' said Anna.

'Even so,' said Addie. 'I'll make something to eat.'

'It'll do him good to eat nut cutlets,' said Anna.

'What about Eveline? And Oscar? What do the children eat?'

'Anything. Breakfast cereal most likely,' said Anna.

'Will Eveline manage the flight?'

'Doctor Bhalla thinks so.'

'I should have done better,' said Anna. 'You'd have done better...'

The sound cut out and Addie's face froze on the screen.

~~~

Anna had not been concerned when the asthma attack first started. They had been walking back from the park, Eveline dawdling, Oscar sucking a lolly, scuffed and satisfied. Hazy sunshine blurred through the chestnut leaves dressing the edges of the common.

Eveline had trotted from behind and asked, 'When is Daddy coming home?'

'When he's hungry,' Anna had replied.

Eveline had frowned.

'What if he doesn't get hungry? Or buys a sandwich?'

Anna hadn't replied, intent on crossing the road. By the time they were at Wollstencraft Terrace Eveline was wheezing and dragging on the buggy handle, head drooping. The blue inhaler gave no relief, she was caught in the catch 22 of not being able to inhale. Time was lost finding car keys, scrambling for change and pacifying Oscar. His sister's lips paled, then became a shade of lavender that made the ground fall away under Ann's feet. Her strength had sapped as the urgency of the task increased.

She had arrived at the hospital carrying Eveline, dragging a wailing Oscar, shoulder bag spilling out.

'Help. I need help.'

The accident and emergency admissions nurse had abandoned her officious manner, and when she saw the oxygen reading she had quickly set aside the admission paperwork. A mask had been placed over Eveline's face and they were escorted to a cubicle. Anna thought about that moment, how suddenly life and death it had become.

~~~

The call re-connected and Addie became animated again.

'Me?'

'You've rescued a three-legged animal that's being eradicated,' said Anna.

'Look, I have to help Oscar on the toilet,' said Anna, her movements fast-forwarding. 'Apologise to Harriet that we'll disturb her peace.'

'Oh, I've already done plenty of that,' said Addie. 'She needs it.'

The video feed went blank.

~~~

Martin had used the moment of relief when Eveline was out of danger to tell Anna about his affair with Harriet. An attack of guilt, brought on by the stress, he said. He wanted to give her the truth she deserved, to tell her, and to swear it wouldn't happen again. He pointed out that until the crisis with Art Harriet had hardly been in touch anyway. Then he had said Anna shouldn't feel guilty about Eveline.

'Jesus, along with buying your mother a birthday card that you won't bother sign, I sort out the finances of your botched 'Drive em Wild' commercial, take a toddler who is potty train-ing to the park and try and bring some joy to a daughter who spends far too long cooped up in the house and you think I'm feeling guilty?'

'Well it's just after all your nagging, you're the one who forgets the inhaler. It shows you're only human.'

Anna swallowed hard, balled her fists, but kept them by her side.

'I love Harriet. I don't understand what she was doing with you. But it wouldn't have been to make herself happy. She really doesn't deserve the misery.'

'Creates enough of her own.'

'She fell in love,' said Anna.

'Love doesn't get an enforced sabbatical.'

'Shut up.'

Anna had taken out her phone.

'What are you doing?'

'Harriet, it's Anna. Eveline's in hospital again. I hope you don't mind, but Martin was saying how much he'd like a break, some quality family time. Can you believe it?' To Anna's frustration her voice vanished to a croak and her eyes filled with tears. She'd stayed on the line until she could speak again. 'I wish you'd pick up. Call me, If you can. I'll try later.'

Now she had made contact and Addie knew they were coming Anna felt a small knot untie beneath her ribs. She returned to Oscar perched on the toilet. He was mashing a toothpaste tube between his fingers.

'Are you done?'

Oscar shook his head; there was a moment of concentrated quiet.

Anna wondered where the hell Martin was. He had been at the revised shoot for the hatchback commercial, but since then there had been a stand-off between the creatives about what 'picturesque grime' actually meant. An emergency meeting had extended into the night and Martin had stayed with Peter Beachcroft rather than come back home.

'Finished?' said Anna.

'Near-ly,' said Oscar.

He grimaced. Anna turned her gaze to the bathroom floor,

her thoughts drifting back to the accident and emergency room and the laboured sound of Eveline's breathing, her eyes rolling back.

She stood up and faced the bathroom mirror. Her skin was ashen and drawn like her daughter's. They had to escape the city, leave the heat and invisible toxins in the air. She would go without Martin if she had to.

'I've got to change Daddy's dental appointment,' said Anna. 'Don't move.'

Oscar nodded.

As soon as his mother's back was turned Oscar reached for the toothpaste again. He liked the way it bulged and flowed and always wanted to come out. He pushed hard and released the lid, a soft white worm of paste escaped. It stuck to his fingers as he tried to rearrange its shape on the handbasin.

In the hallway, Anna picked up her phone. What was she doing? Why did she look after him? She caught her breath and held back tears.

'Mum! Oscar's squeezed out the paste again!'

Eveline's voice was croaky, like she had grit in her throat.

Anna returned to the bathroom.

'He's very naughty, isn't he.'

Oscar shook his head. How could he explain the paste always wanted to come out?

~~~

At twenty-three Regent's Crescent a cardboard box waited on the hall table.

'For you,' said Peter.

Martin raised his eyebrows.

'Please, take them. Give them away if you don't want them.'

Martin's gaze lifted from the box and to the disordered hallway. One of the ink drawings was missing and the hallway appeared longer.

'I don't know why you're altering anything,' said Martin. 'It's a period property.'

'Time for change,' said Peter.

Martin let the box lid close. His gaze travelled upwards over the details of architrave and the brass light fittings. The gilt geometric surround of the mirror caught them together in its reflection. It was original art deco, valuable, but Peter was determined nothing would stay.

'I've decided to take a flat until it's finished. I hate hotels.'

'I thought you liked room service,' said Martin.

'It's never worth it,' said Peter. 'For the loss of privacy.'

Martin placed his hand on the other man's chest. The edge of his thumb drew down along the seam of Peter's shirt as he turned to open the door.

When Martin left, Peter lifted a hand in farewell and watched him slip behind the railings carrying the box beneath his arm until he was out of sight. This was the last time.

Peter breathed deeply and closed the door. Grateful Martin was gone. After the electrician there could be no more pretending. The adventure was over.

He faced back to the mirror. His eyes were dark, their colour indistinguishable. He resolved to resign from the production company. He must not hurt himself anymore. When Martin was in a room he couldn't think clearly, he acted against so many things he deeply believed.

Peter moved away from his reflection and stood before the remaining framed image. Julia had been so complimentary about the sketches. He was glad to have given her the other picture. He examined the antics of the carnival goers he'd invented, the masked men and women, the grotesque satires and faeries.

'Why did you ever stop taking your art seriously?' she'd asked.

He had been about to say, 'It was a punishment,' but instead he shrugged and said, 'It just didn't seem to go anywhere.'

She had found a job on her renovation team for the electrician without asking questions.

~~~

Martin inhaled the dust and dirt of the underground and shifted the box to sit snugly on his hip. He thought about Harriet and Addie, both at Erskine. He thought about Harriet caught in her affair with a student. He wondered what they did together. He wanted to know where and when? In libraries? Between the book stacks?

Harriet, Harriet…yes, the doors of possibility.

He hesitated at the edge of the platform as the tube arrived, then stepped on board. Anna would be waiting.

11

The clouds shifted, briefly revealing a gibbous moon setting against the pale sky. Showers moved rapidly over the islands and the sky darkened over Erskine. Rain could arrive at any time.

In the kitchen Harriet chopped chicken into fine pieces.

'I should be marking dissertations,' she called over her shoulder. Her voice echoed around the empty room. A minute later Addie came through, a saucer in her hand.

'She turned her nose up at the dog food. But the mince has gone down. '

'How do you know it's a she?'

'Clem, told me. I like him. Anyway, of course it's a she,' said Addie. 'Anna's coming by the way.'

Harriet scraped the chicken from her board into the empty dish.

'Well, then she has to go.'

'Anna didn't say that.'

'You told her?'

'Of course.'

Addie picked up a tourist magazine, perched on the sofa and started browsing a feature on jewellery. She pointed at a photograph of three colossal stones. The vertical thrusts split the blue and green landscape of West Mainland with their rude presence.

'Have you been here?'

'I haven't been anywhere,' said Harriet. 'The car's too unreliable.'

'We should go tomorrow. Five thousand years…can that really be true? I thought Stonehenge was the oldest…you know… thing.'

'What about the stoat?' said Harriet.

Addie shrugged.

'It's a funny bathroom. What was it? A larder?' said Addie.

'It used to fit a bed.'

Addie raised an eyebrow and went to the window. She turned and faced northwards.

'And what's that structure?'

'Ernest calls it a floatel, for oil workers.'

'Ernest?'

'One of the stoat murderers.'

Addie stayed at the window, staring over the sea, holding out the dish of chicken on her fingertips like a waiter about to cross a dining room. The clouds were drawing up their skirts and the sky clearing.

'You'd never think the water would be so blue,' said Addie. 'It's like the Caribbean or somewhere.'

'It's the light,' said Harriet. 'It changes all the time.'

12

Clem studied the concrete bollards by the garages. They looked like stubby fingers, poking upwards, casting thick shadows. He was keen on the action at the garages. A man with a garage could stand and talk with a pal. He didn't have to sit on a bench alone.

Balfour Rise had parking bays and front gardens, the terraces had yards and garages. He watched the boy with the red bicycle; Sigurd fandangled the machine in and out of the bollards without putting a foot down. All jigs and jags of energy, guffawing and kicking a ball. Sigurd rummaged the sweetie racks and slipped them into his pocket without paying.

Clem had seen Sigurd stand by the Subaru on the corner. He'd nod to the driver and take a package then return with money. Clem could see he didn't like his bicycle half so much after being in the car.

Clem had no car. He walked where he wanted to go, day or night.

Once he'd tried to walk back from Finstown after the summer gala. He had been drinking, feeling full of friendliness then the police had been there and told him it was best he went home He'd lied about having ride. No one wanted him in their car. Thick fog had wrapped like a damp blanket around the coast as he straggled along, he'd had to wipe his eyes to check they were not becoming defective. The police had caught up with him and dropped him home.

Auntie Meg had said he deserved a clout, even though he was over a foot taller than she was. There was a shake in her voice. The worry hurt her badly that night.

'He needs tae move oot,' she had said soon afterwards.

Ernest had patted Clem on the shoulder and said, 'Aye.'

Clem thought about Auntie Meg whenever he heard women

calling their bairns or saw a buggy peeking out through the parked cars. He felt sick in his heart wanting to go back.

~~~

The harled walls turned deeper grey as night fell. Clem was restless. Not with thoughts of cars. It was the cutting away the animal's foot—and the woman who was light as air.

He put on a jacket over his pyjamas for a night walk around the scheme, touring the lanes that stretched to Inganess Bay, coming back around by the rust-scabbed play park. He walked as he'd learned to do in school corridors, eyes down as if he were going somewhere, like the incomer boys who'd taken a beating.

He stood at the top of the mound by the swings then stumped his way down trying to mind the sapling trees. He could hear his own blood, like he was moving at a hundred miles an hour.

As he drew back to Balfour Rise his breath shortened. He quietened his footsteps, and came to stand by the blue car. It was like an aeroplane cockpit, with all the dials. The metallic odour of clutch and brakes transported him to Ernest's workshop. Ernest mending and Auntie Meg bringing tea, him sitting comfortably and handing over the tools.

He lightly ran one finger along the spoiler. The coolness ran up his arm as if the energy of the car was travelling inside him. Clem's hand slipped to the car door handle, paused, then pulled gently. A high-pitched alarm sliced through the air. His heart jumped.

Clem convulsed as the sound cut into his chest.

He heard Ernest's voice, 'Run, beuy, run!'

Clem staggered, struggling to make his legs move. He lumbered into a bollard, cracked his knee, threw his arms forward and saved himself from falling then hustled towards the blackest shadow he could see. It was where Sig smoked and rubbish was thrown. He stood behind the garages, hands clamped over his own mouth.

Whee-whee, whee-whee.

His hands wet with breath.

Whee-whee, whee-whee.

The tick-tick indicator lights splashed the scheme with bursts of orange. He waited, pulse breaking against the inside of his skull.

No one came and no one went. The blue lights did not come. He stayed still a long time. His hands became cold, his breath even. He imagined the police, still searching until they found where he hid. He surveyed the empty scheme and turned his back. He wanted his bed. Clem moved sideways and towards a row of bungalows, the moon unnoticed above, and shambled along the pavement. Past the bench, up the bank and down the concrete path, he pressed himself into the shadow of the porch. The night fell quiet.

Clem was alone, knees weak, hands shaking and taking out his key. He shouldna touch. Shouldna want to touch. It wasna his. He shook of his coat and rolled into his blankets.

Sleep came quickly, spiced with vivid dreams. In one Clem cut open a blue car with a knife that could cut through anything. He hid it in his pocket and said he would only show it for a kiss. And then he said he wouldn't show it after all, and laughed instead.

13

In the past, Erskine saw its own share of sleepless nights. James Poke had not the same stomach as his sister Janet for open family living. When his mother passed away, his duties as a husband and desire for privacy when inevitably bairns arrived, inspired him to take his parents' bed in the alcove.

'It's a space for butter and cheese,' said Gudrun as she surveyed the space newly vacated by her mother-in-law.

'No, hid's a place fir sleepin,' James replied.

The couples' marital bed had up to that point been a narrow box bed, boarded around three sides with a roof and shutters that could be fastened for warmth and privacy. They had performed all their intimate relations in this small space, except for once or twice when the lapwings danced and the peat bank deserted. James had taken the straw mattress out of the alcove to be burned and fashioned a replacement. The wooden box bed had been dismantled and the pieces moved to the storehouse.

When Thorn had been at Erskine two years Gudrun suggested the box bed be rebuilt. 'He's outgrown sleeping by the hearth,' she told James.

'Aye, past being a child,' said James. He muttered something about having the appetite of a man and drew on his pipe.

Slaters scuttled as the old planks were uncovered, rats had left toothmarks in the wood and droppings from birds spotted the upper timbers. Everything was cleaned—Gudrun working with sleeves rolled up and cheeks reddening from effort—then left to dry in bright sun. James worked with gouge and hammer to fashion replacement sections. Thorn assisted where he could.

The sleeping platform was erected and gradually enclosed. Finally the top was lowered down like a lid, fitting neatly into place. The bed box was finished with a double-grooved trim and was sturdy enough for items to be stored on top and beneath. James stood back and admired the shutters facing into the room.

'It'll be more privacy,' said Gudrun to her husband.

James nodded in agreement. Unseen, Gudrun and Thorn caught each other's eye.

Nowhere had been private in Thorn's parents' house. Daily and nightly family activity was an open book in Storrtang.

Whether it was quarrels, laughter, or his parents' grunting and grappling in the dark, everything was in common. No treasure was safe, each nook of the rough walls regularly searched by curious, perfidious fingers.

'Go on, beuy, try it fur size.'

Thorn dropped his gaze to the floor. His uncle and aunt waited. There was fresh straw and heather in the mattress and a woollen blanket of brown and grey folded neatly over the top. Thorn turned away, lips pressed together.

'It's no time to rest.'

Thorn had stepped away, and in return Gudrun had lifted her chin. James shrugged and glanced between his nephew and his wife. It was a solid structure and clean. The blankets washed and dried. Far more had been done to prepare the bed for his nephew than for their wedding night.

Gudrun shifted her weight and cast her eye over the cosy inside. She unclasped her hands, then moved from her husband's side to the opening between the shutters. She turned on the spot and perched on the base inside. She viewed the two men standing before the hearth, then pushed the shutters further open and scooted her haunches backwards.

Inside the enclosed space the sounds of the croft were softened. Gudrun curled her legs beneath her skirts and rested on her elbow. It would be quicker to warm than the stone alcove.

Thorn paused and looked back over his shoulder. His eyes caught the light coming down through the open lum and Gudrun felt his gaze fall upon her hip and the scoop of her waist.

James did not look at his wife, but to the row of planks either side of her, each one fitted tight to its neighbour as it should. It had been a fine bed.

His mind cast back to the memory of their early married life, Gudrun's breasts as rounded as Wideford, his moving hands while she lay still as the islands beneath, feeling the coolness of her except for the one slit of heat. He was unsure that his hands were the right tool for the furrow yet it often gave her pleasure before he put the rhythm of his own body inside her. Those had been miraculous moments, better than any whisky, better than the thrill of high cliffs. The closest thing to the feeling he could name was the tullimentan, stars so deep and miraculous in the night sky that he felt his feet float clear off the ground.

Looking at the old bed again James became conscious of the cloth of his breeks around his thighs, he remembered his roughened skin against the smooth dampness of his wife's form.

'You've done a fine job,' said Gudrun.

James nodded.

She reclined backwards. A lazy ache grew in her head and she turned on her side and closed her eyes, imagining the warmth of another beside her. Her muscles relaxed. The sensation of no longer being alone became more real until she wondered if she had fallen asleep and gone into a dream. She reached behind and found softness, then the nip of canoodling teeth. The sound of laughter rose from James and Thorn.

Without invitation the cat had joined her in bed.

Blood rushed to Gudrun's cheeks.

'I kent thou art a witch,' said James.

Gudrun swivelled upright and pulled the animal into her arms, then swung her legs down between the shutters. She rose pertly to her feet and strode across the room and landed the cat outside the door.

'Damned freck.'

James followed her footsteps, chuckling. He picked up a spade and went to clear the burn from its yearly choking of flag iris. Gudrun stood at the door, cheeks flushed, watching him walk away.

'How did you find the bed?' said Thorn in a low voice.

The breath on her ear made Gudren shiver. She went to step

away, but Thorn's hand restrained her from behind. She watched her husband set to work, a small figure, halfway down the brae.

'Cold,' she said. 'Awful cold.'

A length of heat grew at the base of her back where Thorn pressed.

'I doot you'll sleep well in there,' she said.

'Sleep?' said Thorn.

Thorn had breathed in the burned sweetness of Gudrun's hair and pictured his aunt leaning on the pillow. Gudrun moved as if to slip away, yet Thorn moved like her shadow. The kettle swung on its chain caught by their passing. He reached out and touched her hair. His aunt turned aside, her laughter mingled with the rising smoke.

'I'm not your cat,' she said.

Thorn shrugged. He had taken leave of his aunt without another word, gathered up tools and went to join his uncle. He drove hard into the bank.

The blush deepened on Thorn's cheeks as he worked. His chest felt it would burst with each drive, yet he must keep pace. Even the most taxing work did not fatigue his uncle's stoney forearms. He glanced at the clearing already completed and re-membered how well everything was always done at Erskine. He was never bullied, or called work-shy or weak like at Storrtang.

'No need to kill yourself,' said James, seeing his nephew's thrusts.

Thorn laughed and breathed the raw spring air deeper into his lungs.

'I suppose not,' said Thorn.

His glance travelled back to the croft. His throat tightened. There was a shadow at the window. The time had gone when physical exhaustion dispelled the restlessness of his heart.

Inside, Gudrun had taken up the bucket of milk and poured the cream carefully into the butter churn. With slow, steady strokes she began her work, now and again adding salt as she saw fit. Her arms moved freely, their rhythm sure, flowing with easy strength. Her secret mind already dreaming of a child, first a son and then forgiveness from her husband.

14

Smoky lines of rain obscured the distant horizon, but Harriet saw in her mind's eye the sky as it stretched away at dusk, the dying melody of shades fading one into the other. Now she could recall the azure of fine days during her rain-pelted walks, she noticed the changes on the shoreline, how sand washed away to expose flagstone shelves that tilted into the sea.

Addie leaned against the window watching the clouds, her head in a birdlike pose that accentuated the fleeting nature of her attention.

'It can be beautiful,' said Harriet.

'It is. I really should have brought paints.'

'We have to get the stoat out of the bath,' said Harriet. 'Before Anna gets here.'

'She never said.'

The phrase, often spoken by Addie in childhood, transported Harriet back to the day her sister had broken a vase. It was burgundy with curved shoulders and waist, kept in the centre of a dresser in the drawing room, like a small red woman on an altar. Addie had been bored and ricocheting a bouncy ball against the walls. They had laid the pieces in a shoebox as if they were a skeleton bones. Harriet had made Addie go and pick some flowers from the garden.

'Why?' said Addie.

'You've got to show you're sorry.'

'But I'll say it.'

Harriet had insisted. Addie had chosen their mother's favourite flowers—peonies, skipping from one plant to another gathering the ruby heads.

When their mother had returned from her client Addie hung back, tearful. Harriet and solemnly presented the box.

'A present? Oh, I see. Was it you, Addie?' said Julia.

Addie had nodded.

'It was such a maudlin thing,' said Julia, fishing around in the box. 'God knows where I picked it up.'

'Here you are,' said Addie, stepping forward with the flowers. 'To show I'm sorry.'

Julia's lips had tightened at the sight of the blooms.

She had held the flowers at arms' length and said, 'Thank you. But really, the vase doesn't matter. You could have just said sorry.'

Harriet had gone upstairs and cried.

~~~

Outside a speckled bird with a long, curved beak flew the length of Scarth's nearest field.

'What's that?' said Addie.

'A curlew. Ernest has been educating me.'

'The stoat trapper.'

'I like him,' said Harriet.

Addie tossed her hair back.

A flock of starlings flitted along the shore, became a volley of black arrows and disappeared over the rocks. Out of sight, waves yawned onto the sand while oystercatchers and herring gulls skipped forward, red-legged turnstones foraged in the tangles.

In the bathroom Stoat vomited, then retreated to the cardboard box Addie had upturned at one end of the bath.

'What about Art?' said Addie. 'I suppose it was interesting

for you, but…'

'He wasn't an experiment.'

'Mum says you've caused him a disadvantage. For him, it'll be harder.'

'I didn't damage him,' said Harriet.

'What about his prospects?'

'His prospects are fine. He's bright. Practical,' said Harriet. 'I won't make a difference in the long run.'

'It's not up to you.'

'No, it's up to him. He'll finish, celebrate and leave—then neither of us will be there.'

Addie tapped her fingers against the glass.

'Why is it my fault people can't mind their own business?' said Harriet. 'Oh, stop that will you, it's getting on my nerves.'

It had been a mistake to invite her sister, thought Harriet. How could she explain that Art was sick of other people's approval, sick of acting a part.

'There's nothing to eat,' said Harriet. 'What time did you say Anna arrives?'

'The last flight from Aberdeen. She sounded flat as a pancake on the phone. Have we at least got something to drink?'

'The gin's dead,' said Harriet.

Addie raised an eyebrow in the direction of the earthenware bottles arranged on the side. Empty bottles on display, along with sheepskins and dried flowers, were on their mother's banned list.

'Let's have lunch out,' said Addie. 'I'd like to see the town. We can shop.'

Harriet forced a half-smile and went through to gather warmer layers. A message had flashed up on the laptop with an invitation from Professor Paracchini. Harriet skimmed though the contents. Messages, when they reached her, caused attacks of nervous tension and procrastination that forced her to lie on her bed, staring at the beams and following the scars in the grain. The rafters, darkened by decades of peat smoke, stood out against the fresh plaster, a clean map.

Addie checked Stoat and concluded the animal would sleep a long time. She flushed the vomit down the toilet then squirted Anna's perfume in the air.

As the weeks passed Harriet's routine had all but disappeared, including replying to emails. The only thing she must do each day was walk. Whether she wanted to or not. It was a simple win, one more step. One more stone. Exposed to salt spray, walking beneath white wings, feeling the visitation and withdrawal of the sun like a grace. This is what she did.

Addie grimaced at the sight of Harriet's navy coat.

'Believe me—it's practical.'

The day was cool and breezy, the car stuffy. The roadsides were changing, bright green verdure covered the worn-out ivory stems of the previous year.

'This is Scapa Flow...pronounced Sca-pa not Scar-pa,' said Harriet. 'There's an oil terminal on Flotta...you can see the gas flare at night. And...that's a house for the peedie folk?'

'What?'

Clem's description of peedie folk and trows had been difficult to follow, but Ernest had nodded in agreement which lent the words the weight, but Harriet hesitated to explain further and let silence fall in the car.

After a long, straight road bordered by pasture and barley they passed a cluster of houses on the top of a brae and Kirkwall came into view. Below there was open water and the islands of Rousay and Gairsay floating like green cloaks thrown upon the sea.

A small cruise liner was berthed at Hatston; bullet-shaped, low in the water, it delivered a few hundred rather than thousands of passengers. Ernest had said that the town became crowded when the big liners came. His face serious. The idea had seemed absurd to Harriet.

'A rainbow,' said Addie.

It hit on the low land that ran from Scapa beach to the new hospital. Ahead, grey houses clustered around St Magnus Cathedral and streets gradually wound to the harbour. Harriet noticed the gardens were weeks ahead of Erskine, where until the middle of May daffodils had still bloomed.

'Why is it red when everything else is grey?'

'I don't know,' said Harriet. 'God knows how they managed to build it. It's nine hundred years old.'

They took a table in a modern-looking cafe bistro on Albert Street. A young man with a groomed beard and clear complexion came to take their order.

'There's another table if you'd prefer to be away from the door.'

'No, this is fine,' said Addie. 'I like watching.'

'Thanks, Iain,' said Harriet.

They were handed two menus and left to deliberate.

'Iain?' said Addie.

'Steven's son. Our neighbour.'

Harriet looked at the menu, then without warning the present dropped away and she remembered another menu at The Bull. It was a pub where she thought no one would ever find them. The trail of memories unwound and she was back in Oxford, in her flat as they had been afterwards, in her bed, Art binding her arms so all she could do was move her head side to side and laugh.

She must stop thinking about him. Always.

Iain returned.

'I'll have the soup. Is it vegan?' said Addie.

'I believe so,' said Iain. 'Packed with nothing but leek and potato.'

'No, actually I've changed my mind,' said Addie. 'Asian salad, and cappuccino with soya milk.'

'I'll have soup,' said Harriet. 'And some water.'

She gazed through the window into space. What did it all matter? What did it mean? Eating and drinking and being with someone? How could she ever do it again? She wanted crashing waves, pounding and oblivion, until the memories were gone, until there was nothing left.

A warm hand covered her own, Addie smiled.

'It's okay.'

Harriet came back to the present, wiped her tears and steadied her breath. They sat without further conversation and watched the passers by on the street.

15

A familiar gait caught Harriet's eye. It took her a moment to recognise Ernest; his shoulders were bowed and his gaze fixed on the flagstones ahead of his feet. The defeated pose reminded Harriet of the story he had told her about how he acquired his nickname–One-shoe.

He had been on a trip to Westray for a football competition, a full day away from changing tyres in his father's garage by the Peedie Sea. A pair of second-hand boots had hung from his shoulder as he boarded the boat. He had admitted he had been considered good at moving the ball.

'We wir aal haddin wir boots over the side, swingin them roond by the laces,' he said, shaking his head. 'Somebody grabbed had o mine an soon enough wan wis in the water. I had tae play wi wan shoe and wan boot. Scored a blinder.' His grey eyes glinted. 'No wan minds that on.' He smiled wearily then pressed down the lid on the bucket for the dead rats, then added, 'They niver let me forget playin in wan shoe.'

There was a burden Ernest carried that she didn't understand; not Clem, it was something else. Whatever it was haunted him now as he walked, she had an impulse to go and speak to him, to ask if there was anything she could do.

But why was she getting involved with these people; why should she care if Ernest was unhappy?

'I must see the jewellery,' said Addie. 'I want to get something for Mum, so I can borrow it. Oh, cheer up, Harriet. Let yourself enjoy something.'

'Sorry. It's just I'm starting to recognise people,' said Harriet. A woman with fair hair and freckles ran past. 'That's the dentist who inserted Martin's tooth.'

Addie diverted her gaze to the young woman.

'You seem to know everybody.'

'He looked sick as a dog after she did it,' said Harriet.

Harriet received her soup from Iain and smiled.

~~~

Ernest's focus shifted from one thing to another as he followed the sinuous contours of the main street. There goes One-shoe, they'll be thinking. Since losing the money he went from being unable to move at all to feeling he would drop as freely as a rock. He felt too far from the ground, dizzy and light. He stiffened to keep his balance. He remembered the electronic payments flying out, a few thousand pounds at a time, free as a bird.

Gone.

Here and there a modern shop front interrupted the small, stone-surrounded windows. The bank was one of them with its shiny surround. There was a poster of a woman laughing and clapping her hands at a man who was working at a topiary figure.

Why wis she laughin? Whit the hell kinda shape wis hid

meant tae be?

A sensation of falling rushed up through his shoes, and with it such flowing weakness that it felt as if the stitching that held his body together was on the verge of pulling open.

What had he been livin fur? Meg? Clem? What was he living for now?

His memory dragged him back to his attempt to tell the bank what had happened.

'Did you authorise the transactions?'

'Aye.'

'Customers are repeatedly warned never to give out account information or personal details. Did you receive the one-time passcode and enter it yourself?'

'Aye,' said Ernest.

'You are the one responsible for giving permission.'

Everything at the bank had been cancelled. He had told Meg he had lost his wallet. Her blue eyes had looked up from knitting.

'Where?'

'I dinna ken, or I'd hiv hid.'

'Hid canna hiv got far,' she said. 'Let me look.'

Ernest let her search the whole house even though he knew the wallet and his cut-up credit cards had been taken away by the council refuse collection lorry the day before, tucked at the bottom of a bin bag. He'd slipped out three photographs into a plastic packet and laid them at the bottom of his sandpaper drawer.

He could neither bear to look at them or part with them: Meg on the beach with Clem holding out a crab, all of them on the back of his motorbike at the vintage rally, his hair not yet grey and Clem grinning at the fun.

He'd told Meg she would have to manage housekeeping from the account where she put money from selling ganseys until he made arrangements for a new account. It would have been better if thieves had come and emptied the house, then at least he could still have pride in himself.

A gap inside was widening. He had lost more than money.

Ernest suspected most of his nephew's thoughts were about the lass with golden hair rather than any car. The idea would come back to him though.

He looked at the door of the bank, sick at the thought of going in. He should try again. There were stories in the newspaper about money being recovered, and he'd heard a programme on the radio that ferreted out financial things done to folk and made them right. This week another pamphlet had been put through the door warning of scams; it had a number to call.

A voice interrupted his resolution.

'Whit like?'

Clem's reflection shadowed the glass. He smiled broadly, a can of drink in one hand and a polystyrene container in the other.

'I said tae gae hame,' said Ernest.

Clem's smile drooped.

'You widna put the trap back tae Erskine withoot me?'

'No, beuy. I widna.'

Clem bent down and applied his teeth to the container so it opened, then juggled his drink so he could pick out a roll.

'I'd better off and fix things,' said Ernest.

Ernest eyed the bank door and turned away. The air was softening to rain. Ten minutes later Clem was also back at the office, drops of rain hanging from his hair and a hangdog expression on his face.

'I dinna want tae gae hame.'

'Tak yir weet claes off.'

Ernest sighed and turned back to a map he was overlooking with Kieran. His hands moved slowly, pausing now and again as things came to mind.

'Walt's been using kitchen weights to calibrate his trap,' said Kieran.

'Aye, Walt's a good beuy,' said Ernest. 'He's the skills for it. A set o calibrating weights in the van is whit's needed.'

Kieran pointed at a spear-shaped piece of land connected to the Mainland by a narrow strip of land.

'What about here?' said Kieran.

'Deerness?' said Ernest.

'Mull Head Reserve.'

'Ah'll drive oot and see.' Ernest turned to Clem, 'And I'll gae you a lift hame.'

'He's all right,' said Kieran. 'Plenty leaflets that need putting in envelopes. I'll set him up, no worries.'

Ernest turned to where Clem was struggling to shrug his overalls away. He stepped over to his nephew and took hold of the collar and tugged it down.

'Still needing help wi his claes,' he muttered, and walked to the door. It was no good Clem being there all the time, he'd wear anyone's patience.

Kieran's brow furrowed. He watched the door close then returned his thoughts to the map, he hoped his right-hand man wasn't thinking of leaving. It was as if Ernest had a sore tooth nagging away.

~~~

Ernest drove out of town towards East Mainland. The land ebbed and flowed in gentle rises and falls. Reeds dotted the low pasture and newer houses sat a stone's throw from the old along the main road. The water of Inganess Bay was lost as the skein of land grew, a few minutes later the road dipped down and around the old mill at Sebay and the water was visible again. The high tide had risen over the ankles of the stock posts and bulged towards the land in the thrust of the incoming flow. In the southwest towards Hoy a few patches of blue survived in the sky.

Ernest knew a good number of the farms on East Mainland, his mother having come from St Andrews parish. The school she had attended was now abandoned, its windows entrances for birds. There was pleasure revisiting some places even as they decayed because of the history they held. The future was a place he couldn't bear to visit.

What would his mother think of him being such a fool?

It would be easier to push his motorbike over a cliff than sell it without it being common knowledge. And the insurance money would only be a fraction of what was taken, but it would stop them being like Clem's neighbours, living week to week on what they were given. Over a cliff. The thought circled like a gull.

The sight of a vehicle coming in the opposite direction planted a seed of dread in Ernest's mind. What if someone saw through the windscreen that there were tears in his eyes? The hands on the wheel felt like another man's, automatically following the road until the van reached the empty carpark at the Mull Head Reserve.

Nothing stirred at the farm.

Ernest held onto the wheel long after the engine was silent. A word came to his lips, stayed there, held as long as he could hold his breath, then finally released.

'Mither.'

Ernest covered his face with his hands. Tears flooded and ebbed until finally his breath steadied.

He fixed his attention on the worn world outside: the car-park sign was badly in need of repair, the mound of black bags waiting to be collected had drawn rats, the barriers around the Gloup needed repairing. Time had passed. The shades of green were softening into grey. He set off to walk the trail around to the brough.

At the overhang to a cleft cut by the long, soft knife of the sea he detoured to the wooden viewing cradle. The bridge spanned the entrance to the sea. Eventually the inlet would widen into a bay. A new path would be needed.

At the brough Ernest looked over the water, beneath his feet grasses eased their way over the cliff edge as if there was no drop beyond. On the far side of the cove's amphitheatre white seabird guano stained the vertical cliffs. A tidal pool echoed with trapped swell.

The mauve sky pressed heavily, grey, going to purple as the night came. A herring gull soared close, its white arc sharp against the rain-weighted clouds. He stood and stood, never wishing to move again. Anger flushed through him. The wretch who had done this should be thrown into the sea.

How could he go on like he had before? How could he bear it?

There was a sound like a human voice. Ernest saw no one, just a low hill and a wind turbine turning in the distance. He turned back to the sea. A single cormorant skimmed the water. He remembered the story of the family at Erskine. The loss of a man to despair grieved the whole community.

He turned away and lowered his head into the wind, trying to block out the uncanny sounds. One step after another he took himself away from the edge.

~~~

When Ernest returned to the van The Wildlife Trust mobile glowed on the dashboard. There was a missed call from Kieran and a message.

'Ernest, there's an issue over at Erskine. Can you meet us when you're done in Deerness? I'm taking Clem. He's all riled up about something over there.'

Sweat broke over Ernest's forehead. He reached for the keys. Was it worth getting away, when the return was so hard? He sat frozen in the driver's seat. A minute passed, an imaginary Ernest drove away, one whose life was still good, who drove over the stone bridge, past the kye and back to his old life.

But Ernest remained where he was, longer and longer. The brightness behind the clouds waning and the reeds swaying and hanging low.

Finally, his hand moved. The key turned and the engine started. He must see about Clem, and make things right.

'Wan thing I can dae.'

The words released, and afterwards there were tears, less bitter than before.

16

At Erskine, Addie was making coffee for Kieran and Clem.

'Soya?'

'Regular's fine,' said Kieran.

Clem touched his fingers against Addie's coat hung on the chair. She was smiling at him and passing a warm mug. It hadn't been bad so far. No one had found out about cutting the stoat free.

'There's reasons they're not kept as pets,' said Kieran.

Addie sighed.

Harriet was the one who had discovered Stoat was gone. She'd pushed open the bathroom door, complaining about not being able to take a bath after getting drenched at the standing stones of Stenness. She had stopped in her tracks and cursed.

Kieran took the cup Addie offered and listened.

'I couldn't ignore any wounded animal,' said Addie. 'Father wouldn't forgive me. Anyway, it looks like a ferret.'

Harriet shrugged as if she didn't care one way or the other. But it was true. She knew what their father would have done, either care and freedom, or a comfortable death.

'It must have escaped,' said Addie.

'Yup,' said Kieran.

Addie laid a hand on Clem's arm. The warmth of her touch banished the cold better than the coffee.

'You're one in a million Clem,' said Addie.

Harriet noticed the smile spread across Clem's face and sent a warning glance to her sister. It went unnoticed.

'Can you catch her?' said Harriet.

'Have to find it first,' said Kieran. 'My money says it's outside already. The wound's going to make hunting hard. But it'll know there's food around here. We can set the trap like before. '

There was a flash in Addie's eyes.

'And death?' said Addie. 'Death will wait for her again.'

Harriet interrupted, 'Listen, the builders told Anna about rats coming up the burn. Every hole in the place is sealed. I think she's still inside. What about Ernest? Where is he?'

Clem looked towards the driveway. Steven Scarth's tractor moved across an elbow of land by the shore, its wake alive with gulls.

Clem felt in his pocket. There was the knife, still unwashed.

'Why d'you put a box in the bath?' said Kieran.

Addie raised an eyebrow at the intonations of his accent. Everything was a question. Somehow it made it harder to take him seriously.

'She needed somewhere to rest,' said Addie.

'Didn't it occur to you that she could climb?'

'I don't suppose you have humane traps?' said Addie.

'No,' said Kieran.

'Anna can't arrive with a maimed stoat running around the place,' said Harriet.

A brief silence fell. Kieran turned his head, as if he had heard something.

'Will you have another look?' said Harriet.

'Might as well,' said Kieran. He gave her a half smile. 'Did it like the chicken?'

'She was sick,' said Harriet flatly.

'Trust me, it'll have found a small dark space to die in, sooner or later you'll smell where it is.'

Addie's eyes widened.

'Joking,' said Kieran. 'I'll look, okay? I might find it...I mean her. You gotta realise these animals have no place being here.'

'We understand,' said Harriet. 'I'm sure Ernest will help when he gets here. Anna needs some time out, that's why she got the place. This is hardly repaying her for letting me stay.'

'Anna will understand,' said Addie.

'We need it out of the house,' said Harriet.

She put down her coffee and picked up a pair of oven gloves.

'You go and look. I'm staying here,' said Addie.

'I thought you were the one that rescued it?' said Kieran.

'I'm going to sketch Clem if he'll let me. Would you do that? Sitting by the window? Landscapes are so dull without something in them. I've spent all this money.' She gestured at the new materials on the table. 'I promise it won't take very long. Can't all be searching.'

Clem was nodding before she'd finished speaking.

Harriet tied an apron around her waist and picked up a spatula. Kieran put down his mug.

'We're not bloody cooking it,' said Kieran.

Harriet shrugged.

'Well, I might as well look as ridiculous as I feel,' she said.

Harriet caught her sister's eye and smiled. For the first time in months she felt like laughing. The sensation teetered inside her, like the need to cry. She pressed it down, and refilled her mind with the importance of being responsible. Yet she knew now, as she had gradually discovered on the clifftop paths, that whatever happened in the future, she needed to laugh.

~~~

They began searching upstairs in Oscar's room. Anna had insisted on a bunkbed. Martin said a cage would be better. Anna had been right though, the novelty of the bunk kept Oscar in bed far longer than his bed in London.

Harriet wondered what Art had been like as a boy; he'd had a cook, a piano teacher, a certain amount of freedom, prestige. Harriet imagined him running through a tea plantation, back to the old colonial house and one of his parents' drinks parties. He said he felt separated from the 'real life' of Port Louis. Despite all his parents' connections he didn't belong, and he sometimes wondered if his father felt the same.

At first the thought shocked Harriet that she'd already finished her degree the year he started at the Gladstone International School in London. The age difference rippled through her mind as she shifted the stuffed toys from the duvet. Kieran dropped to his hands and knees and peered under the bunk. He sniffed, then reached out his arm.

'Anything?' said Harriet.

'Nothing,' he said.

He pulled out a cross-eyed Loch Ness monster.

What had she been doing with Art? Had she wanted to be young again? No, it wasn't that. She didn't want to return to her youth and he wasn't a child. They were lovers.

'Next,' said Kieran.

'What?'

'Are you all right?'

Harriet straightened her apron, pushing away the thoughts that flooded her mind.

'Yes. Eveline's room. This way.'

Anna had restored a kitchen dresser and installed it in her daughter's room. It was dotted with Eveline's possessions and displayed a drawing of a black cat with a long tail.

As Harriet searched the corners of the room the opening bars of Chopin's nocturne in G drifted through her mind, sad, ambiguous in direction, restless. It occurred to her that Art had never once invited her to hear him play piano. She had seen his name in the music room bookings repeatedly.

She had wondered if it was a sign of composure or discomposure that he should go and play the piano the day of the hearing. Other male students had been celebrating a cuppers football win, braying and carrying the odour of horse and field into the lodge. The traditional communication hub of the college was still an important place to visit once in a while.

One her students had been handing something over the counter to Ancient William who had taken the reins from Ancient Harold.

'Doctor Wolf? I'm sorry it's late. I lost track reading Lévi-Strauss.'

She briefly made eye contact .

'Gift exchange? That's fine Zineb.'

The young woman had leaned over the counter to make herself heard without having to raise her voice.

'I had to include it, the idea of women as gifts. It's really interesting, and since it's our last tutorial this term.'

'Yes,' said Harriet. 'It will be.'

'I'm looking forward to the next topic…'

A cheer had gone up as the goal scorer entered through the archway. Harriet's eyes had begun to water. The chaos, the striped jerseys, the stones worn smooth.

'I have to go.'

Harriet had left via the staff exit, not into the open quad but into a run of dim corridors that would take her to the music room. She had stopped outside and listened. Art was playing jazz and for a moment the rippled improvisation glued her to the spot. She tried the handle, hoping to quietly enter, but it had resisted her touch. She had knocked and he had unlocked the door.

'We must have been seen at the village.'

'Who by?'

'I don't know.'

'What does it matter?'

'There are rules I didn't follow.'

The ground felt like liquid beneath them. Giving way utterly. Art struck his fist on the door jam.

'Putain. Can't you fix it.'

'You've not told anyone? I'd understand if you had.'

'Stop. Why are you talking like this?'

Art had checked both ways, as if crossing a street, and then had taken her in his arms. She had spoken through her tears. "All the time I have to pretend. And hope you're not embarrassed, not ashamed. Because I…'

'I'm not embarrassed,' said Art.

The sound of voices had approached from the Garden Quad. He had released her and stood back abruptly.

'You can fix it. Tell me what to do.'

She had shaken her head and withdrawn.

'I have to see Paracchini. So should you.'

She had to put distance between them. She had known that from the moment she had left the hearing. It had been foolish to seek him out.

She still regretted never asking if she could hear him play, she dreamed of his elegant fingers, meticulous and generous, moving in the dark. Their lovemaking had reminded her of Grandmother's footsteps or…no….what was it called? The game where children scattered.

'How many other women?' she'd asked him once.

Art had lowered his eyes.

'Seven.'

He'd replied without hesitation or coyness. No details given.

~~~

'There's nothing here.' Kieran brought out a screwed-up piece of paper, scrawled with the words 'I am rubbish at drawing.'

Harriet came back to the present.

'I said there's nothing here. Are you sure you're alright?'

'Sorry, I'm not being helpful.'

Kieran was on his feet looking down on her.

'Things on your mind?' he said, then diverted his gaze. 'It happens.'

'Sorry,' said Harriet. 'Hard to shake myself out of it.'

They came back to the mezzanine. They could see headlights meandering along the coast road. Below, Clem was sitting with his hands on his knees, gaze fixed on Addie who made sweeping movements with charcoal over paper. She skimmed the surface, then after half a dozen lines tore off the sheet and started again.

'In here?' said Kieran turning into the master bedroom.

Harriet followed.

Addie's possessions were strewn around the room. Martin's T-shirts had been appropriated for nightwear—the one thing her sister needed she had forgotten.

One morning, Harriet had put on Art's T-shirt while she made their coffee. It draped softly around her shoulders and skimmed her hips as she'd walked. She'd caught sight of herself in a mirror and wondered who was looking back at her, and had hurriedly replaced it with her silk dressing gown.

On the rare nights that Art had stayed it was the moment she first opened her eyes that she felt the age difference between them most acutely.

'Can I have a shower?' he'd asked once.

'You don't need to ask,' she'd said.

Why hadn't she just given him a towel? Why had he asked,

and why had she made a point of his not needing to seek permission? Why did she wave when he walked away from the flat? Like a mother seeing off a schoolboy. Why? Why? Why? Why had they met?

She sighed.

'No. She's not here,' said Harriet.

They returned downstairs. The table was covered with sheets of paper and broken charcoal sticks. Addie smiled and tore off another sheet of paper.

'I have to make mess,' said Addie. 'I can't concentrate otherwise.'

'You'll have to tidy up,' said Harriet.

'I'll do it while you're at the airport,' said Addie.

She dusted her hands, leaned forward and rearranged one of the grey curls on Clem's forehead with her little finger.

'That's better. Look, here's someone.'

The lights swung around and soon they could hear Ernest crunching up the driveway. Harriet felt a desire to go out, to walk, to be alone. Yet, people keep arriving. Why did I invite Addie? She attracts people and then she forgets them all.

'Now we'll get on,' said Kieran. 'He'll have gloves and a pole.'

'Why won't he ever park closer to the house?' Harriet muttered as she left the room, but when she finally saw the familiar blue overalls through the door her shoulders relaxed. Here was help at last.

17

'Sorry you had to come,' said Harriet.

'Clem's no been any bother?'

'No, he's fine. Addie has him sitting for a portrait.'

Harriet began to chuckle, thinking he would join her, then quietened as Ernest's mouth drew into a line.

'Ah'll get the pole.'

Harriet looked after him. Did she say something wrong? Was she still missing some sort of code? Her understanding of human societies provided no clue. Or was it just Ernest? The way he came and went.

Harriet left the door on the latch and went through to the kitchen. She saw her bedroom door had been opened and followed the sound of voices.

'What are you doing in here?'

Kieran stood beneath the old opening for the lum, chin tilted upwards to the exposed beams. For no reason Harriet could logically explain the hairs on the back of her neck rose as she followed the direction of his gaze.

'It's not up there, is it?'

'Nah, I was just thinking. What did Anna know about this place?' said Kieran. 'Before she bought it.'

'I don't know. All she said was it deserved a second chance.'

'There's a rumour...' He paused, 'But maybe it's the other place by the shore. Not here.' A flush rose on Kieran's cheeks and his gaze dropped. He spoke in an undertone. 'You know, people used to be born, live and die in the same house.'

Harriet sensed life and death had passed through the old house. She had felt it from the very first morning when she had been woken by the wind. She was another life simply passing through. Kieran's face remained impassive but she guessed the direction of his thoughts. She wanted to say she understood, but she wasn't sure if there was anything in common with the grief she was dealing with and his own. After all, it was her fault.

Did they have to pass through everything alone? What had made sense when she and Art were together was being dismantled by distance and time. Yet it had been real.

There were footsteps. Ernest stood in the doorway holding rubber gloves and a pole. He followed Harriet's glance to the beams and frowned at Kieran.

'Where's yin stoat?'

The sharp sound of scratching came from behind the bathroom door.

'Right where it started,' said Kieran. 'If it ever left.'

'I checked before,' said Harriet. 'It had gone.'

The sound came again, stronger.

Ernest took the blanket from the end of the bed and handed it to Harriet.

'It's mohair.'

Ernest raised his eyebrows.

'Hid'll do no doot,' he said. 'Mind on.'

'Give us the other end,' said Kieran.

They moved into position, grasping either end of the cloth. Addie arrived, her hands clasped together, eyes bright.

'Oh, you've found it. Clem! They've found it,' she called. 'Come and see.'

'Had on tight,' said Ernest. 'We'll scoop hid up.'

Harriet and Kieran pressed the blanket to the floor with their feet while Ernest released the door.

Stoat flew headlong into the woollen material. Harriet let go at once and the collapsing blanket covered the animal's twisting body. Ernest dropped to one knee and drew up the edges, rolling the animal in the fabric. Fresh red drops marked a trail on the floor. The pungent smell of spray filled the room.

'Thank Christ for that,' said Kieran.

'Oh, well done. You've got her,' said Addie. 'You see, Clem, we've caught her.'

Clem smiled broadly.

'Can you get it out?' said Kieran.

Ernest secured the blanket on the floor, then foraged beneath until he had a grip on Stoat's neck and pulled her out. The wiry body circled around, attacking his hand.

~~~

Memories of fledglings and bloodied nests came in flashes. The sharp metallic warmth of killing and pain. Attack until all is still. Leave behind what cannot be consumed.

Where was the egg? Where was its glowing body and nourishing yolk? She wanted it. She wanted satisfaction.

No surrender until there is no strength, until there is no lust for another kill, another mating and another birth. Death, then rebirth. The fear and ecstasy.

~~~

'She's terrified,' said Addie. 'She needs a vet.'

Addie stretched out her hand towards the ermine coat.

'Ah widna,' said Ernest.

Stoat's black eyes bulged and she bared a jaw of tiny, wolfish teeth.

'Let's get her outside,' said Kieran.

Ernest was first, everyone else followed in procession, Clem close to Addie. The sky was heavily overcast, the green of early summer fields luminous and rising in the low light. The sweetness of grass swelled in the air.

'What are you going to do?' said Harriet.

'Put the poor creature oot o hid's misery,' said Ernest.

He addressed her without taking notice of the others in the group.

'You can't,' said Addie.

Clem came to his uncle's side. He gestured with his ungainly hands for Ernest to release his hold.

'She's not gonna last long,' said Kieran.

Stoat curled up her back legs and began pushing with her

undamaged leg at Ernest's glove, twisting, seeking ways to use her teeth.

'Let her go,' said Harriet.

Her voice flat as the turn of a dead tide.

Ernest felt his mouth dry, caught off guard by her tone. Harriet's eyes were dark and she held herself still. He felt the weariness of killing fall heavy upon him, the weight of another burden he could not carry. Slowly, he stooped down and let the animal touch the wet earth. Its muscles tensed and its remaining paws clawed at the soil. Ernest released his grip.

~~~

Stoat's ears pricked up, a great swell of freedom and wildness ran in her blood. She flew like an arrow away from the place of pain, her blood hot at the thrill of being loose, moving with pain but without obstacle. She heard the soft rain advancing, and the wing-beats of the sparrows flitting in the hedge, and in the restless rustle of the sea. She felt the wounds inflicted by the black cat open and itch and the throb of her missing limb.

Stoat turned and bared her teeth, circled around and eyed her captors for a final moment then bounded unevenly to freedom.

~~~

'She'll be easy to recognise,' said Kieran. 'I'll put the trap back.'

'No,' said Harriet. She faced Kieran squarely. 'Take it away. I don't want it here.'

Ernest avoided meeting her eye. Harriet's stomach muscles tensed. They must see it was wrong for her to let it happen again. Couldn't they all see it was wrong?

She felt that the world would never understand her and she would never understand the world; that was her fate, and the division was as inevitable as the sea and the land.

A low drone came from the sky. The red and white blinking lights of a small twin-engine propeller plane were visible above

South Ronaldsay.

'Harriet!' called Addie. 'The plane. You've got to pick them up.'

Harriet took a deep breath and walked away. If the stoat survived, that would at least be something. Every small step, that was something, some small proof of continuation. Tears rose in her eyes as she climbed in the driving seat. It came back to her all at once—the way everything had finished with Art.

In the end, they had not been brave enough to defend each other. They had run away wounded. Free.

18

High above the pinch of land of Dingieshowe the plane's wings tipped and it began its final descent. Petrol-coloured water swelled white over shelves of rocks as the tide advanced, submerging limpets and floating bladderwrack. The glow from the sky kissed the skin of the water silver as it drew back and came again on the breath of the evening breeze. The sands, pitted by the impact of earlier rain, resisted in their minute way the return of the water and the erasure of the past.

The Churchill Barriers gave Anna her bearings, yet from above the position of Storrtang eluded her and she struggled to pick out Erskine on the twisting cloak of green below.

Eveline had drifted to sleep in her seat, exhausted without having done anything. She slept poorly when her father stayed away at night as he had before they left.

The air inside the London house was musty and dead, windows closed to keep out pollution, humidifier kept whirring. Anna had listened to her daughter's raspy breath through the open bedroom doors. She remembered how her mother had sat in a chair by her bed night after night after her father died. It had been the only way she would sleep. If she woke and even found her mother dozing she would rouse her so she could stay watch over her while she slept.

It did not disturb Anna anymore when Martin was away. What was ahead except slow suffocation as the years passed? She felt her chest tighten. She must leave, find more. Fresh, cold air.

~~~

Earlier, as they had bundled into the taxi for London City Airport, Eveline had started wheezing.

'Where's Dad?' she had said. 'Where is he?'

'He'll meet us there,' Anna said. 'We can't wait any longer.'

It surprised her when Martin had been actually waiting for them at the gate. Both children had run towards him and jostled to gain his attention.

As they leaped up into his arms, suddenly oblivious of her presence, she had recalled the phone call she'd overheard between Martin and Peter Beachcroft about paying off an electrician. The narrative of exactly what her husband had done was unclear, but she knew he had been more than unfaithful.

On the plane, Anna had watched Eveline half-open her eyes, search for her father then drift back to sleep. Sitting by her side, Oscar had traced diagonal droplets as they skidded down the outside of the window, leaving mist marks with his fingers on the glass. Drawings of wild cows with bloody mouths rested on his knee.

Anna had leaned forward and put her hand on her husband's shoulder. She raised her voice above the drone of the propellers.

'Will they miss you?'

'What?'

Anna had repeated the question.

'I shouldn't think so,' he said. 'We're beyond the stage I do anything useful. I'm not like you, darling.'

'What?' said Anna.

'Indispensable.'

She looked back at him blankly.

It had struck her as an odd word to use. How was any person dispensable? How could anyone be thrown away and replaced as if they didn't matter? There had been no replacement for her father. Life had simply continued, poorer.

Oh, God. Poor Harriet.

Had it been tactless to offer her the house? Would it have been better if she'd stayed in Oxford and brazened it out? Would it have been better if she'd stood in the centre of Gloucester Green and proclaimed from a soap box 'I am not dispensable!'

What exactly was Harriet accused of that could not be accommodated? What was sordid or indecent compared with what passed for tolerable in other circumstances? From what Harriet had told her of the committee hearing the reptilian Dean Neeley couldn't even put his prejudice into words.

Not like Professor Paracchini. Paracchini would give Harriet anything she asked for, if only she'd ask. Anna remembered being introduced to the professor; he had taken her hand and raised it to his lips.

'I wish for a mathematical mind like yours,' he had said, after discovering Anna's profession. 'My world would be many times simpler. It should be a scientist, not a philosopher, who is organising this collection.'

It was early February and the skylights let down diffuse light on the galleries below. The army of newly installed LED lights illuminating the crowded cabinets garish in comparison. Harriet had passed the professor his cane.

'No one knows half as much about the collection as you,' said Harriet. 'Really, Anna, you could ask him anything.'

Professor Paracchini had shaken his head.

213

'Don't worry, I won't,' said Anna.

They had skirted the maze of displays on the ground floor to the exit into the Museum of Natural History. Professor Paracchini sighed heavily.

'Someone is interested to speak to me about the museum's founding collection.'

Professor Paracchini raised his cane to a glass cabinet.

'This museum's origin required such a diverse and complicated combination of events that it was either pre-destined or nearly totally improbable.

'This poor, shrunken face, with its pursed lips, and eyebrows and hair that still seem to grow, this person's whole life, every misadventure of youth, survival from disease, the construction of their psychology that made them a warrior in battle is all so chance. And for the victors to then take this head and preserve it with such consummate skill,' he emphasised these two last words as a politician might, '...to produce this marvel, this most popular exhibition of a head the size of a tennis ball, whose recovery, possession and guardianship is equally unlikely, is so preposterous that we must be astounded. We must consider the infinite.' He looked from Anna to Harriet, letting the force of his words settle, then he had added in a conciliatory tone, 'We must consider the divine plan.'

His head bowed slightly and he had leaned more heavily on his stick, a small tremble echoing along its length, then moved away with priest-like steps towards the visitor rooms on the ground floor.

~~~

Outside on Parks Road the brick stripes of Keble College echoed a faux industrial past in the gritty, late-winter air. The moan of buses on Banbury Road carried through the Lamb and Flag passageway as Harriet and Anna made their way to lunch.

As they had cut through the graveyard of St Giles' Church a

slight young man with tawny skin and groomed black hair had stepped out, almost as if he had been waiting for their approach. He had looked from Harriet to Anna and hesitated.

'How was the tutorial?' Harriet had said.

'Interesting, I think.'

'You think?'

'Game Theory's not my passion.'

Anna had looked past the brash yellow forsythia towards the restaurant. The window seats of the restaurant were filling up with students, some being dined by generous relatives, others absentmindedly enjoying the privilege of wealth.

'You have to understand it, though,' said Harriet, then added, 'I'll see you in my room at three.'

The young man had nodded to Anna.

'Nice to meet you.'

The waiter had offered them a small table overlooking the Woodstock Road. Students released from morning lectures pressed along the pavement outside, grasping folders to their chests, faces like uncertain spring flowers.

'Martin said the last model was recalled because of a fatal flaw in the fuel injection system, so above all the advert must make buyers feel safe. What about it actually being safe? Does anybody consider that, I wonder?'

'What did you think?' Harriet interrupted.

'Professor Paracchini? You know I like him very much. I've met him before.'

'Not him. Art, of course,' said Harriet.

Anna had been momentarily lost for words. The large clock suspended in the glass lantern ceiling seemed to pause, the clink of plates and background chatter quieten.

'That was Art?' said Anna.

Harriet lowered her voice.

'You didn't know?'

'How was I supposed to know? You didn't introduce us. I thought he was one of your undergraduates.'

'He is.'

Anna had looked away, the line of her jaw tightened.

'He's from Mauritius,' said Harriet.

'Oh, I see. I wondered.'

Anna had reached out across the starched cloth and taken hold of Harriet's hand, the fingers pressed warmly into her own.

'Oh, Harriet.'

A flush grew on Harriet's cheeks.

'It doesn't matter to me where he's from.'

Harriet let out a breath that turned into a sob. Anna had offered her a napkin.

'I really couldn't have guessed he was 'the one".'

'He's so good for me, to me,' Harriet had said. 'In all the ways he can be. And you'd like him.'

The corners of Harriet's mouth had hovered between a smile and a frown.

'I don't know him. But I like him if he makes you happy,' said Anna.

'He does,' said Harriet.

Anna had loosened her hand when the waiter returned with their drinks. Harriet had wiped her cheeks.

'How did it start?' said Anna.

'He came to hear me sing.'

For the rest of lunch Harriet had talked at double speed, barely touching her food. The longer they sat the more Anna noticed the smile lines around her friend's mouth and the creases in the corner of her eyes. Harriet had laughed when the waiter came to collect her plate.

'I don't seem to get hungry anymore. You see?'

Anna nodded. Her friend had changed, she had lost all perspective, and she called it love.

19

Ernest watched Harriet's tail lights disappear. He had noticed her shoulders shake, a tide of grief had opened as she reversed and pulled away. The woman he had got to know, who showed signs of recovery, was falling again. Without knowing any details he understood humiliation dragged at the soul like an undertow.

He trudged to the van with his head down, barely breathing. He must get rags and tidy the bathroom, and leave on better footing. The chances the animal would survive were as small as being rescued from the sea.

As he returned he heard raised voices inside.

'What gives anyone the right to annihilate a species?' said Addie.

Ernest entered the kitchen to see Harriet's sister turn sharply and face Kieran. Her eyes were narrow, a dark glint in their centre.

'We're actually saving wildlife,' said Kieran.

He itched the stubble on his cheeks and met Addie's gaze head on.

'What about the stoats?' said Addie.

'They don't belong.'

Addie held her frame taut, cheeks flushed.

'You don't belong. At least…' she paused, '…at least Clem has the decency to save a creature in distress.'

'You don't know what you're talking about,' said Kieran.

He stepped towards Addie so she had to tilt her head upwards to meet his eye. Kieran's hands rose in frustration, fingers curling as if trying to grab words from the air that would finish the argument.

From a distance Clem watched Kieran's hands. They moved with the same sharpness he used to dispatch stoats and rats;

they were close to Addie now.

Clem reached onto the kitchen counter and something came to his hand. He saw Addie with bright eyes, pleading eyes.

'I'm…Jesus. Trying to explain…it's nothing personal,' said Kieran.

Addie held up her palms, 'You're nothing but a heartless…'

Kieran shook his head and drew a deep breath. His hands reached out, coming close to touching Addie's face.

Clem lifted the wooden chopping board and landed it against the side of Kieran's head with a sweeping movement. The tall man staggered sideways, bent over from the blow.

Clem's face fell into repose as Kieran caught the back of a chair to prevent himself from falling.

'Oh, Clem, what did you do that for!' said Addie.

Clem upheld the board for a second blow aimed at Kieran's back.

'Put hid doon beuy.'

Ernest's voice filled the room. He stood at the door, the rags dropped from his hands. Ernest's eyes were wide, as if he'd put on a mask.

'He didn't mean it,' said Addie. There was a tremble in her voice.

Ernest strode towards his nephew.

'Yir a bloody menace. And I'm a fool for puttin up wi you.'

The chopping board wavered in Clem's hand.

'Jesus, what's got into him,' said Kieran. 'Nearly knocked me out.'

A welt was rising on Kieran's cheek and his ear blazed. Clem stepped towards Addie, wanting to be closer to her, the board still raised in his hands.

'Clem, step back noo,' said Ernest.

'He was protecting me. He wouldn't hurt anyone.'

Addie stepped forward and lay her hand on Clem's arm,

then went up onto tiptoes and kissed his cheek.

'I'm okay,' said Addie. 'You're being very sweet.'

Clem's gaze drifted. Ernest had seen the look before—whenever Clem saw the flashy blue car belonging to the beuy always in the sheriff's court. He was wanting something. Clem thought of the peedie folk, always feasting, a fiddler playing a tune so they could dance. He saw their faces, glistening from heat and whisky, and he wanted to be dancing and merry with his own lass and never return to Balfour Rise for a hundred years. And here was a faery, kissing his cheek. He lowered the board and reached to hold Addie to dance.

He kept coming closer until he had her in his arms and held her against the cave of his body and squeezed tight. Addie pushed against his chest. The smile dropped from her face. Clem started to sway.

'Clem, let her go,' said Ernest.

Clem knew he must hold her tight and keep her. The fiddler's tune in his head gained pace, twisting and turning like the stoat to be free. A tune so wild that the dancers could think nothing except going faster, faster and faster, until they started to fall one by one by one to the ground. He must hold his partner tight, tighter and tighter, and keep her from falling.

Ernest was next to him now.

He pulled at his nephew's shoulders to release their grip, remembering how Clem had nearly killed a boy at school, fresh as the day it happened. It had been winter. A blaze of snowballs had flown in Clem's direction as he walked up School Place. He had caught hold of a boy years younger by the scarf and dragged him behind a wall. They were only alone together for only seconds before another child saw the boy lifted off the ground, blue and slack, and gave the alarm.

Ernest dug his fingers into Clem's neck muscles and levered backwards.

Still Clem didn't turn.

The tune in his head was madness now, the fiddler dripping with sweat, music crashing inside Clem's head, a storm of rushing and crashing blood.

Ernest breathed deeply, released his grip on Clem's shoulders, then drew his right elbow back from the shoulder as if pulling the string of a bow. He braced, twisted at the waist, released and let fly.

The punch flicked Clem's head clean sideways. The flesh on his mouth deformed on impact and the neck muscles twisted until they could twist no more. Clem recoiled, stared at Ernest, jaw slack, eyes blank. Ernest formed another fist and drew back his arm.

The boy in the playground, a Spence, had purple fingerprints on his throat and burst blood vessels in his eyes. They had stayed red, then yellow for weeks. For a short time the bullies had left Clem alone. But it didn't last. It never did.

Ernest delivered another blow, following through with the strength of his shoulder, connecting with the underside of Clem's jaw. Clem staggered and brought his hands up to his face. Addie was free. Ernest breathed hard though his nostrils, sweating under his clothes, and prepared again.

The headmaster had been right. The boy could have been left dead.

He swung his left and landed another hit between Clem's hands. Blood burst from his nephew's nose. Arrows of pain shot through Ernest's knuckles and a wave of unwanted exhilaration washed over him.

Addie raised her arms.

'Stop! Stop!'

The boy had to learn. He couldn't do things like that to a woman. He had to listen when he was told. He had to stop himself. Ernest swung again, this time an uppercut to the chin.

Clem's teeth churned against each other like shingle.

'Please,' said Addie. 'He doesn't know.'

Blood flowed freely down Clem's face from his nose onto his chin. Ernest formed another fist. He looked up to take his aim, and for the first time saw what he had done.

The fist hovered.

'That's enough, mate,' said Kieran.

Clem's eyes were dull, his lips hanging swollen. He had one hand cupped beneath his nose, catching drops of blood that escaped with ease onto the floor. Clem watched the blood trickle through his hand.

Addie turned away unable to watch, sobs escaping her throat. Ernest's arms dropped to his side. He stepped back, stood still for a moment, looking at no one, then picked up the rag from the table and held it out to Clem.

'Tak the cloot,' he said.

His voice was quiet.

'Pity's sake, tak the cloot beuy.'

Clem gingerly took the cloth without touching his uncle's hand. He pressed it to his upper lip and nose. He looked quickly at Addie then back at his uncle.

Kieran stepped forward, wincing from the pain in his head as he moved. The expression in his eyes softened.

'He's going to need stitches. I can take him?'

Ernest shook his head.

'Get in the van, Clem.'

Clem held the cloth to his face and began lumbering to the door. Ernest turned to follow, arms pressed at his side.

'Clem? It's okay,' said Addie. 'I'm okay.'

Clem didn't turn. He didn't want dancing anymore. He wanted his bed. He'd go back to Balfour Rise, be on his own.

'You shouldn't have hit him,' said Addie.

Ernest's steps paused, but he did not turn.

'He's no a bairn,' said Ernest. 'He's a man's body an strength.'

Kieran opened his mouth to speak, but Ernest moved away. It was time for night and home, and honesty.

~~~

Kieran and Addie were left alone. Addie went to the window and watched Ernest's van disappear into the dark.

Kieran ran his fingers over the pile of sketches on the table. The broad sweeps of charcoal caught the landscape, In the foreground, Clem's portrait remained a simple sketch, yet Addie had captured his essence. He was there, unfinished yet complete.

'Why'd you have to get so bloody involved?' said Kieran.

His voice trembled.

Kieran had a flashback of Ernest's expression, a kind of love, love mixed with pain. It remind him of his father the first time he'd gone from the top of the hill without trainer wheels. Addie swayed slightly and leaned her forehead on the glass.

'Will the stoat really die?' said Addie.

'I don't know. She might make it,' he said.

Kieran took some water from the tap and offered it to Addie. She gave him a half smile.

'Thank you,' she said. 'I should get you some ice.'

'Nah, I'd better go.'

As he drove away to the west, head pounding, he wondered about the stoat's survival. It all depended on the strength of its life force. Some animals went on and on. They just wouldn't let themselves die.

An eerie, blue-green light filtered through the clouds. The barley whispered and waves lifted the seaweed from its bed. Swirling currents flowed between the arms of kelp as they lifted upwards and forwards in the cold, salty water. The tide was coming swiftly now, engulfing the rock pools, wakening the limpets from their clamped slumber and bringing the wetted rocks back to life.

20

The passengers disembarking at Kirkwall airport were greeted by moist, meadow-scented air. The coolness and openness roused Eveline from sleep half way down the steps from the small aircraft. She twisted down from her father's arms and walked groggily across the apron to the squat terminal building.

Reunions were taking place, kisses and embraces between women and nods between men. They waited by a black conveyer that coiled from one hatch to another. Anna gripped Oscar's struggling hand and looked for Harriet.

'Where is she?' said Martin.

'Oscar, don't touch,' said Anna.

Martin reclaimed a cardboard box from the horseshoe of bags and parcels and hugged it to his chest.

'What on earth's in there?' said Anna.

'She's there!' said Eveline.

Anna turned and saw Harriet, breathed and steadied herself.

'Sorry I'm late. It took longer than I thought,' said Harriet.

Her cheeks were flushed, there were so many things to say, but it could not be done at the airport. Harriet crouched down to Oscar while Anna collected suitcases. The boy's face was narrower than she remembered, his limbs longer and stronger in just a few weeks.

'I was racing the plane in the car,' she said.

The boy blinked and inserted his thumb.

'It's not a very good car,' said Harriet.

'As long as it gets us to Erskine,' said Anna.

She took Eveline's hand, then manoeuvred closer to Harriet and kissed her friend on the cheek.

'It's been a very long day.'

~~~

Martin took the front passenger seat, box on his knee. He pictured the china dogs as they had been in Peter's bay window, the room as it had been before the wallpaper had been stripped and the furniture covered. The night before he and Peter had thrown back the protective sheets and unearthed brandy balloons. The room had swum in green darkness illuminated by a single lamp. Alcoholic vapours rose, sweetly and darkly into the summer night. He had been struck by a sudden notion of wanting to be seen with Peter.

'What about a balcony?' said Martin.

'No chance of planning,' said Peter. 'Not here.'

Martin had been aware of Peter watching him over the rim of his glass, become aware of his greying tooth and an unwelcome sense of change. Outside, the cherry trees in the square, which had frothed gloriously in April, were now heavy with summer foliage. Their leaves drew a curtain around the Georgian row.

'Ready?' said Martin.

'Nearly.'

Peter had drained his brandy slowly, and for a brief moment Martin wondered if something might be ending. And if it was, what could he do about it? The thought flitted into the shadows, only to be replaced with an impatience to go to bed. Peter did not demur and yet the feeling of unease persisted.

~~~

Martin glanced over to Harriet. She did not look at him, her gaze instead shifting between road and rearview mirror. It was the wrong way around, Harriet picking them up like this and acting hostess.

The Orkney landscape, which had been confined to muted grey and green during the day, was awaking into richer shades as night fell. A band of peach was widening in the west as the sun descended beneath the clouds.

'Addie's getting food ready,' said Harriet.

'Who's Addie?' said Eveline.

'My little sister.'

'Don't worry, Pumpkin, you don't have to eat it,' said Martin. He laughed at his daughter's puzzled expression.

'By the way, I've a present when we get there.'

'In the big box?' said Eveline.

Martin nodded.

As they turned past the war memorial the undersides of the clouds grew brilliant, shimmering pea-green in the near distance, then drawing back in a line of ivory and gold. The tide was climbing the rocks, waves piling up one on another like the bodies of the dead in the trenches. The Orkney landscape was studded with remnants of war, distant events that stole its sons and returned the names on memorial stones.

Harriet had walked over the slabs of a collapsed bunker eroding onto the beach, rusted metal bones protruding from within. It was an ugly intrusion, yet over time, she had come to view it as belonging exactly where it was. If it had been removed she would have been dismayed.

A gull with black wing feathers and a bright yellow beak perched on the roof of Storrtang. As they passed it arched its head back and let out a sharp cry. Harriet turned the car away from the shore and towards the glowing lights of Erskine.

Red campion glowed brilliantly at the base of the pillar where her collection of pebbles marked the success or failure of her days. Tyre marks were all that remained of The Wildlife Trust vehicles that had been in the driveway.

Ernest had seen it was right to let the stoat go, wounded as it was. The animal did not deserve to be killed. It must find a way to survive. She tried to put it out of her mind. Anna was here and they were together again.

When the engine silenced Oscar was asleep on the backseat between his mother and sister. Martin left the passenger seat, carrying his box, and began walking to the house.

'Can't you come back for that?' said Anna.

'He's not going to wake up,' said Martin.

Addie stood at the door, arms hugging her waist and shifting from one foot to another. Her hair had been tied into a loose bun and there was a furtive quickness to her gaze.

'I haven't had time to cook,' she said. 'Come in Anna, it is your house after all. Sorry, my things are still in your room.'

'Don't worry, let's get inside.' She kissed Addie on the cheek. 'Martin, are you going to fetch Oscar?'

'Going,' said Martin.

Eveline moved quietly, sliding her hands along the walls, making sure she knew the place again. Addie, Harriet and Anna stood together in the hallway.

'What is it, Addie?' said Harriet.

'There was…'

Tears filled her eyes.

'What?' said Anna.

Addie glanced at Harriet.

'I think…oh, you'll hate me,' said Addie. 'I hadn't meant to do anything except be kind.'

21

Addie described the scene that had occurred without sparing herself. Harriet leaned back against the kitchen counter; she imagined Ernest leaving, knuckles bloody. How was it possible to explain to Addie exactly what she had done?

'He'll need stitches,' said Addie.

Harriet looked away.

'Don't do that,' said Addie.

'I didn't say anything,' said Harriet. 'How could you not see what was going to happen?'

Martin appeared, Oscar in his arms.

'Put him upstairs,' said Anna.

For a moment Harriet saw Anna's birdlike features shed their elegance, the fine nest of creases around her eyes deepened, her mouth hardened. When Martin was out of earshot, Harriet said, 'What's wrong, Anna?'

'I wish he hadn't come,' she said. 'But there it is…wishing doesn't change anything.'

The words echoed a conversation they had had as undergraduates. Anna had been speaking about her father. 'For a year I wished he would come back,' she'd said. 'Over and over again in my head, I wished and wished he was not dead.'

They had been sipping tea and sharing a chocolate bar.

'Then one day I stopped. He was really gone and everything I had held back rushed in …I felt I was going mad.'

She had cried, and Harriet had held her.

The same memory had returned to her during the desultory taxi ride back from The Red Lion after she gave way to Martin's persuasion. She had stared into the fog-blurred night, dreading the self-pity that waited for her in Jericho and desperately hoped her friendship with Anna would survive.

Harriet wished she could take away the shadows that crossed her friend's face.

'Anna?'

'Not now,' she said, opening the kitchen cupboards. 'Is there anything to eat, Addie?' But before Addie could reply a scream rang out.

'Christ,' said Anna. 'Eveline.'

Harriet's heart heaved. The gull-like cry repeated, then Eveline began shouting for her mother. Anna met her daughter half way across Harriet's room.

'Darling, calm down. Ssh please. Take a breath.'

She crouched with the girl in her arms. Eveline pressed her face into Anna's shoulder.

'Do you need your inhaler?'

The distressed child rolled her head to and fro. She pointed to the bathroom.

'Go and look, Harriet,' said Anna. 'Please.'

Addie whispered rapidly into Anna's ear. 'Maybe there's still blood, from the stoat.'

Eveline shook her head and stayed glued to her mother's side.

'Was there a mess in the bathtub?' said Anna.

'No, Mummy. The cat.'

'The cat?' said Addie.

In the bathroom, Harriet's gaze ran over the gritty trail that looped around the bathtub. An irregular line of mustelid footprints led over the top of the cardboard box, indicating how the stoat had escaped. She didn't think the stoat's trail would be terrifying to a child. But then what did she know about children?

She turned around and noticed the vanity drawers were open. Harriet crouched by the bottom drawer, knees folding awkwardly in the cramped space. She reached back for balance and her hand brushed something soft. It didn't make sense, had the stoat come back in? She tipped onto her heals and peered between the silver claws of the bath.

Sleekit was curled on his side, green eyes staring blankly ahead, a deep wound on the back of his neck. Harriet looked up, face pale. Addie was at the door.

'See what your stoat did.'

Addie's gaze followed her sister's gesture.

'It can't have done,' said Addie. 'Look at the size.'

Harried rose to her feet, lips drawn.

'Please, out of the way.'

Martin was standing by Anna and Eveline, hands on hips.

'Well? What is it?' he said. 'What's the drama?'

Harriet stooped down. She addressed Eveline directly, her voice steady and low.

'That must have been a horrible shock,' she said. 'We didn't know he was in there. Addie thinks he came in…maybe chasing a mouse and then fell.'

Anna caught Harriet's eye.

'Oh dear. Poor thing,' said Anna. 'Poor Sleekit.'

She kissed the top of Eveline's crown of hair. Her daughter's breaths extended. A frown creased Eveline's forehead. How could a cat could be so clumsy? Oscar was clumsy. He fell over just running down the hall. But a cat? Maybe it was not a very good cat.

'Something, the mess, might have given him a fright,' said Addie, corroborating Harriet's lie.

Martin looked up and squinted at the beam above him, hands in pockets, then smiled down at Eveline.

'I've got something for you. Take your mind off all this.'

Eveline shifted in her mother's embrace.

'For me?'

'Martin?' said Anna..

'Don't worry. Trust me. This is just the thing.'

He held out his hand. Eveline reached up and let herself be led through to the kitchen.

'I'll get rid of it,' said Harriet.

'I'm so sorry,' said Addie. 'Anna, are you okay?'

'Oh, don't worry,' said Anna, her voice breaking. 'It was basically feral. A bloody nuisance really.'

'Anna, please. Let me apologise.'

Anna tipped her head back to drain away her tears. 'Just ignore me. I need a drink. I expect you will too, Harriet.'

She met Addie's gaze briefly and then left the room. Through the open door the sisters overheard Eveline's chirped questions and then, 'Mummy, they're pugs!'

'I know you're sorry,' said Harriet. 'Go, help Anna. I can do this.'

~~~

Harriet slid the cat's body out from under the bath, then arranged a carrier bag. She lifted the animal inside, sliding her hands beneath its ribs and supporting the legs. Its whiskers wavered as if the animal were still alive, as if it sensed the enclosing plastic. Beneath the thick dark fur the animal's body was stiffening and cooling. Sleekit was no longer the sinuous creature that had curled upon a woven chair. He was gone.

She pulled up the sides of the bag, unable to banish the thought that the animal might come alive and start to protest. But there was no movement, just a not-too-heavy weight in a bag, that was all. Harriet crossed the room to the old door and unlatched the catch. She stood in the dusk, plastic bag in hand.

The sensation of the living world stole around her as she carried out her task. The sun and rain had encouraged new grass, damp and lush. She found a shovel in the outbuilding and made her way to where a sycamore broke the line of the rosa rugosa.

The land glowed orange and gold as she worked, the house martins darting to and fro and the rumble of Steven Scarth's tractor carrying on the breeze as it fired silage into a trailer.

Harriet felt the strength in her arms as she worked. The manmade plastic bag became more and more of an aberration as it waited by her side. When the hollow was ready she eased the plastic bag away and briefly held the dead animal close, breathing the sweetness of the grass she laid the body down. Her tears began to flow; for the cat; for Anna; for every ending. The flush of anger dropped away into a deeper sadness, one with the capacity to heal.

22

The final ruin of Storrtang came in the whip-crack of a spring storm when the new century was still in its infancy. The temperature dropped, a wind ripped southeast across the tip of Deerness sweeping into Scapa Flow. Ewes in search of shelter, heavily in lamb or recovering from birth, gathered on the land behind the croft.

The neglected steading had already partly flooded. Marram grass that held the dunes together tore and tumbled onto the stony beach. The storm, which had been foretold by Betty Scarth's leg pains, found the house ill-prepared. The ballast holding firm the roof turf was cutting through its ropes in the grappling wind. At the side of the house the peat-cutting implements, the tusker and luggie, toppled against the untidy remains of the previous year's stack.

Janet had been again with child, fatigued before the quickening. Her face was puffy and grey and she suffered dizzy spells.

Rain streamed from Robert's shoulders as he opened the door.

'Where is Issac and Jimmo?'

The wind hammered behind him, whirling a pail across the flagstones. Janet held a hand to her forehead. She was certain there must be something wrong with the unborn child that it made her feel so wretched.

'We'll lose the turf,' said Janet.

Robert cursed and fixed the door closed. He crossed to his chair and took out the whisky from its drawer. He swigged a mouthful and held it up to his wife.

'Have some yourself, Janet.'

His wife took a cup from the shelf and poured herself a measure and matched it with water from the jug. There came a child's cough from the blankets in the bed box. Robert eyed the shutters and was about to speak when Jimmo, who had been charged with corralling the ewes, threw back the door. He leaned over on his thighs catching his breath then pressed against the door to keep it closed.

'The dyke's given,' he said. 'The ewes are washing away.'

Robert rose, shoulders hunched, head hunkering down as if the already battling against the wind.

'Get Uncle James. And your brother if he can be mustered. We must drive them up higher.'

Janet swallowed her cup, took a shawl from where it was drying and wrapped it around her shoulders ready to go outside.

James arrived down first from Erskine, Thorn and Gudrun coming behind with tools and a barrow. James, Gudrun, Jimmo and Issac worked with the animals, picking up strewn lambs and driving them to higher ground while Thorn and his father shifted rocks to plug breaches in the dyke. Blisters formed and then fell away on Thorn's palms, stinging in the seawater. His muscles burned as he worked replacing boulders awash with icy water.

A ram tangled in the mess of seaweed tumbled in the surf, head caught fast while its body flailed. The high bleating noise contrived to cut through the storm when even a point-blank shout could not be heard. Pink lightning painted the sky overhead and set the ewes in a panic. Some abandoned lambs, while others abducted their neighbour's offspring trampling yet more lambs.

The sky flashed a peculiar violet-grey. A hellish vision burned briefly, then was lost. Rain whipped sideways across the croft. Robert looked up as the torrent passed over with renewed force, drops beating like a schoolmaster's cane. Spray ran through his beard and his hair caught and tangled over his face so he was hardly recognisable.

James battled towards the dyke and clapped his nephew on the shoulder. 'Tak them up. Go with your aunt. Herd the ewes to Erskine. I'll build the dyke.'

Thorn winced at the shame of his uncle offering a gentler occupation. He saw the look in his father's eye, mocking his weakness.

'These two are healthy!' shouted Gudrun, driving a pair up the brae. 'Ready to lamb.'

Thorn glanced towards his aunt, her figure caught in a flutter of distant lightning, her clothes slick against her body and her eyes fixed upon him, wanting him to follow.

'Go with the woman,' said his father. 'Your uncle's twice the hand you'll ever be.'

He spat on the ground and turned.

Thorn cursed his father and yielded. A moment later the sea sent over a rock as big as a man's head to where he had recently stood. It would have knocked him dead. As he retreated Thorn despised himself for cowardice and leaving his uncle and father.

He grabbed up a lamb scrawled away in the peat stack, tucked it under his clothes, grabbed another ewe by her scruff and followed Gudrun up the hill. They worked together, Gudrun with a stick in her hand, driving the animals to Erskine, Thorn calling from behind, shouting and whistling to his father's dogs.

They sheltered with the ewes in the byre, procuring hasty adoptions between orphaned lambs and bereaved ewes, until at length Gudrun said, 'I must have something to eat.' She wiped her red hands. 'Come into the house and warm yourself.'

'While everyone works on?' said Thorn.

'It would be foolish not to,' she said plainly.

She had dipped her head through the entrance and was gone.

As Thorn wiped clear the yellow sack from the face of a new-born he felt the weight of his coldness and hunger. He watched a lamb stagger and find its mother's udders. He winced at the remembered sting of his father's look and the sense that he had abandoned his family when most needed.

He rinsed his hands in a pail and limped across the steading. Inside Erskine, the kettle was lowered and bannocks lay on the table. Peats glowed crimson on the hearth. The cruisie lamp's flame cast a yellow glow, its shallow sides glistening with whale oil. The lum rattled overhead, a quiet regular noise compared with the racket outside. Gudrun was half out of her clothes and wrapped in a blanket. She held out the cup she was drinking to Thorn.

Thorn drank the mixture of whisky, honey and hot water and handed it back empty.

'Take off your wet things,' she said.

Thorn had undressed to the waist, felt the warmth of the whisky, the heat from the peats on his goosepimpled skin. His aunt lay her blanket on his shoulders. He noticed the coolness of her hand as it brushed away a frond of dulse papered to his skin. When it was removed her fingers began to play over his chest. She was close enough that he could feel the ebb and flow of her chest as she breathed.

The tiredness of his limbs faded, and he had turned around into Gudrun's embrace. They lay together in the bed nook and fulfilled each other's need. As the storm passed its peak, fatigue lured them into the temptation of sleep.

~~~

For every two stones Robert and James replaced three were washed away. The tide stayed high as if forced unnaturally onto the land by a monstrous hand. Only at dawn did it finally begin to retreat. Bonxies floated above, eyeing the corpses on the beach. The crude remedial work on the dyke held nothing back except clean, clear air.

When James returned to Erskine his fingers no longer felt anything they touched. His thoughts wandered to the dashed ewes along the shore, their heads dunked in the sand, fleeces tugged out like rags into the tangles of seaweed.

He was past hunger, but knew he must have something to sustain himself. Only when the numbness of the body had passed would he sleep.

The croft had appeared empty, the hearth dead. He entered and listened to the creaking of the timbers and the rattle of the lum and felt a sense of bittersweet contentment that at least here everything was secure. If only Gudrun had stacked the fire a little better.

A sigh had caught his ear.

He was not alone after all, Gudrun was in bed.

James had stepped forward to see into the bed nook. There she was, head thrown back, breasts exposed. Thorn's arm, slack from sleep, lay across her waist. His nephew's lean back glowed in the dim light, shadows ran down muscles to his narrow waist.

James moved slowly away, careful not to disturb Gudrun's spinning wheel, careful not to tip the water in the pail, careful not to scrape the door he closed behind as he went back outside.

He had returned to the byre. The animals were agitated, among their crowded bodies were two stillborn lambs and one dead ewe. James moved them away, then sank against the wall onto his haunches. A deep weight filled his limbs, heavier than he had ever known. It could have been ten minutes, ten years or a ten thousand years that he sat there. It made no difference. Hunger and thirst ceased to exist. When he moved his fingers it was as if a puppeteer pulled the strings. So Gudrun, there you lie, he thought. Over and over again, the same thought. James lost sense of his heart beating, of his breath coming and going. All was still and infinite.

A sound came, his nephew had come out of the house and making water against their midden as was his morning habit. The young man's footsteps drew away down the hill.

A smile played on James's lips.

He no longer noticed the smell of wool and iron as he rose to his feet. The bleating, orphaned lambs no longer troubled his ear. He straggled from the byre to the house.

Sickly yellow, the after storm light followed him though the door. Now he noticed every detail, and how a single cup had done for two. The peat embers had suffocated themselves completely. The kettle cast a weak shadow onto the stone wall.

Gudrun slept on, ebony hair flowing around her apple-shaped face as it had when she was his bride. Even after such a night her skin had the shade of midsummer dawn, all peach and rose.

'Ah, lass,' he said.

They had waited a long time for that bed, worked hard for Erskine. He moved sideways, keeping his eyes on his wife in case she woke. He leaned in and took Thorn's pillow from inside the box bed. He remembered how hard it had been to silence their lovemaking with his parents so close, the pillow muffling first his and then her cries. He would stroke her hair and think in his mind 'I love you. I love you,' twice over to show that it was not an idle thought passing. It was the very feeling of his body and soul. He always imagined she was replying in her own mind, 'I know. I know,' and that was their bond for the days that followed. The bond that took them through the hard times of nursing his father and mother who became as needy as children. The bond that took them through storms and harvest when they would catch each other's eye and he would again think 'I love you' and she would answer with her eyes 'I know'.

But in recent years his mind had begun to ask, 'Where is our child? Where is our child?"

James drew up, became straighter and taller and then took two swift steps forward. He held the pillow aloft above Gudrun's face, making sure no shadow fell upon her eyelids, then swiftly lowered it down. A great current ran through his body, like the current of life that had once passed between them in the night.

His voice was soft, as she struggled.

'Even though we had the better croft we never could get you caught with a bairn.'

She raked the air with her nails, arms and legs tangled and caught in the blanket. He spoke quietly, soothed and held her down.

'Why was that? Why? Did I not work hard enough?'

There was no answer. Gudrun's arms lay limp.

James sighed and put the pillow back in the box bed. He turned back to Gudrun. His face became blank. Why did she not move? Maybe she was still asleep.

Out of habit he hauled the kettle up on its chain before going away outside. Yet, still she did not stir.

He must go and survey the ewes; they would bloat and become maggoty on the sand. Time and action was with him again, what he had seen and done forgotten.

Thorn stood alone on the cliffs of Rose Ness overlooking the land.

Storrtang was sodden and desolate, the sands where he had landed the day his father threw him over the dyke were washed clean away. He saw his uncle walking down the brae. He thought of Gudrun, and to his shame wanted her again.

23

On the drive back to Kirkwall Clem's nose swelled and the cut on his eyebrow opened, raw and seeping like a burn. Ernest stayed silent. Clem's fingers explored the wound, withdrew, then explored again, dabbing now and again with his cloth.

The silhouettes of farms on the evening turquoise sky became black paper cutouts, a collage on a fantastical background. On the eastern horizon, a line of crimson washed upwards and faded in the cold embrace of the blue above.

Habit brought Ernest home. The final light from the sun cut through the blind and onto the kitchen wall as Ernest and Clem sat and waited while Meg found disinfectant and cotton wool.

'Hid's an aafil mess,' she said.

Clem grimaced as she dabbed his cheek.

'A'hm sure hid wis whit you deserved,' said Meg. 'No like yir uncle tae lay a finger on you.'

Ernest kept his gaze on the fortifying pot of tea Meg had made. He pictured Clem young and small, sitting at the kitchen table, having his knees dabbed and disinfected.

'You ken your uncle niver had a temper,' said Meg, wiping the dried blood from Clem's eyebrow. 'More patient than I ever wis.'

She twisted two pieces of tissue and laid them on the table.

'Maybe hid's the reason I never took wi a bairn. Maybe my body kenned I widna manage.'

She looked at the damaged face in front of her, then carefully inserted the twists to dam the remaining flow from Clem's nose. She leaned back to inspect her work as she would her knitting. After adjusting one of the twists she took up a fresh cloth and began to ease away the dried blood around Clem's chin and lips.

'Gettin grey hair noo, Clem,' she said. 'No gittan any wiser though. I suppose that's you.'

She smiled more softly.

'Hid wisna because o the money,' said Clem.

'Wisna?' said Meg.

Ernest looked up sharply.

'I wis haddin her,' said Clem.

'I ken,' said Meg. 'The young sister stayin at Erskine.'

Ernest cleared his throat and spoke. 'She didna ken how

238

personal he'd tak her bein friendly.'

'No.'

'I couldna let him carry on.'

Meg nodded.

'You've been told aboot haddin,' she said to Clem.

She stooped down and pressed the cool cloth to his mouth. Clem winced.

'Whit wis the money you were spaekan aboot?' said Meg.

'I canna tell,' he said.

'No secrets, unless hid's a good secret,' said Meg.

Clem fidgeted his hands, curling the fingers out and in, then clasping them together on his lap. Meg stopped working and looked at her nephew.

'Did someone tak yir money?' said Meg.

Clem's cheeks darkened and he cast his gaze down to the tiles.

'No,' said Ernest. 'Hid's you. You married a damn fool.'

Meg turned to her husband.

'Whit's this?' said Meg. 'You're no a fool beuy.'

'Wan phone call.' Ernest paused. 'Wan call. An I wis stupid enough to fall for hid.'

Ernest continued, speaking rapidly, his gaze fastened hard on the teapot. He described first the email and then the call, and then how the money had been sent away. His stomach sickened as he laid out what had happened.

The worst was confessing the double shame of trying to do some secret good for Clem and failing. When Ernest finally finished speaking he raised his eyes to his wife.

'I niver lost me wallet. I lied, I couldna stand anyone findin oot.'

'Not even me, beuy?' said Meg. Her voice was low. 'You couldna even tell me?'

Ernest wished he could screw himself shut, anything to stop the bite of shame. Meg watched her husband closely, she saw his hands grip together and the water gathering in his eyes. She chose her words carefully so they carried as they needed to.

'I didna tak you fur bein full of pride,' she said. 'No when money's involved. Pride fur yir motorbike, pride fur yir nephew, pride fur yir work and havin knackyhands, but fur money?'

Ernest bowed his head, a penitent man.

'Did I gae you away?' said Clem.

'Aye,' said Ernest.

Clem stayed still as a mouse, let the time grow around the truth. Ernest raised his head a little, looking first to his nephew and then his wife.

'You did me a favour, beuy.'

'We must mind on tae try an get hid back,' said Meg.

'Hid's gone—spent no doot. I might as well have given them my breeks too. The bank's no goin tae help, they ken I broke aal the rules.'

Meg set down her cloth in the basin of red water.

'And whit aboot this, beuy? Who you've hardly laid a finger on aal his days and noo come's home fit fur hospital. Hid's no his faalt.'

'No,' said Ernest, slowly. 'No, hid's somebody's though. God knows somebody's made a fool o me yet.'

'Weel then. If hid canno be helped we'll aal be poor togither,' said Meg. 'You can keep yir pride if you want, but it'd be better to try and get that money back.'

She reached out and grasped Ernest's hands with her own.

'Dae you think I wis yir wife on the promise of a fortune?'

Ernest stared at the hands covering his own, he saw tides of wrinkles around his wife's fingers, the gold band that nipped in like a belt.

Meg sighed.

'And noo yir too deep in yir own misery tae get back whit's rightfully wurs. Hid's a damn pity.'

She shuggled his hands to and fro, then lowered her head so he could not avoid her eye. She held his gaze a while, then rose and looked at her nephew. Clem's eyes were round and serious and his cheeks drawn flat, so his lips came down in a line. A purple-blue bruise was rising across the bridge of his nose.

She touched the grey hair at his temples. He'd been the most handsome baby she'd ever known once the bruising of birth had healed. He had become stuck by the shoulder and been a half-dead blue rag when he was finally pulled free of her sister. They tipped him backwards and forwards, blowing on his face to bring breath before he was given to hold. Her sister had him in her arms a minute or two, then the pains began again. She had doubled up, held out the baby to Meg and said, 'Take him a peedie minute.'

Her sister's life had drained away in seconds.

The baby had gone back with his father, who decided a name after the Prime Minister. He gave the care he could with his mother doing the rest. As the boy was finally learning to walk his father had died from a heart attack.

'The bairn needs a hame,' Ernest said after the funeral. 'Hid wid upset the grandmither if we had him,' Meg had replied. Clem had grown rowdy in his grandparents' house as they declined and grew infirm. The year Clem turned six both had died, the grandmother from pneumonia and grandfather from lung disease. Clem had come to their house and stayed, and became their boy. Meg had given up on a child of her own.

'I'll be damned if I canna get Clem's money returned, whether you'll help me or no,' said Meg.

She brought across the cake tin from the counter and put a glass of milk in front of Clem.

'Hot drinks will scald fur a few days,' she said.

Clem nodded and reached for the tin.

'And only soft food.'

Clem nodded and solemnly dipped his biscuit.

Ernest glanced at his wife, his chest tightened. She turned and headed towards the spare room, he heard the snap of ring binders.

'Ah'm sorry,' said Clem.

Crumbs dropped from his swollen lips.

'Nothing tae be sorry aboot,' said Ernest.

He patted Clem's knee and then folded his arms and fixed his gaze to the west.

The bars of golden light blurred into each other as the sun declined below the horizon. Moisture gathered but did not fall from Ernest's eyes. By the shore, the harbour grew shadows and a clear evening sky stretched tight over the isles.

24

After Kieran left Erskine he returned to Kirkwall. The fiery dusk drew him to detour towards The Ayre. There was a ripple of electronic sound then the vehicle was silent. The carpark was now empty, the snack wagon closed. In the distance the Shapinsay boat was gurgling a haze of diesel into the egg-shell green sky. Close running waves caught the pale iridescence above and broke into inky triangles. Three oystercatchers crossed from right to left casting shrill whistles.

The image of Ernest striking his nephew returned.

What would Mish think? Would she like Harriet and Addie? What about their accent and education? She'd laugh, of course she would.

Kieran tapped his fingers on the wheel. His face fell into repose as he watched the chop and rebound of waves on the breakwater. He opened the window to hear the murmur of the evening sounds, then took out his phone and searched for Mish's number.

He heard her yawning. 'At least it's morning. How are you?'

'Did you know my sister had a rabbit?' said Kieran. 'Blackberry.'

'What?'

'She used to feed him long bits of grass to see him eat it like spaghetti,' said Kieran. 'Got away one summer. I had to go under the house to find him.'

He pictured the dark hole where his arm had reached and could not reach the bottom.

'I thought you were calling about your dad,' said Mish.

'This is.'

He drew breath, tasted diesel on the air.

'Mum told me to take out the trash. It was a nor'wester, and she was packing for Tekapo. I thought I found it.'

'Found what?'

'Blackberry. But maybe I didn't. Maybe it was just I heard Dad say something about the hassle of getting someone to look after the rabbit and put things together in my head the wrong way.'

'You're not making sense,' said Mish.

'I thought Dad put him in the rubbish can,' said Kieran.

'Kieran?'

'Why would I do that? As if I wanted to believe the worst of him.'

'I don't know.'

'All those memories. That summer—' Kieran's words became rapid, '—the lake being perfect, swimming with Toni, and Dad fishing. But I don't know. Was it really like that? It's easier most of the time to not to think back at all, or to think that it wasn't so great. But why would I think that about the rabbit?'

There was no reply.

'I wish I could have told him that I didn't mind that he wasn't perfect. That it didn't matter. And to say sorry for thinking that. I want to remember him how he really was. How can I do that without being too much one way or the other?'

His ear tuned into the lapping water, the soft loss and gain of sound.

'It's hard remembering being happy, when things change,' said Mish.

Tears welled up in Kieran's eyes.

'What do I say to Mum? I don't know how to start.'

'You're talking to me,' said Mish.

Her voice was low, fading away. Kieran's eyelids started to droop, an irresistible urge to sleep fell on him.

He saw himself and his father standing face to face, each mirroring each other's movements, hesitating. Then they were walking together, not on water anymore but surrounded by green light, working silently on some task, passing tools to and fro. He heard a voice, and it said 'I love you.'

Kieran started upright against the seatbelt.

'Still there?' said Kieran.

'Still here,' said Mish.

He steadied himself.

'Is it okay if I keep calling?'

'I'm right here. You're not alone—you never are.'

The call ended. Kieran sat back in the car and watched darkness take its gentle hold on the islands.

25

Stoat's whiskers brushed through the grass. She hunkered low, cantering on three feet. Her sharp senses followed a vole trail to a still blind litter. Stoat moved quickly, kill to kill. Her teeth tore and held until the nest was silent; blood and silence bought peace.

Stoat picked up one of the dead in her teeth. She carried it back to the burrow where she had left her small selves. Stoat circled and sniffed the kits, then abandoned the site, the vole still in her teeth. All was still. They had starved while she was away, all except for the weakest—killed by its siblings. She returned to the vole burrow, secreted her scent and made it her own. She ate and rested.

She survived, to begin again.

~~~

The lights of Erskine were coming on.

'But why can't I? I want them in my room,' said Eveline.

'They're for downstairs,' said Anna. 'So we can all see them.'

'Dad said they were mine.'

Anna brushed tangles from her daughter's hair; unwashed, it was the dark grey-blonde of a wild rabbit. Eveline wriggled free, and hid beneath the covers.

'Let me kiss you goodnight,' said Anna.

'No. I don't want to be kissed. I hate you.'

Anna waited. She remembered saying the same thing to her mother, and believing she meant it. She hadn't meant it at all. It was all wanting, and wishing and needing. Anna sighed and began to run the brush through her own hair. A voice came from beneath the covers.

'Mummy?'

'Yes, Pumpkin.'

'Why do we live in London when it's so bad for me?'

Anna touched the top of her daughter's hair where it peeked from the blanket.

'I have to work, and you have to go to school, and Daddy…' Anna's voice trailed.

'Can't we live somewhere else?'

Anna's throat tightened.

'No, darling,' she said. 'We can't.'

Eveline turned over and held out her arms.

'Sorry, Mummy.'

'It's all right, darling,' said Anna.

'I love you.'

Anna felt her daughter's body relax as they embraced. Grey shadows still remained beneath her daughter's eyes, but her lips were pink and she breathed without wheezing.

Dusk was so long here, as if the day begrudged ending at all. She kissed her daughter on the forehead and closed the curtains to block out the remaining light. She checked Oscar had not rolled out of bed and then paused on the landing to gather her thoughts.

~~~

Downstairs, Addie and Harriet were casting a critical gaze over Martin's gift.

The pair of pottery pugs sat on the dining table. They leaned shoulder to shoulder, a mirror image, with wrinkled snouts and black glass eyes. Gilt collars crimped their necks and bat-like ears perched either side of their heads. The high-gloss shine gave an impression of wetness, increased by the animal's disgruntled expressions.

Martin sat on the sofa reading the back pages of a newspaper, glass in hand.

Anna descended and Addie held out a gin and tonic.

'You have it. I'll make another.'

Anna took a sip, eyes watering at the strength.

'Our mother gets through a bottle a week,' said Addie from the kitchen counter.

'She doesn't really,' said Harriet.

'That's nothing compared to some people,' said Anna, glancing toward her husband. 'How is Julia?'

'Her client list is ever longer and more prestigious,' said Addie from the kitchen counter. 'People want whole houses done, everything out, everything in. It used to be a room or two.'

'What do you think of this place?' said Anna.

'You know it's perfect,' said Addie. 'Apart from one thing.'

Anna raised her eyebrows, then understood. The pugs.

'He says he picked them up at a flea market,' said Anna.

Addie leaned on the counter, sipping her drink.

'Do you go to many flea markets, Martin?' called Addie.

'All the time,' he said. 'Makes up for the terrible new things I'm constantly promoting.'

'Does it?' said Addie under her breath, then more loudly, 'Let's go outside. I want to watch the sky.'

Harriet replied with a shrug and the three women left through the French doors.

The weird call of eider ducks carried up from Kingsgarth Loch, and at the shore Storrtang was at once picturesque and sinister, gradually blending into the darkness. The Churchill Barriers stretched between the southern isles, concrete cubes and lines of steel chaining the supine bodies of Lamb Holm, Glimps Holm and Burray, and in the distance the long finger of South Ronaldsay.

The three women moved away from the doors to where they could see out to Scapa Flow and no longer be overheard. 'It's like they're melting,' said Addie.

There was a pause as the sinuous shapes of the islands blackened and slid into the water.

'Thank you,' said Anna, touching her shoulder against Harriet.

'For what?'

'Burying the cat. God, it's like something out of an awful comedy.'

The smiles on their lips faded as they watched the darkening sea.

'Martin's lying to me,' said Anna. 'I think he's in trouble.'

She looked to the bright room where Martin was turning the pages of the newspaper. She wished she could always be outside and never have to go back to him.

'You know something, don't you, Addie?' said Anna. 'And Harriet, you see through it all. I don't want either of you to tell me though. When I have to I'll bear it.'

Harriet wrapped her arm around Anna's waist and they drew closer. They watched the glow on the water, the illusion of light rising into the dark.

The soft bubble of curlew song broke the nocturne.

'It is a special place sometimes,' said Harriet. Her tone low and soft. 'But it's not an easy place.' Anna's arm tightened around her friend. 'I wonder if it might have helped if Art and I had been frank about what we were doing.'

'Mum said it was predictable no one would support you,' said Addie. 'She went though something similar with Dad. There was an age gap, although they were both older, they were from different worlds. She didn't fit.'

'I'm in your corner,' said Anna.

The chill was beginning to settle, seeping into their skin, cooling the blood.

'What about Clem?' said Anna. 'What did you do to make him love you, Addie?'

'Clem didn't stand a chance against Addie,' said Harriet.

She chuckled and looked at her sister.

'No,' said Addie firmly. 'I won't have anyone laughing at him. And I won't have you making me feel better.'

'I wasn't laughing,' said Harriet.

'He didn't deserve what happened,' said Addie.

'Ernest loves him,' said Harriet.

'He can't have wanted to hurt him,' said Anna.

'It doesn't need to be said,' said Harriet. 'He's struggling with something. I don't know what it is. He's a good man.'

She stopped.

'Clem sat so well for me,' said Addie. Her speech quickened and rose. 'I wasted my time trying to fill in the background, trying to capture all this.' She opened her arms. 'He waited and waited, not even looking one way or the other, and I hardly made a start.'

Addie bit her lip to stop it shaking.

'Addie, it's okay.'

Harriet released Anna and they moved either side of Addie.

'The sketches are…they're moving,' said Anna.

'Are they?' said Addie.

'He's in the landscape,' said Anna. 'You saw that. Part of the place.'

The sky overhead had become a blue Anna had never seen before, so intense she almost couldn't stand it.

'God, what a place this is.'

'I'm resigning my fellowship,' said Harriet abruptly.

'What? It's all you've worked for,' said Anna. 'What about Paracchini?'

'It's not the professor, he doesn't notice personal lives, or the students. They're like skin cells, renewed every three years.' She laughed briefly. 'It's me. I can't face going back to me. Do you ever feel like that? You just can't face yourself. Not in the same place, doing the same thing.'

'Are you feeling guilty?' said Addie.

'Yes. No. It's everybody else's guilt. I didn't hold a knife to his throat.'

'Why resign?' said Addie.

'Father changed career. He felt too guilty to carry on without being more humane.'

'It's not the same,' said Anna.

'You don't deserve it,' said Addie.

'Have you told Art?' said Anna.

'No. He'll think it means something it doesn't.'

Harriet turned towards the faint glow in the northwest imprinting the scene on her mind.

'He doesn't need me,' said Harriet.

'There's nothing wrong with wanting somebody,' said Addie.

'Isn't there?' said Harriet. 'Isn't there something here, inside me, that isn't right?' She pressed a hand against her forehead. 'They've imagined us naked. Tell me they haven't. Thought about me with him, and me like that.' Harriet let the tears fall that had been gathering. 'And I see myself with their eyes.'

She looked towards the gate post, the tiny patches of darkness against the pillar.

'You have choices,' said Anna.

'I'm not you, Anna. I don't have your patience, or kindness. And Addie…' said Harriet.

'Ssh. Darling, don't. You know I'm a fake. God knows me and Mum, we both are. You and Dad, you're the ones in the real world. Ssh, don't cry.'

'I didn't know what Art was,' said Harriet. Her voice dropped away. 'What he would be to me, afterwards.'

A breeze came, brought on the breath of the high tide. In the distance a twinkling cluster of orange lights marked the harbour of Stromness.

'You know, how I've always said, "If it was right then it's right now." Well I was wrong,' said Addie. 'It's a trap. I'm not the same today as I was, or one day hope to be.'

'You're sounding philosophical,' said Anna.

'Blame the gin.'

Addie raised her empty glass. Harriet stayed silent, gaze fixed in the mid-distance.

'More drinks, we need more drinks,' said Anna. She turned and looked inside, then added, 'And Martin needs sending to bed.'

Her husband's chin had sunk onto his chest. It will catch up with him in the end, she thought then turned back around for a final glance of the night.

The brightly lit room had robbed the landscape of its subtlety. She could no longer make out the outlines of sea, land or sky, only the brilliance of distant orange lights and the pulse of the red and green shipping lane markers in the dark.

~~~

Martin blinked himself awake and followed the women's movements as they passed inside. The warmth stripped the moisture and coolness from their clothes. Anna took an ice cube into her mouth from her glass and crushed it between her teeth to relieve the sense of sudden, suffocating warmth.

All three women felt his gaze, and all thought how much they would like to smash the pugs. They wouldn't, of course. They never could—for Eveline's sake.

26

A queue of students wearing black tie waited for the college doors to open and the ball to begin. Gowns were full length, and verged on theatrical, the whole spectacle conspicuous next to the everyday attire of passers by. Close inspection revealed small differences in the young men's attire. Hired suits shone from wear and fitted imprecisely, while tailor-made suits sat neatly and had greater depth of black. Art had been given a suit by his mother; it had been kept in the embassy for formal functions. It was Dior, four buttons on the sleeve, one to fasten the jacket. The increased width of his shoulders further improved the hang of the jacket and the sharp white shirt collar glowed against his skin.

The Oxford summer sky, briefly blue in the afternoon, had bleached and dulled as the sun sank. Leaves hung limply like silken green flags on the hazel branches. The queue stretched along the high stone wall of the Master's garden. Wild flowers seeded in the cracks, grown swiftly in spring, thirsted under the flat white sky. Art longed for a breeze, for the smell of the sea.

With Harriet gone he noticed that there had been a change in the way he was regarded. The speculation on his relationship trumped the exoticism of his childhood and his father's position in the diplomatic service. He felt younger, lonelier.

He felt someone brush against his arm.

'E'scuse me.'

He stepped backwards to make room and his sleeve caught against the sequins of an aquamarine dress. A blush rose on the first year's freckled cheeks.

'You could wait here,' he said.

'But they've got my ticket.' She gestured ahead.

He caught the lilt of her faint Irish brogue. It was enough to place her as Cassy, a geography student. The young woman's red hair was coiled into a chignon, a free curl deliberately dressed the nape of her neck. The corner of Art's mouth rose.

'I'm sure they'll leave it at the door.'

Cassy hesitated.

'I didn't mean to push in.'

'If they are behind us I'll wait with you,' said Art.

Art shifted position and made space, a couple of his friends introduced themselves, although it was needless. With less than three hundred students college members knew each other, either by name or reputation.

'I'm looking forward to the band,' said Cassy.

'Yes, they should be all right,' said Art.

Cassy felt warmth bloom where the gaze of his almond-shaped eyes lingered on her neck and shoulders. She had heard the rumours. They seemed unlikely, although the tenseness of Art's bearing held promise lacked by other young men.

When they reached the head of the queue they were welcomed with champagne and ushered into the temporarily transformed college. The iconic grass quadrangle was hidden, the turf boarded over, and a stage erected along one side. Affixed to the ancient stones there were neon signs illuminating attractions, arrows pointed into gardens and cloisters. The four-hundred year old facade was like a naturally beautiful woman decorated with cheap trinkets—she bore it well and in the morning she would be herself again.

Art and Cassy walked side by side for a short distance, taking in their changed surroundings. The sequins of Cassy's dress returned the light like fish scales in shallow water under sunlight. Art's elegance of movement contrasted against the brazen enthusiasm of his peers as they strode towards the bar.

Cassy caught sight of her friends heading to the dining hall for the first sitting.

'Where will you be later?' said Art.

'I won't be hard to spot.'

She smiled, swept up her skirt with one hand and sashayed away.

Art cast his gaze up to Harriet's study window. He remembered another evening, another dress. It had been unusually humid, waves of warmth rising from the stones mingled with moisture from the flowerbeds. He had been punting in the afternoon and returned to change clothes before going to the pub. The sound of string instruments tuning up had flowed along the chapel cloisters. Harriet had been waiting to enter the chapel, studying a page of music, the activity at odds with her bare shoulders and the black dress synched tightly around her waist. Something about her reminded him of home and his first taste of rum.

'Performing?'

She had looked up and smiled.

'Hello, Art. We start in ten minutes.'

'Are you nervous?'

'More than usual. I have a solo. '

She had looked at his rumpled clothes.

'I suppose you have better things to do than a concert in the chapel.'

'Yes,' he said.

Her cheeks had flushed.

'Well, have a nice evening,' said Harriet.

As she had turned and walked away Art realised two things. Firstly, that he had hurt her feelings, and secondly that he did not have better things to do at all. Who would notice his absence from The Turf?

When the candlelit performance had come to an end he clapped just for her. And when the audience moved from the chapel into the Master's gardens for refreshments he had delayed his departure. Harriet had been speaking with other members of the choir, but she had noticed him and smiled. He nodded from a distance, then slipped away without interrupting her conversation. He had felt her gaze on his back as he retreated. At the door he had turned and again their gaze met and held. The incident had provoked a physical sensation he had never expected, not erotic in a sordid sense, but like water was flowing through him, a sense of weakness, nausea even, that increased whenever he thought about her.

~~~

The sensations had changed the more he got to know her, became more complicated. His head ached when he tried to reconcile the events of the past year with who he was, and who he'd promised himself he would be. Part of him would always be hers, he would not apologise for the fact.

He walked restlessly around the college and found himself in a tropical-themed bar, draped with fake bougainvillea. He ordered rum and coke, flavourless compared to Mauritian rum, yet he stuck with the drink. He turned his gaze to the amusements, willing himself to forget walking the same paths just to catch a glimpse of Harriet as she moved between tutorials.

Darkness fell. A green dress flashed in the shadows.

He left his friends and followed the lure of its sequins to a yurt in the walled garden. The weeping willow had been hung with lights and cast teardrops of shadow. Fabric with intricate geometric patterns had been hung around the walls of the tent and mint tea was being served in small tulip-shaped glasses. Speakers piped a jazz tune, and straightaway Art had a yearning for his piano and the old villa, almost forgetting why he had entered.

'You found me,' said Cassy.

'I did.'

'Have you tried the baklava?' she said.

Silver platters rested on the low, round tables and three large hookahs with flavoured tobacco were being freshly prepared. Cassy patted a richly embroidered cushion by her side.

'Where are you from?'

'London.'

She raised her eyebrows.

'That's not what you meant, was it?' said Art.

Cassy drew up her legs and leaned sideways on an elbow. Art mirrored her position and fulfilled her somewhat predictable curiosity about his history.

'My parents are from Mauritius, and I was born there. They're in the diplomatic service.'

Harriet's curiosity had been more nuanced, more particular, at once more removed and more intimate. The ambiguity of their interaction had left him in a limbo that made any time away from Oxford tortuous. In the long vacation he had resumed an affair with a girl from the international school. He'd barely touched the piano or looked at the books for his dissertation.

He had returned to Oxford believing himself deluded and determined to think more clearly. The second week of Michaelmas Term a text from Gregory had arrived just before their tutorial. He asked Art to say he had flu, rather than a stubborn hangover.

Harriet had made out she was displeased.

'We'll have to manage as best we can without Gregory,' she said. 'But maybe we won't last an hour. Was there anything you were particularly interested in? '

'I don't mind,' said Art.

He had tried to avoid eye-contact, yet something was magnetic about her gaze.

'Taboos,' said Art finally. 'How they work. And how can physical paternity count for nothing legally?'

'Let's start with paternity. Physical paternity does not necessarily represent commitment or good sense. A different approach takes away uncertainty,' said Harriet. 'Creates stability.'

He had misconstrued her meaning deliberately and forced her to explain in more detail, and then said things to make her laugh. The sound of the college bell at five o'clock had rudely intruded on their time together. He remembered the echo of the last stroke, and wishing time did not exist.

Harriet sat in her chair holding eye-contact. She made no motion to indicate he should leave. Eventually, she had said in a low voice, 'Why don't you kiss me?'

Art leaned forward.

'Really?'

She'd nodded.

He'd stroked aside a curl of fair hair. His fingertips had travelled over the delicate muscles of her neck. He'd watched Harriet close her eyes and then gently put his lips to her cheek.

~~~

In the Arabian Nights tent, Art ran his finger along the length of Cassy's arm.

'Why are you taking geography?' he said.

'I wanted to come here,' she replied.

Cassy tilted her head to one side and Art leaned forward and kissed her on the lips. They stayed together from then on, walking from entertainment to entertainment, catching other people's eye as the night passed.

Close to midnight Cassy said, 'I need to change my shoes.'

Her room was in an accommodation block tucked away from the main quadrangle. A wisteria plant swept in a wave along one side of its facade, the heavy fragrance drifted through the open bedroom window. She sat on the bed, lifted her gown over her knees and removed her heels.

Art sat beside her, and they kissed again. His hands explored the level of her acquiescence while his mind swum in darker waters and memories of Harriet. A few moments later she paused his hand and slid open the drawer by the side of the bed and removed a packet of contraceptives. She passed them to him and reached over to extinguish the desk lamp.

~~~

Before they moved to re-dress Cassy spoke. 'How many women have you been with, Art?'

'Seven,' he said.

She thought for a moment, but said nothing.

'And you?' said Art.

'Boys one. Men three. Women, zero.'

She'd turned on her side, a smile playing over her lips. They looked more fragile without lipstick, more like a girl's.

'You know,' she said, 'you're a terrible liar.'

'Am I?' said Art.

'Yes. But people can't resist you, can they?'

'What do you mean by that?'

Cassy interrupted him.

'Listen,' she said. 'The final act's starting.' She sat up on the bed. 'It's all people will talk about.' She replaced her underwear and dress. 'The bathroom's just across.'

Cassy gestured towards the door.

Art sighed and swung his legs to the floor, while Cassy retrieved her high heels.

'I thought you wanted to change shoes?'

'Oh, they're feeling a lot better,' she said.

A muffled voice on a loudspeaker counted, 'One, two, three, four...'

Cassy applied fresh lipstick and removed her remaining hair pins, auburn hair settled in curls on her shoulders.

'Come on, you're so slow.'

She smiled and reached forward to button Art's shirt.

That was something Harriet would never have done. She would never have called him slow either; and the contraceptives in her drawer were pills. Why could he not help thinking about her all the time? She would have liked the band—she liked music with energy. She'd turn off anything melancholy when they drove, preferring silence.

Cassy held out her hand and led Art out of the room. When they arrived at the ground floor they found the Lucas Mayfly, who had recently been made Junior Dean, entering the building with a female student. Anita, a third year mathematician, leaned heavily on his arm. Although his movements were indistinct, Lucas was clearly less inebriated than his younger companion.

'Amazin' night,' said Anita.

She looked close to passing out, face tilted upwards and smiling broadly, teeth flashing against her dark skin. Lucas opened his door and ushered her inside without comment.

'Leave them to it,' said Casey. 'Let's get a quick drink.'

'I thought you wanted to see the band?'

Cassy shrugged.

'As long as I see a couple of numbers. I don't really mind.' She ordered vodka lemonade and said, 'College'll be paying this off for years.'

~~~

After everything ended, in the faint chill of dawn, Art hung his jacket on Cassy's shoulders and they sat side by side on the great stone steps leading to the dining hall, waiting for the survivors breakfast to be served. They leaned together, blank-faced and pale, listening to a slurred female voice echoing in the cloisters saying, 'Best night ever.'

The survivors photograph was taken through the window below Harriet's teaching room. All the partygoers arranged on the main quad's covered grass. Students who had not attended the ball began litter picking.

'I need sleep,' said Casey.

A shiver of cold air slid between them as she stepped towards her room. Art remained still, unresponsive to the brief pause that asked if he would follow.

There was a frisson of memory, the long line of contact between their skin. He had an inclination to shake her hand

259

and say thank you, or perform another formal farewell gesture.

'I don't think I can,' said Art. 'Not now it's morning.'

Casey smiled, handed back his jacket and they parted.

As Art walked out of the college into the low sunlight he realised they had not given each other anything more than few hours of company. A brief gift of time.

The town was breaking its shell. Piles of cardboard were being pushed out for collection, pigeons rustled in the trees, busses passed The Martyrs monument. It had been built in 1843, in honour of three men burned for bearing witness to sacred truths three hundred years earlier.

In Mauritius a whole mountain, Le Morne, had become a memorial to escaped slaves who were massacred in 1845. It had recently become a UNESCO world heritage site. The unfolding story of the maroons was being more broadly told, the truth of blood commemorated in stone.

Art kept moving, across to the second-hand bookstore and past the neo-classical facade of the Taylorian. His steps taking him towards the railway station.

He bought a ticket without really believing he would use it, the destination was so unlikely, and passed through to the platform. Relieved of the burden of weekday commuters the sheltered area was occupied only by an old woman with a small white dog and a teenage boy engrossed in his mobile phone.

Art felt he could sleep standing up. It wasn't exhaustion from lack of sleep or physical exertion, it was all the pretending. Without Harriet that's all there was—tiredness of the soul.

He looked for a place to sit and found himself looking down at a piano stool. Black-padded and worn it stood by a Yamaha upright, incongruous among the concrete, perspex and steel. A notice above read 'Donated by the Oxford Piano Festival.'

Art sat. He slid his feet to the pedals and rested his hands in the shape of the F major. Muscle memory joined the times he

260

had been himself making Harriet laugh until she cried, telling her how he felt curiously alone except when he was with her. Art's fingers tripped into a tune, running into an improvisation that built in tempo, until it triggered another deeper memory. He heard Rita saying, 'Sometimes music is not performance. It's treatment and cure. And there's no reason you cannot treat yourself now and again.'

27

Under darkness, a fog bank rolled in from the southeast, settling over the airport, spreading around St Ola and into Kirkwall Bay.

For a second night Clem could not sleep. He hadn't been able to swallow the pain pill from Aunt Meg.

He left the bungalow on Balfour Rise, wincing as the damp air made contact with his wounds, and walked through a narrow path that connected the crescent with the play park. Meadowsweet grew in the verge, frothy spears glowing in the fog, their scent lost to Clem's damaged nose.

Only a single swing remained operational, hanging forlornly above the worn padded tiles made from recycled rubber.

Clem watched the haar closing in, blurring the edges of buildings, forming cones of orange beneath the lampposts. Steady steps took him to the harbour, head tipped so that his crown broke into the space ahead.

He was troubled. How was it best to decide about doing one thing or another? Addie had been sure about rescuing the animal. Addie knew best. Uncle Ernest had said the stoats must be trapped. Uncle Ernest knew best. But did they?

At the harbour, the haar was thick and milky. Clem walked

along the quayside until the inter-island ferries came into sight. It was too late for anyone to be fussing with a boat or yapping by the taxi rank. There was no movement, no life, not even a scavenging gull at the bins. He listened to the last wash of the incoming tide as it came and went.

The bungalow was empty without him, always empty except when he was there. He wanted someone to be waiting.

'Sorry for the skelping,' Ernest had said when he'd pulled up at Balfour Rise. 'And I'm sorry fur losin yir money like a fool.'

It had been a solemn thing to receive an apology from his uncle.

'I dinna mind aboot the money. Whit's the good o a car? I canna drive.'

Ernest had returned a small smile.

'I can try teachin you in this. Hid's a big responsibility.'

'Aye?' said Clem.

'Maybe, when thir's no cars aroond at the Mart carpark.'

Clem had watched Ernest from inside behind the window, how his uncle had stayed sitting in the car just staring was a worry. Clem had grown tired, switched the light off and lain down in his clothes, his face bulging and hot, like when it was sunburned at the County Show.

Now he was leaning at the harbour. A fresh flow of fog was coming, enfolding the land, swallowing lampposts and masts. The cold droplets touched the hot healing of his face. Clem turned from the rail and began to make his way back to the empty rooms. He would walk past the car, and not touch.

In the morning they both had to go back and apologise. Meg had said, 'Hid'll hiv upset them,' and Ernest had nodded and said, 'Aye.'

A figure grew out of nothing and strode down the sweep of pavement from the Old Grammar School. Clem hung back by the East Church and waited to be passed.

'Clem?'

Clem glanced up. Kieran pulled air through his teeth and whistled.

'You're goin to have a hell of a shiner.'

Without thinking Clem smiled and it made his lips hurt like hell.

Kieran leaned forward on his toes, like if he stopped moving for too long he'd fall off balance.

'I finally called my sister, and my mum,' said Kieran. 'Wanted to do it at a reasonable hour, so had to stay up. Then couldn't sleep.'

Clem nodded, fingered the ironwork of the gate, keeping his face turned.

'Time difference, that's the problem,' said Kieran. He stared into the haar, his gaze following the drifts moving along the empty street. The closed ranks of houses funnelled the fog like a river; it drifted in eddies, the only element alive in the whole scene. 'Can't get away from it.'

Clem wondered what it would be like to have a mother and a sister and not to go back to an empty house. He pulled a flake of rust away and pinched it between his fingers.

'I didn't cry at the funeral,' said Kieran. 'You're meant to cry.'

'Hid's no easy,' said Clem.

'Wasn't ready,' said Kieran. 'I wasn't ready for him to go.' He gave a half smile. 'I don't suppose he was either.'

Clem ran his finger along the railings and looked towards Mill Street.

'Canna always stay,' said Clem.

Clem raised his head, it felt heavy as a boulder, and looked the tall man in the eye.

'I apologise,' said Clem. 'For the clout.'

'No worries. It all got a bit excited didn't it. You take it easy, get home.'

Kieran moved away, long strides cutting through the mist. Rather than going up The Willows Clem headed past the big square houses on Bernstane Road, all penned in their plots by country dykes even though they were in the town. He followed the bus route back to the scraggly saplings and the open field.

The car was there on the road, sapphire blue beneath its film of moisture. Why, he thought, why did he want a thing so much? It did him no good.

He lay his hand gently on the spoiler to feel the coolness of the dew.

The alarm triggered and knifed through the fog.

'Hoi!'

The man was very close this time.

Clem pushed his legs hard into the ground. One, two. One, two. He heard Ernest's voice, 'You've great strong legs. If thir efter you, run!'

Past the bollards and away. Clem bounced in through passageway behind the garages. Cold sweat poured down his back and his heart ran wild.

One, two. One, two.

'Run, Clem. Run!'

He flew hard to his own front door, froze in the shadow of the porch, knees barely holding, pressed against the grey wall. The alarm drilled through the fog and found him. But there were no footsteps, no blue lights.

Clem promised himself that if he wasn't caught this time then he would never touch again.

He stayed still, afraid to move. The haar came down even thicker, so he couldn't even see the bench or beyond. He listened for footsteps then took a chance, opened the door and scooted inside. The alarm stopped.

He lay on the sofa, damp and weary. He remembered fragments from his father's funeral. He had stood in the line of men with Ernest and shaken everybody's hand as they'd come to the cathedral. There had been nineteen cars in the parade to St Olaf's cemetery. Or had that been his grandfather's funeral? It was all mixed in his head now.

As he melted into sleep, he remembered a photograph there was of Ernest and Meg with his mother and father. They had gone together to the sports awards. All young and smiles. It was all smiley before he was born. Smiles and dancing.

Auntie Meg loved his mother so much, she hardly spoke about her without a tear. He was what her sister had left behind, she'd said once. She had smiled and held her hand on his cheek, and said she was glad. He always remembered that.

28

The mantle of fog drew over the linked southern isles in the early hours, clouds of fine vapour pressed against the windows of Erskine.

Anna did not sleep. It was not the gin—more nor less would have brought rest. She went into the garden night-walking and searched for the stoat, following around the dykes that rose like old ships in the haar. The closeness of the fog played tricks on her mind, objects appeared as if she brought them into existence. She bent low and scanned the ground. She could easily pay for veterinary treatment if she found her; the creature must be in pain.

She crouched into a ball, preserving her warmth, and hunkered down by the mound of earth where Harriet had buried Sleekit. It was an un-Harriet thing to do, taking the dead animal and putting it in the earth. She should have done it. She had adopted the creature. Anna remembered the cats wheedling affection, but her eyes remained dry.

Anna looked back to Erskine and recalled the forlorn remains she had bought. She'd thought that she could bring it alive again. Only once had she noticed Harriet raise her eyes to the beam in her room. Had someone told her? Ernest? Steven?

Anna stood up quickly from Sleekit's grave, needing brightness and unsure where to look for sunrise. How could anyone tell in such fog?

Had she seen what she wanted to see when she first came? Didn't she always? She shivered and a notion she should take care of herself more rose in her mind.

Anna was sitting still in Harriet's coat when Martin came downstairs thirsty in the early hours. A fresh cup of coffee by her side. The smell of cut grass hung in the air. She held one the statues and stared into its black liquid eyes..

'Are you coming upstairs?' said Martin.

'These,' said Anna, gesturing at the pugs, 'are unspeakably ugly. Take them away.'

'They're Eveline's,' said Martin.

'I don't want them here. Do you understand?'

'What's to understand?' said Martin.

'They don't fit.'

'We can take them back to London,' said Martin.

Anna's tone hardened.

'No. Not in our house. They'd suit a bay window.'

'What did Addie say to you?' said Martin.

Anna scrutinised her husband.

'You don't remember that I ever went to Peter's,' she said. 'Three years ago, you were celebrating the frozen foods commercial? I was pregnant with Oscar, and you laughed when I needed help up from the couch. Peter offered his hand.'

'He did?'

'He said it was a terrible couch, and that the whole place needed refurbishing, but his mother wouldn't have anything changed.'

Martin avoided his wife's gaze.

'I took a taxi home with Eveline and left you to stay overnight,' said Anna. 'You said you had an early shoot.'

'If you say so,' said Martin.

'I want you to take them away.'

'This is ridiculous,' said Martin, avoiding eye contact.

'I won't have Eveline fawning over them. I won't be reminded.'

'Why, Anna? Why do I offend you so much now?'

Anna stiffened.

She remembered how Peter had seamlessly passed her husband refreshed drinks, an invisible tether had stretched between them. She saw how Martin's gaze rested on Harriet's hips and on Addie's hair. Sometimes he looked at her in the same way. It was anyone. Everyone.

'Knowing I know, isn't that enough to stop you?' she said.

'I never intended...' he began, tone flat.

Anna held up her hand.

'I know you're not sorry. Don't lie to me.'

Her breathing eased. Their small store of drama was finally being spent. It really had very little to do with Peter. He was simply a proximate cause. It was absurd that Martin had given the ceramics to Eveline.

'The box is in the hall,' said Anna.

'Is this it?' said Martin.

'There's nothing else.' she said.

'I'm going back to bed.'

'I will not see it differently in the morning.'

She turned and spoke to the haar-pressed windows. 'Leave.'

Martin took the animals by the neck and left her alone.

Anna began thinking how much she loved Harriet, and Addie. Addie should be included, despite everything with the stoat. It was right, and yet also wrong, to let it go away injured. Anna's fingers pressed around her coffee cup.

From the old heart of Erskine, there came a sound, a distressed voice tumbling out words. Harriet, caught in another dream. Anna shivered at the sound. Harriet had not been hurting anybody. Art had moved her, and Harriet had had the courage to welcome the risk. Did she know what it would take to recover?

Outside, the haar obscured the waves washing to shore, there was no witness to their one and only arrival and departure. Anna kept vigil and the house again fell silent.

29

While the newly crowned Edward VII travelled Europe, the spring storms abated in Orkney. Relentlessly wet weather had persisted through June and July. Water lay in great grey lakes in depressions on the fields. Fog came in August and with it an outbreak of measles.

The untimely death of Gudrun heralded a poor harvest for the crofts at the entrance to Scapa Flow. It was a bad sign that a capable woman could die in her bed after a single night working out of doors. She had been happily cutting peats with her nephew the week before and there had been no previous sign of illness.

Robert had offered James a new bottle of Scarth's whisky when he came to offer his condolences.

'I'm at a loss tae explain hid,' said James.

The memory of what he'd done was now preserved only in his darkest dreams, an act committed when mind and body dwelt in a world that was once again locked.

'Aye,' said Robert. 'And the ewes drowned as well.'

Thorn sat away in the shadows. He looked over to where Gudrun's spinning wheel gathered dust. What foolishness had drawn him to his uncle's wife? The question tormented him as he worked at the peat edge, cutting and flipping with the tusker. His mind turned the night of the storm over again and again, looking for another ending as he toiled stacking turfs.

Thorn's sister Alice came and to take away the churns of milk and returned with pats of butter and cheese. Her efforts a poor substitute for his aunt's produce. Neither Thorn or James had appetite. Silence reigned as they worked on together, half-heartedly coaxing a harvest to survive the winter.

Once or twice Thorn saw his uncle stop and stare at the bed nook. His lips moved as if he were addressing someone lying there.

Thorn wondered if any other woman would have done the same. Was it a particular sin to themselves? The thoughts circled around his head—they could go nowhere else.

Late in autumn, a gale hit with an icy edge. This time nothing could be done to staunch the flood and protect Storrtang. Robert stood braced in the steading as great plumes of froth erupted and the sea cracked and rolled over the stones. He would not be persuaded inside—it was the end and he would see it. Janet and the sickening children huddled together as water flooded beneath the door. The baby at her breast slept limply, red spots on its cheeks.

Up at Erskine, the lum spat and James stared wearily into the hearth. A sea trout skewered through its gullet hung from the rafters, stiffened and yellowed.

'If only we'd had a bairn,' James said. He looked up and gazed perplexed at his nephew as if wondering who he was.

The pressure of the storm grew, squeezing the walls of the croft, pushing out the words Thorn had wanted to say a hundred times since his aunt had died. His heart clamoured as they burst out, 'She was alive when I left her.'

His uncle seemed not to hear over the storm, dull eyes resting without acknowledgement on the dangling kettle. In a lull between gusts Thorn spoke again, even louder this time. 'She was alive and breathing, asleep in the bed that morning.'

Thorn could not tell from his uncle's expression whether he had been understood.

'Uncle. Do you suspect me?' said Thorn.

James stirred and said, 'Why break a trough and leave yourself nowhere to lap?' he said. 'Be a dull thing tae dae.'

He glanced to the bed nook. A look of fear grew in his eyes. Thorn followed his gaze. He imagined his aunt in the shadows, plump, winsome skin the colour of seashells rubbed by the waves, lids half-closed, dark eyes turned slantways towards him. Thorn started in his seat.

'Have a dram,' said James, and filled his cup.

Thorn took what was offered. He sat spellbound with his uncle as the sleet caned the windows. The cruisie lamp guttering as the wind harrowed the land.

Now in his mind's ear Thorn thought he heard the rhythm of Gudrun's needles in the creaks of the croft, her sighs in the moan of the wind. He saw his uncle look again into the rectangular opening of the bed nook still guarded by its huge piece of flagstone.

Thorn stared into his cup and saw a blackness into which he longed to fall. His eyes slowly closed. How hotly their limbs had entwined, how quickly their fatigue and hunger had been forgotten. If she had fallen quickly with a child the sin might have been made well.

270

Thorn lurched in his chair and drew awake again. A devil danced in the embers.

James sat stupefied, cup in hand, watching the shrinking glow beneath the peats.

'I must go to bed,' said Thorn.

'Stay,' said James.

'I'll leave here, find a passage away.'

'Do you see her?' said James. 'Tell me?'

'I don't see anything that isn't there.'

'So you say. So you say.'

James's voice was flat.

'Once and for all. Uncle, do you accuse me?' said Thorn.

'Of what?' said James.

The pitch of the wind rose and gusts scuttled beneath the slates, straining the ballast that held the roof. Thorn could not answer. The orange glow, the eye of the croft, flattened into grey ash. The hearth was dead.

His uncle started in his chair.

'Thorn! Where are you?'

'Here,' Thorn replied from the dark. 'But I'll be gone to-morrow.'

In the east, a dirty light began to separate the grey of sea and sky. The night was passing. Thorn moved stiffly out from his chair. He collected the bottle of whisky from the table and his stick from the nook by the door.

'The devil will find you,' said James.

Thorn put his hand on the door and paused.

'Well, he won't find me here.'

Thorn took a final look around the interior. Dawn was break-ing, and without the glow from the fire to soften its poverty each item stood in shabby isolation: the spinning wheel, the butter churn, the kettle, the box bed. Once broken they would never be repaired again.

Thorn stepped into the wind and cut himself loose from Erskine. He felt the breeze on his back as he passed the sycamore saplings, and heard the hurrying bleat of sheep.

He set his uneven steps towards the jetty at St Mary's, where he might find space on a fishing boat once the storm blew out. The coast road was awash and he was forced to scramble behind Storrtang and through his father's fields. He kept his head turned from the dim light creeping from the sills of his parents' croft.

A memory came back to him, sitting with his sister Alice in a nook long since washed away. He had picked a posy of thrift and handed it to her. She had plucked the heads from their stalks and tossed them between her hands, humming a dancing song. It had been a breathless day, the water rising in Scapa Flow as if the land were simply a filling basin. They had stayed out of their father's sight, determined to enjoy the sun. He remembered envying her going to school, and belonging to the world of small delights he had left behind. She had the measles now, and a poor chance. Thorn wiped his coat sleeve across his eyes; it was a pity he would see her no more.

~~~

In the croft, the devil slunk around the hearth.

James saw Gudrun's lips twist and become sly.

'Whit did you ever want o me? Have you no had hid aal yet?' he said.

There was no reply. Why could a man not be at peace in his house and take comfort in his whisky?

He began to stride restlessly, pacing around the hearth with its gawping, shrivelled fish, feeling the rain spit through the lum.

'Why must you stare and stare? And no go doon to the devil whar you belong?'

He talked on as he fetched the skein of mooring rope from its place on the wall.

'If you will no leave me alone then I will go.' He tested a knot for fastness on his arm and seeing it held firm cast it over the rafter. The sound of his voice rebounded from the walls. 'There were times we loved,' he said and pointed to the bed box. 'And where you lie, there was no sin in that.' He pointed to the nook where his wife stared. 'No sin in a man having his wife as often and as plainly as he wants and as he needs, even if a child does not come. Is there?'

He secured one end of the rope to the peg where animals were tethered when they shared the same roof. His voice mimicked the minister's: 'A woman is not to be trusted. She is a devil who simply wants what she cannot have.'

He fetched Gudrun's spinning stool beneath the beam. His gaze returned again to the shadows of the bed nook. Gudrun looked up at him with her bright Spanish eyes as he climbed on to its seat.

'Mercy, you're determined, once you get a thing in your head.' James paused.

A greater, deeper silence fell on the room. He looked up through the lum and saw the sky. Blank. Nothing but darkness and deeper darkness. Thorn will find me, thought James. He sighed softly and lowered his head, slipping the rope beneath his chin. He can take the croft, maybe find a wife. And then he'll see how hard it is to get any rest, and know well the penalty of a promise.

He proclaimed the secret oath: 'My flesh be torn to pieces with a wild horse, and my heart cut through with a horseman's knife, and my bones buried on the sands of the seashore where the tide ebbs and flows every twenty-four hours, so that there may be no remembrance of me amongst lawful brethren.'

He whispered, 'Both in one,' and flicked the stool away with his foot, believing himself to be a man unmourned.

He saw a spume of white as he dropped. The salty foam suspended for a second in the air, then the weight of water crashed down on the shore.

30

Ernest switched off the engine and dropped his hands into his lap. Meg held out her hand and warmth slowly grew where they touched.

'Hid's like gaan oot wi no breeks.'

The corners of Meg's mouth twitched upwards, at the same time her throat tightened. Another car pulled in next to them and the moment was over.

'I'll get the ticket,' he said.

Ernest buried his hands in his overall pockets and kept his head down as they walked through the car park. He sensed rather than saw the haar that clung to their clothes. Meg was in her light summer coat and carried a bag with a zip-lock freezer bag full of documents that related to their accounts.

Three people were already waiting in line for the bank to open. All were familiar one way or another, yet neither Ernest nor Meg joined in conversation. At nine the glass-panelled door swung inwards. Orla Spence secured the latch, nodded in greeting, then walked to a podium where she directed customers to the cashier or offered help with the cash machine.

Meg stepped forward.

'There's been money taen from wir accoont.'

Meg placed a statement down and pointed.

'This eens and this eens. Hid wis a scam.'

Orla placed on her spectacles.

'This wis April?'

'Aye,' said Meg.

'You need tae speak wi Kellie. Come through-by.'

Ernest kept his gaze down on the tiles and his mouth shut. The night before he'd watched Meg sorting though the files, checking every piece of paper, back and front, like she had never done once in her life before.

Kellie smiled warmly and invited them to sit down.

'Not much of a summer, is it?'

She spoke with the rising intonation of the Midlands. Her shiny black hair was held in a long flat pleat that stayed in place down the centre of her red uniform jacket.

'I'm still in tights.'

Her nails were as bright as the bindi between her eyebrows. She rocked from side to side, making herself comfortable behind the desk then addressed the computer.

'Let's have a look at your account then.'

She took the April statement from Meg and compared it with what she saw on the screen.

'They were all authorised.'

Ernest's stomach clenched.

'They said hid wis because me accoont wis compromised.'

'Who was this?' said Kellie.

Ernest looked down at his hands and Kellie waited for him to speak.

'I didna ken they wisna the bank. Hid wis the right number on the handset.'

Ernest suddenly wished Clem were there with him. It was a strange thought to have, to want him out of all people to be there with him.

'Did you give them your password?' said Kellie.

'Aye.'

'And did you give them any other details?'

'Whole lot o details.'

Kellie took her hands away from the keyboard. Her deep-brown eyes turned from Meg to Ernest, lips pressed.

'The bank cannot refund transactions when payments have been authorised by account holders. I'm really sorry.'

'Where did hid go?' said Meg.

'It's a bank a policy….' Kellie stopped and started again. 'In most cases the transferred funds are moved within hours. It's really important to act quickly.'

Ernest stayed quiet, watching figures behind the frosted glass passing by.

'The accounts are unlikely to be traceable. But the fraud office will try,' said Kellie. 'Looks like twenty-thousand pounds was transferred from your joint account and fifteen thousand from the saving account for a Mr Clement Rawson.'

'Aye,' said Meg. 'Wir nephew, Clem.'

Ernest's thoughts began to drift. A fog had grown inside him, a milky whiteness, a trap that brought ships to rocks, that made captains turn the wheel the wrong way in good faith. Ernest thought about the hazards he'd seen coming in life, but there were always ones he didn't see, the cliff edges that crumbled, the ground falling away before danger was sensed.

'Everything needs to be reported to the police right now. They'll give you a crime number and the case will go to be investigated by Action Fraud.'

Kellie pulled out a leaflet and circled the important information.

'Here's the information, and this is the helpline number.'

Ernest came out of his reverie. He stared down at what was being offered.

'How can I ken whit's true?' he said. 'How can I ken who is at the end o the line? I might as well hiv given my keys tae a stranger an said "Help yirsel".'

Ernest's clenched his hands and watched Meg take the leaflets and then they waited while Kellie made a phone call. An appointment made with a police officer, but what good would come of it all?

When they left, Orla Flett cast a pitying gaze towards them. Aye, thought Ernest, everyone will know. Blood came to his cheeks and he quickened to the door.

On Albert Street, buildings loomed as if it were a strange town. Ernest's breath shortened. It was all damn vanity and pride. There was nothing to be done except to feel a fool.

Meg took hold of his hand and drew it to her side. The touch brought him back to himself, the pavement moved beneath his feet again. The town became recognisable.

They reached the car park at the back of the co-op.

'I've a few peedie messages,' she said, quietly. 'You go on wi the car and see Clem. I'll be fine.'

Droplets had caught in the fair grey of her hair, each cast the world in miniature. He thought of all the things he'd wanted to put into her hands.

'Tak better care today,' said Meg. 'And bring him back for tea. No doot he'll need somethin easy.'

The haar was thinning. Ernest reached up and brushed the moisture from her curls. Her eyes were as blue as the summer sky.

'Aye,' said Ernest. 'Hid'll lift noo.'

Meg searched his face and he held her gaze. Life continued.

It was in his mind to drive by St Nicholas Kirk. He had a need to pass the stone in the far corner where James Poke was laid. It was from the actions of forebears that lessons were learnt, one way or another.

31

Kieran loaded cleaning materials and a fresh punnet of eggs into the car. The walk from the new flat on Buttquoy Loan had woken his limbs, but his mind was still slow from a poor night's rest. He yawned, climbed into the driver's seat and shook himself warm.

The haar was close against Wideford and persisted as he drove east. Cars were hidden until they were almost upon him, looming like ships as the electric vehicle cut a tunnel through the moisture-soaked air. He eased his foot from the accelerator and economised on miles. There was no hurry.

The fog pressed closer as he crossed the barriers after St Mary's towards Burray. He could have been anywhere. He wiped his eyes and steadied the wheel and eased his speed again. As the weeks went past he had started hearing his father's voice, like he hadn't died and they were simply having a conversation, one they'd always needed to have but never did. By the time he stopped at the entrance to Walt's drive he could only see a few meters of road. Kieran composed himself then headed toward the polytunnel where the trap was snug behind a line of willows.

Walt raised the kettle at the kitchen window as Kieran passed the house and nodded.

Kieran pushed through the grass and began to loosen the top screws, pausing before opening the lid of the rectangular box. He lifted the lid and revealed a carcass, the stoat limp and bedraggled beneath the kill bar. The smell caught in his throat and released the tears that had been welling up in his eyes.

Kieran steadied his breathing, withdrew, then secured the kill bar. He set to work, cleaning away the matted fur and blood with short, efficient brush strokes, and letting his tears fall. They were frequent now, and he let them go. He hadn't known it would take courage to grieve.

The cold hand of the fog pressed lightly on his shoulders as he worked. He checked the mechanism ran smoothly, hands moving methodically like his father's. When everything was clean and set he placed new eggs inside and replaced the screws. He wiped his eyes, and took a deep and steadying breath.

'You're only human.'

It was his father's voice. He'd used the exact same words after the carpark accident and then added, 'Just don't be human in my car.' His father had laughed, the load lightened.

Kieran stared down at the trap, wondering why it all mattered so much. When he looked up Walt was there, holding out a hand to help him up, 'Come on, beuy.'

He gestured towards the corpse.

'Shall I put hid in the wheelie bin?'

Kieran shook his head and raised his hand to wipe his eyes again, staying crouched over the newly set trap. Walt waited, his gaze casting around to the shapes in the fog, the familiar old dyke and faint line of the road. After a pause he laid a hand on Kieran's shoulder.

'Oh, hid can bide. Come on inside,' he said. 'He's no gaan anypiece.'

He showed Kieran where he could wash his hands, then went through into the kitchen and made two mugs of coffee.

When Kieran joined him they talked about mousetraps.

'My dad swore peanut butter was best bait,' said Kieran.

'He might be right there,' said Walt, dipping a digestive.

'He died,' said Kieran.

'Aye,' said Walt. 'I heard. It's a pity.'

'I'll get used to it.'

Walt nodded.

'No doot. Gae yirsel time. Plenty o time, beuy.' Walt turned to the long window.

'See noo, we'll get a better day yet.'

Faint clusters of blue were growing over the haar and a fresh wind was coming.

32

James Poke had had a private burial. Now three of his nieces were also in the ground. Measles had left the baby lifeless in its basket, and Alice had woken one morning, her fever gone, both her sisters cold beside her. Storrtang was filled with January darkness. There had been no cleaning of the house to welcome the year, few neighbours stopped past.

Janet had moved listlessly around the croft shifting greasy dishes, picking up and putting down soiled cloths. Issac, kneeled on the rug, head bowed and facing the embers. He glanced at his parents, rose and wandered to a bench by the wall, lay down and turned his back.

'Stop fussing, woman,' said Robert.

'Hid's awful quiet.'

'I've sold the sheep to Scarth.'

'Must we go?'

'What's not ruined will be soon. I'm speaken to Bannatyne the morn.'

Robert had spat into the fire. Janet's gaze ran to the curling edges of the illustration of Queen Victoria surrounded by the miniature portraits of her children

'Remember how Gudrun nursed my folk, and we were glad to have this place.'

'I kent they'd last a peedie while.'

Robert pulled open the drawer beneath his seat and pulled

out a near empty bottle.

'Hudson's Bay will take me.'

The croft roof trembled as a wash fell against its roof, sending smoke down the lum and into the interior. The tilly lamp flickered low as Robert raised the bottle to his lips.

Robert patted his knee. Janet moved slowly towards him, sluggish as water under a leeward cliff.

'Never fear a storm, lass. A dram will give you a bit o warmth, and so will I.'

Her husband reached up and pulled at the top of her dress. He passed an arm around her waist pulling her downwards. He offered her the bottle then reached inside her skirts loosening his trousers.

'I won't be beaten,' said Robert.

The hard thump of water sounded on the disintegrating cliff, hail tatted on the window.

She had laid the bottle down and cradled her husbands head against her breast, still sore from missing the nursing baby. Her gaze strayed to the picture on the wall, as they moved. A flush rose on her cheek as her husband shuddered beneath her. She wiped away a tear afterwards, for this was the end.

'Us'll get something better,' he told her as she straightened her skirts. 'To hell with this place.'

33

Meg's plan had formed on the threshold of the craft shop. Rather than going inside and completing her business she turned around and hurried to the Travel Centre. The bus to the Hope passed through St Mary's and from there she would walk to

Erskine. She remembered it being a short stretch, past the chalet accommodation and onto the coast road.

As the bus made headway the fog lifted from the heathland and fields, coiling backwards like freshly carded wool. The walk made her blood run, put energy into the task ahead. When she reached Storrtang crowds of sand flies rose, and a penetrating smell warned that something dead was nearby. She held her breath, gulping only the smallest amounts of air and strode past.

It brought back a memory of Clem running away from dead things on the beach, slipping on bright green sea lettuce slathered over the rocks, and then to a day she had been with her sister poking at a mass of stinking whale blubber, washed up on the stones by Greameshall.

She spotted a heron balanced on one leg spying for small fish in the rock pools crowned with bladderwrack. The water winked as she passed, the depths green and still, the tang giving off reek as the sun worked itself into warmth.

She had the leaflet and card given to her by the woman in the bank tucked into her bag. Its strap was beginning to cut and a carrier bag knocked against her legs as it was caught in the breeze.

The fog was lifting its skirts over the southern linked isles, stretching like a long green arm towards the coast of Scotland. Soon it would be possible to see the beaten edges of Caithness.

Meg paused and eased the stitch that ached under her ribs. She could see the outline of her destination.

The story of Erskine had been retold half within her hearing by her grandmother. After the worst of the tale was finished, voices would rise and a second cup poured out. The decline of the farm would be chewed over.

'Left twathree bairns in the kirkyard before they flit.'

'I mind hid wis Toronto.'

'No doot, seeking better fortune. The eldest boy niver back

afore he wis away tae fight.'

'Got his name on the memorial owerlookin the flow. And a medal to boot.'

'Reports said Thorfinn Poke made good a bridge, single-handed under machine gun fire.'

'Mercy.'

'Canno hiv been aal devil.'

'I ken, a Military Cross. Life's some twists.'

The modern extension of the house was not at all what she expected from Ernest's brief descriptions. The lines followed the landscape, echoed maritime shapes that held strong in the face of storms, but it was bold.

The car Ernest had fixed up for Harriet sat in the drive. Meg pulled up the strap of her bag and tucked a strand of hair behind her ear. She rang the bell then clasped the plastic bag with two hands and waited.

Meg recognised Anna from Ernest's description. Dark-haired and bonny as a lass.

'Hello. Can I help?'

'Meg,' she said. 'My husband comes, checking the traps.'

'Oh? Did he leave something?'

Meg shook her head.

'I thowt the peedie bairns would have wan o these.'

She retrieved two woollen hats from her bag. One was finished with a green bobble, the other had ear flaps hung with bright red tassels. She gave them into Anna's hands.

'Wash them lukewarm.'

Meg pushed her feet a fraction deeper into the driveway stones.

'I've heard you work in London, with a bank. Ernest says you've a knack with numbers.'

Anna managed a smile. A hand at knee level indicated the presence of a child hiding behind her legs.

'I'm sorry, we're all upside down this morning. Do you want to come in?'

'No. I'll no bother you long.'

Meg fished inside the plastic bag again.

'Somethings turn out so weel they're too good to sell. It's a Fair Isle pattern. Leftover wool. For being patient with Clem when he's here, and an apology for Ernest. Sometimes folk come as pairs.'

The knitted sweater danced in the air, whirling its hips as Meg held the garment for inspection. Seeing Anna's gaze run over the pattern she pushed it forward into Anna's hands.

'The weather is all kinds, even on a peedie dander. Your friend can have a lend of it. '

Meg looked with soft eyes on the sage green and sky blue bands, a band of red and orange in diamonds and chevrons ran through a background of sand-coloured thread. It would last a lifetime if loved well.

'I crochet, but nothing like this. Thank you.'

Meg pinched out Kellie's card from her handbag and held it out to Anna.

'She gave me this. The woman at the bank.'

Anna took the card and read the local branch manager's name.

'I don't understand,' said Anna.

'It was a scam,' said Meg. 'He can hardly spaek aboot hid. Looked fit for the grave when we went to the branch this morning.' Meg pointed at the card. 'Told her all the details he could muster, that he gave out his security details and had all these codes for permission. She said it's been left it too long and she thinks the money is long gone. All of it.'

The wind eddied through the slates and the whistle of oystercatchers looped up from the shore. Memories came to Meg as she built up steam to ask for help, walking the lanes with

284

her sister, Clem as a baby, when everyone loved him as perfect, Ernest determined to teach him to swim.

'He's like a drowning man,' said Meg. 'It wasn't just ours, it was Clem's too.'

'Meg. I'm sorry,' said Anna.

The pressure grew behind her ears, she needed to speak straight but all that came were tears, like a burn finding its way out of an underground channel to the corners of her eyes.

Meg turned away, feeling the cold tracks on her cheeks. A cool bank of air swept over the house. She took a deep breath and pushed out the words she had come to say, 'I'm sure this Kellie knows well enough, but I thought if there was someone this woman could speak with, to help her, and who knew how banks worked, we might get back some of what's taken.'

Anna glanced at the card again.

'I could try.'

Meg nodded.

'Ernest said you were a good lass.'

'Really? I don't know about that.' Anna gave a short laugh. 'Will you see the house?'

Meg looked upwards then leaned to the side to catch sight of the original stones.

'No. I have to catch the bus. You get inside now. You look awful cald.'

'Wait. What's the surname? If I call the bank.'

'Manse. Everything aal in the same name.'

'I really don't know if I can help at all. '

'You'll ken better than us.'

As she turned down the lane Meg saw a shadow dart under a spray of hogweed. Stoat no doubt. Meg had seen the cogs in Anna's mind beginning to turn. It was worth the journey, no matter what the outcome.

34

Along the jetty, ropes of water ended their silent approach and grew slack. A listless atmosphere hung around the surfeit shore. The morning drew on. Meg returned to Kirkwall, hope in the nest of her heart.

At Erskine, Addie still slept deeply and radiated heat like a warm stone. Harriet lay awake waiting for her sister to stir, listening for far distant sounds. Finally, Addie stretched and uncurled. Harriet felt a hand on her back.

'What is it?' said Harriet.

'Seeing if you were awake.' There was a short pause. 'You're better than I thought you would be.'

Harriet didn't reply.

'Mum said I should be gentle on you.'

'Hmm?'

'Really I'm gentle on everyone,' said Addie. 'Why did you never bring Art to see us? We could have got to know him. It was only that one time, in the car.'

Harriet remained silent. Her sister's eyes glistened in the half-light.

'It's too late now, but it might have been fun.'

Addie was curled up so they were knee to knee, floating in a grand bed on a sea of flagstones. She felt a yearning for the closeness they had shared as children and at the same time a desire to escape endlessly defining herself against another. Harriet propped up on her elbow and regarded her sister.

'Addie, what kind of world do you live in?'

'I love you,' said Addie.

It was so totally unexpected, Harriet felt tears rise.

'You're not a monster,' said Addie.

'I've never expected to feel that way about anyone,' said Harriet. Her tears fell freely. 'And once it started I couldn't…and I didn't want to find a way back. Nothing meant the same.' She smiled and wiped her cheeks. 'We would have done anything for each other. For a short while, anyway.'

She returned her head to the pillow and looked up into the beams of the room.

'I can't pretend it never happened,' said Harriet.

'You shouldn't. You shouldn't have to. I think we would have liked him.'

The quiet morning rested on the old roof as they lay together. The skin on Addie's forearm glowed around the edges of her tattoo. Harriet's gaze traced its curves.

'I think it was a mistake,' said Addie, noticing her attention. 'Mum says it was cultural appropriation, I think Dad agrees.'

'Really?'

'But there would be a scar, even if it was removed.'

'I like it,' said Harriet. 'I always have.'

'You will forgive yourself, won't you?'

'When I've collected enough stones.'

Harriet smiled.

'And when will that be?'

'No idea,' said Harriet. 'We should get up. Anna's probably been awake for hours.'

The previous night's drinking had left Harriet hungry. She rose, stretched then headed into the main house in search of food. Addie remained where she was, warm as a cat.

Oscar was dribbling milk from his spoon, cereal scattered on the table. Eveline lay on the back of the sofa dangling her arms. The smell of coffee hung in the air. There was no sign of Martin or Anna. The pugs were gone from the table.

'Mum's in the bath. She said she needed to warm up,' said Eveline.

'Oh,' said Harriet.

Oscar scrambled down from his chair and waggled the handle of the French doors.

'Want go out,' he said. 'Out,' he repeated, crisply. 'Go out.'

Eveline slipped off the couch and stood by her brother, eyes eagerly on Harriet. Oscar thrummed on the handle. Harriet moved to open the latch at the top of the door.

The cold stones under bare feet set the children running. A high-pitched giggle trailed after Oscar as he flew past chased by his sister. Something about the sound suddenly took Harriet back to Oxford, to a still, well-appointed office.

'Doctor Wolf, won't you join me?'

Harriet assented.

'Black, please.'

The coffee cups had sailed on a sea of polished walnut.

'You have received written communication from The Academic Disciplinary Committee.'

'Yes,' said Harriet.

'There's no question that you disregarded the staff code of conduct.' The dean looked down his aquiline nose. 'Principals you agreed to adhere to when you signed your contract with the college. The Anthropology and Archaeology Department has its own strictures, no doubt less formal.'

Dean Neeley's sharply tailored suit was the same dark blue as the curtains, a shade favoured by the college following a rowing victory in the early nineteenth century. Harriet had worn a red suit and patent leather boots. The stain of her lipstick marked the coffee cup.

Formerly a pioneer in keyhole surgery, the dean was experienced in leaving the minutest scars. Neeley ultimately controlled the bureaucratic strings that decided her fate. His personal motivation was as disguised as hers was exposed. Sanctioning Art was politically impossible, so it had to be her.

'The recommendations suggested by the committee have

always been approved by Governing Body. This will be no different.' He had stirred his coffee, deposited the silver spoon crisply on the saucer and smiled. Harriet's arms stiffened against the arms of her chair. She took a small unsteady breath.

'And the terms of my return,' she said.

Heat prickled at the base of her spine.

'Will be considered presently, depending on student and external reaction to the certain revelation of these events.'

Art had not been mentioned once.

She tried not to recall the meeting, but it came back to her in perfect snapshot clarity. Her breath faltered.

She imagined Art walking towards her, his deep-bronze skin glistening as if he had been hurrying to meet her, his lips parted. He bowed his head in a reverence and then suddenly he was gone, a figment.

Oscar flashed past the old back door, and swung around the scullery with a hearty 'Huh-huh-huh', each stride sounding through his chest. A sense of responsibility dawned on Harriet.

She stepped out into the mist.

'Oscar! Stop! Come back. Eveline, don't run. I don't think you should run.'

The Wildlife Trust van passed Storrtang's ruins and turned up the lane.

~~~

Upstairs Anna was watching, crying, and then laughing at the three of them chasing each other round and round the house, Oscar out-pacing Harriet towards gateposts. The top of a vehicle was rising over the brae and Erskine was brimming with life.

She unclasped the window and drew breath to call down to the fun. Oscar's head was down. His knees chopped and his feet flew. Harriet's voice called and called.

Abruptly, Anna saw what was about to happen, her arms reached ghostlike out of the window.

Harriet heard Anna's voice from above as she rounded the side of the house. The van was coming around the dyke, Ernest's view blocked by the stone pillars either side of the entrance. He was pointing towards Scarth's farm, attention distracted by a new seed drill.

Oscar ran forwards into the thrill of cold air

'Huh, huh, huh, huh…'

Beneath Harriet's numbed feet the stones streamed, her arms stretched forwards and down as if into deep water, reaching into the low world of children and wild things, fingertips extending and grappling with droplets and rushing air to reel in the space between herself and the boy.

A fingertip caught Oscar's shoulder, another hooked into the fabric of his pyjama shirt. The boy's body tipped and twisted backwards.

Clem lurched forward as his seatbelt snapped. Gravel sprayed from the drive as Ernest stamped the brakes.

Oscar's body pivoted, became briefly horizontal and then crashed down. His head hit the ground like a stone.

Ernest and Clem, slouched forward, held upright in the seats by their belts. Ernest's eyebrows were lifted high, jaw clenched tight. The van idled, halted a metre away.

Harriet was on her hands and knees, leaning over Oscar. His gaze wide and fixed, mouth open.

What had she done?

The boy's eyes were lustreless as they stared up into her face. Harriet's dressing gown fell in a silk tent around his limp body. Ernest turned the key to silence the engine.

She lifted her hand and placed it on the boy's chest. Breath neither came nor left. Ernest's boots and blue overalls were at Harriet's side. Still nothing.

There was a flutter beneath Harriet's fingers. The boy blinked and focused. Oscar examined his cave of silk and the stoat man's shoes. His attention travelled to Harriet's face and he filled his lungs in preparation for the noisy release of pain.

Eveline crouched down. She stared hard at her brother and spoke strictly.

'Oscar, you're very naughty.'

Oscar paused, his cry stifled.

'Mercy he's queek,' said Ernest. 'If you hadna caught had o him…'

'I'll carry him in,' said Harriet. She looked down at Oscar and said. 'If you'll let me? You've hurt your head.'

Oscar caught his breath back and nodded, tears welling.

Ernest signalled to Clem to get out of the van and follow into the house. Anna's face was pale, florid spots on her cheeks as she rushed downstairs. Oscar held out his hands and Harriet passed the boy to his mother's arms.

'He ran away again,' said Eveline.

'Hid looks a good, clean gash,' said Ernest, gesturing.

Clem peered at the boy's bleeding knee and nodded. He had had plenty of bloody knees. Auntie Meg said his mother would like him to be more careful, for she had given him a good body and he was to look after it.

'Stand back, beuy,' said Ernest.

'It was my fault,' said Harriet. 'I don't know why I let him outside. He asked and I just did it. He hit his head as well,' said Harriet.

She stepped away quickly, unable to look Anna in the eye. She felt the chill of drying sweat and retreated to her bedroom, the shame of another unintentional wrong beating in her temples.

'Addie, wake up. Get dressed. Ernest and Clem are here.'

When Harriet returned, a towel with ice cubes was pressed to Oscar's head. His tears were dry and his knee plastered.

'Where are my pugs? Mummy, where are they?' said Eveline.

'Ask Daddy.'

'Can't you tell me?' said Eveline.

'Eveline, would you like to make some pancakes with me,' said Addie. 'Vegan. They're very nice.'

Eveline's forehead pulled into a frown.

'Eveline?' said Anna. 'You've been asked a question.'

'I want my pugs.'

'Well, go and ask Daddy.'

Eveline stalked out of the room. Anna passed her fingers gently over the lump on Oscar's head and winced.

'He'll be okay, Harriet,' said Anna.

'Really?'

'Good large lump.'

Anna's phone buzzed. She fished it out of her pocket, read the message, glanced over to Ernest then sent a reply. Cradled against her chest, Oscar began watching Addie more closely as she stood at the stove.

'Clem'll try a pancake, no doot,' said Ernest to Addie. 'He's wantin tae speak to you, aren't you, beuy.'

Clem stepped forward and took out something concealed from behind his back.

'I'm apologising fur bein too close.'

He held out a box of chocolates.

Addie took the box with both hands. Clem stood eyes lowered, hands at his side. The bruising around his eye socket had turned indigo-black, spreading to green onto his cheek. The cut on his lip had shrivelled to a dark, crumpled line on swollen seashell-pink flesh.

'Thank you, Clem,' said Addie. 'I hope it's not too sore.'

Clem shook his head.

'I dinna ken if they're vegan chocolates,' said Ernest.

'They look delicious,' said Addie. 'I'm sorry too.'

Addie placed the gift carefully on the side and then begin to move with purpose the kitchen. Harriet looked across to

Ernest who caught her eye, a hint of a smile crossing his lips.

35

Upstairs, Eveline stamped her foot outside her parents' bed-room door. She had seen how her mother looked at the pugs, seen that she wanted them too, but didn't loved them. Maybe she was jealous because they were a grown-up present, not a plastic toy, something she could keep forever.

Eveline pushed open the door. Her father was packing the china dogs into his bag, padding them around with clothes.

'Daddy? What are you doing?'

'Darling, I can't let you keep them,' said Martin. 'I had a call from the antique shop. Someone else had bought them already.'

'How could they?' said Eveline. 'I thought you said they were from a flea market?'

He pulled his mouth into a frown, but Eveline could tell from his eyes he was being fake.

'They had paid, and were picking them up later.'

'But you gave them to me.'

'I know,' he said.

'They're mine,' said Eveline.

'I'm afraid they're not.' He picked one of the china dogs out of the case and turned it over in his hand. 'I'll get you some-thing even better.'

Eveline tightened her lips.

'I don't want anything better.' Her voice rose into a petulant cry, 'I don't want anything from you ever again. You'll probably take it back.'

She made her face very plain and then said, 'I hate you,'

and watched his reaction carefully, to see the pain. Her father's features hardened, like a devil was passing through. Then he put on a soft smile.

'I'm very sorry.'

She turned and ran out. On the landing her face reddened and crumpled. She dashed into her room, slammed the door shut, threw herself face down on her bed and wept.

~~~

Alone, Martin stared blankly out of the window. It was lunacy coming to Orkney. Two flights, the second at extraordinary cost, only to be rejected. Anna brooded in Orkney in a way she didn't in town; she was better with a schedule to keep. She needed to be occupied.

He knelt down and prodded a shirt around the head of a pug then flipped over the cover and fastened the bag. He stood up straight and looked out of the window. He saw the white van was on the driveway close to the house, tyre tracks in the stones. What had all the fuss been outside?

The labyrinth of fog lifted and shifted. It was not like London, where the veil over traffic arteries and concrete came as a relief. Here, perspective became confused, he lost his sense of direction.

The stoat catchers, with their a quixotic activity, came as if they had a right to the place. What had Addie been thinking rescuing one of the creatures?

Martin looked across into the mirror and grimaced to reveal his front teeth and sighed heavily. The replaced tooth was definitely greying. He would need a veneer.

~~~

Nobody paid any attention when Martin came to the living room door. The kitchen area was bright and there was the smell of pancakes frying. Anna had Oscar on her knee. Harriet was laughing at something the stoat catcher had said. Addie was at the stove holding out a plate.

'There's a post-production crisis,' he said. Nobody turned. 'They want to put an advert either side of the royal wedding and I need to pull in some favours from scheduling.'

'What a shame,' said Anna flatly. 'You'll have to go.'

Oscar looked up from his pancake and frowned at his mother. She kissed him on the forehead.

'Don't worry, we're staying.'

'The haar'll be gone by noon,' said Ernest, nodding in the direction of the airport.

'I can take myself,' said Martin.

'Yes,' said Harriet. 'We can pick the car up later. Leave the key in the glovebox.'

'Can you say goodbye to Eveline for me?' said Martin. 'She's upset.'

'Yes,' said Anna. 'I expect she is.'

Martin scooped up the keys from the table in the hall and picked his coat. 'Bye, Oscar.'

Oscar wiped a finger through a trail of syrup on his plate; he nodded, sucked at the sweetness, and did not watch his father leave. Anna made no sign of moving. There was no ritual goodbye kisses. They were beyond all that.

~~~

At the airport, Martin had done as instructed and left the car unlocked with its keys inside. He turned back uncertainly, then reflected that if taken the vehicle would not go very far.

At the service desk Martin secured a seat to Edinburgh and then sat in the small cafe area. He tried to order beer, but it was not served. He usually enjoyed waiting in bars at airports, one drink after another, opportunities coming and going. It was different here. These were strangers, but nothing was really anonymous, nothing would be forgotten.

The fog fragmented as predicted by Ernest and flights began to land. When the woman at the gate checked his ticket he noticed her search behind for Anna and the children. She said nothing, just raised her eyebrows and wished him a safe flight.

As the plane rose into the air over the Pentland Firth an ache settled in Martin's stomach. It reminded him of when he had made his mother angry as a boy. 'Why did you do it? Why?' she would say, and he would reply, 'I don't know. I just did.'

The north of Scotland floated beneath, distant hills blue-violet, the ground beneath green-grey. He thought of the pugs in his suitcase; briefly loved by his daughter, despised by his wife. Ugly. He held his breath to keep back a sigh. The ache deepened, and Orkney was left behind.

36

Anna did not indicate any foreknowledge when Ernest related details the scam to her. He'd cursed his own foolishness and wished the thieves a power of ill-luck. He'd shown her a photograph of the motorbike he had planned to sell, with his wife sitting side-saddle and Clem holding the handlebars. A big grin was pasted on the young man's face.

'Meg and Clem's borne the brunt o me ignorance.'

Ernest tucked a bite of pancake into his mouth and looked over to Clem, who sat watching Addie ladling the last of the batter into the pan.

'No bad these,' he had said. 'I should have spoken oot sooner. I ken that. Might hiv got somethin back.'

'It's easier to see afterwards,' said Harriet.

'Aye,' said Ernest. 'Same with most things.'

The fog opened, the shifting labyrinth condensed into scruffy brown clouds that gradually parted to reveal a sanguine sky.

Anna had asked for the new account numbers then excused herself and retreated into the laundry. She scrolled through a list of contacts and made a phone call. A few minutes later she sent a short message, opened her banking app and deposited her annual bonus into the new accounts created for Ernest.

It was a fraction of what had been stolen. The real money could not be traced. In London, when she returned, she had arranged a meeting to interrogate what was going so badly wrong with fraud protection, particularly in rural communities.

An idea had occurred to her as she came back through; it lifted her sense of disappointment at not being able to help more.

'Mum, Mum. Cat garden.'

Oscar pointed.

'He wants to show you the grave,' said Anna. 'Do you mind?'

Clem collected a final pancake from Addie, added jam and folded it in half in preparation for the expedition outside.

'First, I have a question to ask Clem,' said Anna. 'And Ernest. You'll need to agree. I realise now, that the garden needs keeping under better control, grass cutting, ditches clearing, pruning. Harriet can't do it all.'

'I'm not doing any of it,' called Harriet from the kitchen. 'Why do you think I have a flat?'

Ernest looked at Anna then to his nephew.

'Can you do it, Clem?'

'I'm learnin catchin peedie stoats,' he said to his shoes.

Ernest caught Anna's eye.

'I can spaek to the boss.'

'I dinna ken whit's flooer and whit's weed,' said Clem. He shrugged his shoulders.

'You can cut grass,' said Anna.

Clem looked up. His face brightened.

'Still go fir a piece?'

Ernest nodded.

'I'll still tak you in the van, beuy. Wouldna be the same withoot you, buey.'

Oscar was tugging at Ernest's sleeve, dragging him to the door. 'In winter there'd be other jobs, digging offlets, firewood cutting, fixing these.'

They were outside now, Anna gesturing towards the dishevelled outhouses.

Ernest caught a shower of notes falling from above, so rapid his ear could hardly catch them all. He noticed things as he walked, as if stepping outside for the first time in months, how the old slates sat well, how the meadowsweet scented the air, and that Anna's new gansey was bonny. When he thought about it, the pattern was more than familiar.

~~~

Addie and Harriet remained inside, clearing dishes.

'You've proved it,' said Harriet.

Addie stopped, cloth in hand.

'What?'

'I need you,' said Harriet.

'Don't be melodramatic,' said Addie. 'Go outside.'

'I'm going upstairs,' said Harriet.

'Eveline?'

'Yes.'

'Martin's such a bastard,' said Addie. She stated it plainly, then her voice softened. 'Poor Ernest though, losing all that money.'

Harriet nodded. 'I think he'll recover.'

'Like you?'

'Like me.'

37

Harriet paused outside Eveline's door and listened. There was silence. She leaned on the banister and reflected.

She had cared for Art, but had she looked after him? Did she care for any of her students except that they learned what they needed to learn? Why hadn't she come forward to Professor Paracchini and removed herself from having responsibility over Art? She could have fought.

She could have told them she loved him.

Professor Paracchini had emailed to say the Nepali migrant project funding had been extended, including the field trip to Nepal. He had been firm that the grant award was hers. It was an opportunity to walk unknown paths.

Harriet stepped towards Eveline's bedroom door.

Eveline was lying flat on the bed, as if floating down a river.

'They're looking at the grave,' said Harriet. 'Your dad's gone.'

'I know. I saw him drive off,' said Eveline. She drew in a wheezy breath and then sat. 'I suppose Sleekit wasn't even our cat.'

'No,' said Harriet.

Eveline fumbled under her pillow and took a draw from an asthma inhaler. She shifted to make a space for Harriet on the bed.

'Are they going to kill all the stoats?'

'It's their job,' said Harriet.

'Can't they put them somewhere else? A new island?' said Eveline.

'It's too hard.'

The answer rested between them. It was not impossible. Just too hard.

'Are you going to be allowed back to Oxford?' said Eveline.

'I'm going somewhere else.'

'I don't understand what you did wrong.'

Harriet put her arm around Eveline and hugged her close.

Outside the window, the sun had melted the last of the haar from Steven Scarth's fields. In the barn, a new litter was being licked clean by a she-cat. The smallest kitten was coal black.

'Mummy says you sing,' said Eveline.

'Yes,' said Harriet. 'I sang in a choir. I miss it.'

'Why don't you just sing anyway? Mummy hums, when she's here,' said Eveline. 'She copies the bird that disappears into the sky.'

Harriet smiled.

'I'm glad. Humming is better than not singing at all.' Harriet tousled the girl's hair. 'Get dressed, you can see the grave too. The sun's coming out.'

Eveline rose and Harriet followed. As soon as the front door opened the girl skipped away. Harriet scanned the horizon, a soft blueness was growing, the sun was turning from a vague area of brightness to a definite point of light.

Another car was coming up the lane. Kieran. Harriet waited at the front door. There were circles beneath his eyes, but he smiled.

'Sorry about yesterday.'

'So am I,' said Harriet. 'It's hard, once you've cared for something, even a little bit, to see it killed.'

'Yeah, I get that,' said Kieran.

'I understand they have to be caught,' said Harriet.

'Things need a chance to survive, some things belong, others don't,' said Kieran. 'Can't forget that.'

He met her gaze.

'Everyone forgets,' said Harriet, her mind elsewhere. 'Don't you think?'

'You've gotta stay in touch,' he said. He looked her in the eye in a way that implied far more than he was saying.

They reached the fluttering leaves of the rosa rugosa just as the party at the grave was breaking up. Harriet looked over to Scarth's fields, down to the ruined croft, out to the sea and islands beyond. The whistle of an oystercatcher cut through the air.

The wind was rising, enough to lift and press their clothes. Three sharp bursts and a rising trill came from the sky above. Harriet's blood stirred in response. The soft sweetness of the air enveloped her. The wind's energy invited her rather than trapped her inside as it had when she arrived. She felt kin with the blades of grass, that grew and grew again.

There was a touch on her shoulder. Addie was smiling. She lifted Harriet's arm and ducked underneath, twirling around. Harriet laughed, stepped back and Addie bowed. They stepped apart and made space for Anna and Eveline.

The procession from the grave became a parade around to the new entrance of Erskine. Harriet held her head high, breathed in the far horizon, and surveyed the islands nestled in the sea, like a great pod of sea mammals risen briefly from the deep. Time moved forwards, one wave, one step, one journey at a time.

Acknowledgements

I am fortunate to have a friend in Lucy Alsop. I am doubly fortunate to benefit from her skills as a reader and proofreader. I am indebted to her local knowledge and understanding of dialect as well as her sensitive reading and constructive comments on the manuscript. I am also grateful for early comments from Mandy Haggith, the cake had only just gone into the oven and it was nerve-racking to let anyone open the door. It is to her absolute credit that her comments did not cause the cake to collapse, but to continue to bake.

My grateful thanks also go to Liz Coward for useful comments on the manuscript timelines and to Lucy Gibbon for her patience and encouragement while we scribbled notes. The services provided by the team at Orkney Library and Archive are embedded features of many writer's work, including mine and I thank them for their continued service. My thanks also go to Babette Stevenson and Fiona Flemming who reviewed and commented on early fragments of the manuscript. I apologise wholeheartedly to anyone I have neglected to include here. This project has stretched over many years.

I would also like to thank Lesley Affrossman and Jim Campbell for all the unseen hours at Sparsile. The Scotland Prestige Award for Book Publishing Company of the Year 2024 is richly deserved. My particular thanks go to Alex Winpenny for his insightful comments and spotting opportunities for sweetness in the text that I had overlooked.

Finally, I would like to thank my children for their forbearance at having a creative parent. Their lack of discouragement speaks volumes, and the continuing encouragement from my family means everything.

A note on the text

Every piece of writing dates including this manuscript, which was first begun in 2018. Although this is a fictitious narrative I feel it is noteworthy that the shrunken heads or 'Tsantas' referred to in the text have now been removed from display at the Pitt Rivers Museum in Oxford. The stoat eradication project in Orkney has also moved on to new phases. Guidelines institutions use to moderate student staff interaction are also constantly changing. A pandemic has occurred.

Book Club Questions

1. How is Harriet's relationship with Art more or less wrong?

2. Anna knows Erskine's history, yet she still buys the croft. Why? What would you do?

3. Does Thorn have any chance of wholesome life?

4. Ernest and Kieran both experience grief. Is one greater or lesser?

5. Addie should know better. Does she do anything on purpose?

6. There are bad people and bad places. Where does Martin fit in? Where does Dean Neeley fit in?

7. Should Stoat be allowed to live?